THE
GREEN
Ribbons

CLARE FLYNN

CRANBROOK PRESS
THE GREEN RIBBONS

Copyright © 2016 Clare Flynn

All rights reserved.

Published by Cranbrook Press 2016
London, England.

978-0-9933324-2-5

This is a work of fiction. Any similarity between the characters and
situations within its pages and places or persons, living or dead, is
unintentional and coincidental.

Cover photography from Shutterstock.com

Cover design JD Smith Designs

DEDICATION

For my parents
Tom Flynn 1924–1989
Kay Flynn 1928–2016

CHAPTER ONE

I sometimes hold it half a sin
To put in words the grief I feel;
For words, like Nature, half reveal
And half conceal the Soul within.

(from In Memoriam, Alfred, Lord Tennyson)

June 1900

Hephzibah shivered as her parents' coffins were lowered on ropes into the hole in the ground. A squirrel ran across the grass behind the grave. As she watched it scrambling up a tree, Hephzibah bit her lip, fighting back the tears. How did she have any left to cry? They had been tears of shock at first that both parents had managed to get themselves mown down by a tram. Afterwards came the loss, grief and loneliness that she wondered if she would ever shake off, mixed with anger that they had died such a stupid avoidable death.

Hephzibah had been at home in Oxford packing her bags for the six month trip the three of them were about to make to Rome. Her parents had been in London making the final arrangements for the journey. They should have been leaving today and instead here she was, alone, witnessing their interment in a shared grave.

Not only was she now facing life as an orphan, with no other living relatives, but she would be penniless. She couldn't blame her stepfather. His was a sin of omission not intent. He would never have expected to die so young. He'd probably thought there was plenty of time to make provision for the stepdaughter he adored and had treated as though she were his own flesh and blood.

Hephzibah looked around at the crowd of mourners. Professor Prendergast, her stepfather, had been a popular and well-respected man. There was a contingent of students and dons, but the stepbrother she'd never met hadn't deemed it worth his while to make the journey from South America to England to pay his respects, even though she had offered to postpone the funeral until he could complete the voyage. He was an engineer working on the construction of a railway out there and told her that he would leave it to the lawyers to sort out his inheritance. He didn't enquire about her own circumstances. Now he would get the lot – the house in London and every penny – even the money her own late father had left to her mother when he died, all swept up into Professor Prendergast's estate.

Hephzibah didn't care about the inheritance. It was the realisation that she was now on her own, soon to be homeless and without a clue what to do about it. She leaned over the edge of the grave and dropped two white roses she had plucked from the college garden onto the coffins.

Tears pouring down her cheeks, Hephzibah turned away from the graveside and ran out of the cemetery past the mourners waiting to pay their respects.

Over the weeks that followed her parents' funeral, Hephzibah struggled to know what to do. Her friends were as devoid of ideas as she was. All of them offered to keep a lookout for any suitable employment that also offered accommodation, but she sensed they now saw her as an encumbrance and were just going through the motions, hoping she would fade away and become someone else's problem.

The assumption had always been that she would one day marry a don like her father, or possibly one of his students, but marriage had not been a pressing issue. Her father had talked of her studying at one of the women's colleges first and had been coaching her for the entrance examinations – but there was no chance of that happening now that she had no means of supporting herself.

The day she had been dreading dawned at last. She had been summoned by the Master of her father's college. Hephzibah knew he would want to know when she would move out of the house, which was owned by the college and situated within the grounds.

Over breakfast she opened the post as usual – each day brought a diminishing number of letters of condolence and an increasing number of unpaid bills. She added them to the pile to be sent to the solicitors to be dealt with as part of probate. She opened the last envelope and read the letter inside. Perhaps her prayers had at last been answered.

Stuffing the letter in her coat pocket she set off for the Master's house. Ten minutes later she found herself in his office, sitting on the edge of a chair that was too big for her, making her feel small and awkward and out of place. She twisted her hands in her lap nervously as her host spoke the words she had dreaded hearing.

'Miss Wildman, we need to discuss your future plans,' said the Master. 'I do not wish to inconvenience you, but the new Dean will want to move into College House before term begins. Perhaps there is something we can do to help? I imagine you intend to live with a relative? Or will you stay at your stepfather's London house?' He peered at her over the top of his half spectacles.

'I have no relatives,' she said, wondering why this fact made her feel ashamed, when it was not something over which she had any control. 'Papa had a son from his first marriage, but he was already grown up and had left home when Papa's first wife died. My own father had no living relatives and Grandmama, my mother's mother, died last year.' She paused for a moment then added, 'The London house has been let since we moved to Oxford.'

'Dear, dear. That's unfortunate. But at least you can use the rental income to live on and rent a room for yourself?'

Hephzibah lowered her eyes. She studied a shaft of sunlight which had carved a line through the Master's carpet, revealing the previously invisible spatters of ink which peppered its surface. She had never entered the hallowed portals of the Master's house before and felt uncomfortable and out of place. She swallowed and raised her eyes to look at him. 'My father's estate, including the income from his London property, will pass entirely to my stepbrother. Papa had intended to make an allowance to me but had not yet had opportunity to do so.'

The Master frowned. 'I see, I see. I suppose Professor Prendergast would not have expected to meet such an unfortunate and early demise. Tragic. Terrible thing to happen. And Mrs Prendergast too. Quite shocking.'

The elderly man looked flustered. Hephzibah had noticed how some people were embarrassed by death. Losing her own father when she was a child had made her see death as a fact of life. While that didn't lessen the pain, she couldn't understand why people were reluctant to mention it. It was as if discussing death somehow risked tempting fate into advancing the time of their own demise.

'I received a letter this morning from one of Papa's former students, a Mr...' She pulled a folded letter from her pocket and examined it. 'Nightingale. The Reverend Mr Merritt Nightingale. He is a parson in a village called Nettlestock in Berkshire.'

The Master waved a hand in the air. 'Nightingale. I believe I remember him. A good student. Took a double first. I've never heard of Nettlestock though.' He frowned and Hephzibah sensed his impatience.

'Mr Nightingale mentioned in his letter that the local squire there is seeking a governess for his ten-year-old daughter. I wonder if it might be a suitable opening for me, although I know nothing of Mr Nightingale, nor the place.'

The Master's relief showed immediately on his face. 'Governess. Perfect. Just the thing for a young woman such as yourself. Where were you educated?'

'Mama taught me all I know, including French and a little Latin. Then over the past months Papa had begun to teach me some ancient Greek, but I fear we had got no further than the rudiments of grammar.'

'More than adequate, Miss Wildman. An excellent plan. Do you need a letter of recommendation? I will be happy to furnish one. As you know I held your late stepfather in high regard.'

'But you don't know me or my competencies.'

He waved his hand again. 'No matter. I am sure your mother will have prepared you for all that will be required in the upbringing of a young girl.' He chuckled and shook his head. 'No need to worry about the Latin and Greek. Good manners, reading of the Bible and some of the finer feminine skills such as singing and sewing should be more than adequate. And a bit of French never did anyone any harm. If the Reverend Nightingale recommends this family I am sure it will be a good one.'

The Master rose from his chair and said, 'Very good, Miss Wildman, very good indeed.'

She was dismissed.

The packing was almost finished. The furniture had been dispatched to storage, pending the dispersal of the estate. With the solicitor's permission, Hephzibah had sent her parents' clothing to the local workhouse for the benefit of the poor and dispossessed. Hephzibah reflected that she too could almost be classified in that way. Her own worldly goods now consisted of a small trunk, crammed with clothing, her mother's copy of *Shakespeare's Sonnets* and a small daguerreotype of her parents.

She had been tempted to keep some of her mother's jewellery but the solicitor sent a man to make an inventory of the contents of the house and he itemised every piece. All she had managed to keep were a pair of her mother's pearl earrings and the locket her mother had given her when she married Professor Prendergast. It had been a gift to her mother from her first husband, Hephzibah's father, and her mother had felt it inappropriate to continue wearing it once she remarried. Hephzibah raised her hand and squeezed the small gold heart on its chain around her neck and wondered at the cruelty of God in killing them both just as they were all about to embark on an adventure in Rome, where Professor Prendergast was to research his book on the cult of Mithras. Hephzibah had been looking forward to six months in the Eternal City, perhaps learning a little Italian and spending her days clambering around ruins with her stepfather.

What a difference one single moment had made, destroying two lives and utterly transforming her own. She picked up the book of sonnets and as she turned the thin, almost translucent, pages of the small volume, Hephzibah felt the tears well up inside her again. As she glanced over the pages a line caught her eye: *"My grief lies onward, and my joy behind"*. She held the leather-bound book up to her face and gave a little inarticulate cry. Had she the strength to get through this? She had to find it. Nothing would bring her parents back. Nothing would restore her life as it was. Accept that, Hephzibah, and get on with it, she told herself. She brushed a hand over her eyes, took a deep breath and set about finishing her packing.

The last item to go into the trunk was a pair of double-sided green velvet ribbons, a gift from her mother, just the day before she died. Hephzibah planned to use them to trim a hat or dress her hair. Now in mourning, it would be a long time before she would want to wear such bright colours. She thought wistfully of the pleasure she'd felt when she and her mother chose them in the haberdashery store, hesitating at first over whether to choose a safer blue, but her mother convincing her that the green was more vibrant. They were so vivid in colour that she would not have dared to wear them in Oxford, but they would be perfect for Rome. Now, as a governess and in mourning, it would have to be sober blacks and greys for a while.

Hephzibah was to make the journey from Oxford to Nettlestock by train. It was a distance of only around forty miles as the crow flies, but the train required her to travel two sides of a triangle via Reading and involved a lengthy wait between trains.

It started to rain as soon as the train left Oxford and the water ran in torrents down the windows of the carriage, blurring the landscape as the train passed through it. She had lived in Oxford her whole life and felt bereft about leaving her city, probably for ever. As the rain pelted down she shivered in the draughty coach and tried not to think about her parents or her miserable situation. But it was hard to think of anything else, as little icicles of grief had frozen her heart over and made the rest of the world appear pointless and trivial.

Hephzibah took out the letter she had received from the Reverend Nightingale in response to her request that he petition Squire Egdon on her behalf. He had beautiful handwriting: confident, broad, bold strokes in black ink. His letter confirmed that the squire was more than happy that Hephzibah was to take up the position, expressed his delight that he had been able to arrange things to the satisfaction of all concerned and was full of assurances that she would not regret her decision to come to Nettlestock. Hephzibah sighed. What decision? To describe it as a decision implied she'd had a choice. She scrunched the letter into a ball and dropped it back into her bag. It was tempting to dislike the Reverend Nightingale for his unbounded enthusiasm, but she told herself it was hardly his fault that her parents were dead and her life turned upside down. It would be unfair to take against a person before even meeting him, particularly one who had acted as her guardian angel and sent her a lifeline.

The train from Reading was a slow one, a branch line, stopping frequently at towns and villages on the way. When it finally pulled into Nettlestock station and Hephzibah climbed down from the carriage, she stepped into a puddle, drenching the hem of her woollen gown. She looked around the empty platform, wondering what she was to do about transporting her trunk and bags up to Ingleton Hall. She couldn't even see the village, so feared it would be a long walk and it was still raining heavily.

'Miss Wildman! It is Miss Wildman?'

A young man was hurrying along the platform towards her. His black coat billowed out behind him as he ran, then fell back to cling damply around his legs.

'I've been listening for the train. I had a feeling you would be on this one. There are only two a day. Please come and take some tea with me at the parsonage. It's very close. I've arranged for the carter to deliver your bags up to the Hall. He'll be along to pick them up from here in a few minutes. Squire Egdon will be expecting you in an hour. The carter will come back and collect you from the parsonage, once you've had some tea.'

She looked at him. He had a shock of thick reddish-blond hair and a friendly countenance, notable mainly for its rash of freckles. Perhaps she had met him before as he had been Papa's student – but if she had it was not surprising she didn't remember, as, freckles aside, his face was very nondescript. Pleasant enough but unremarkable.

'Mr Nightingale.' She nodded in greeting, then hesitated, looking at her trunk, uncertain how to respond to his invitation.

CHAPTER TWO

Escape me?
Never—
Beloved!
While I am I, and you are you,
So long as the world contains us both,
Me the loving and you the loth,
While the one eludes, must the other pursue.

(from Life in a Love, Robert Browning)

The parish of Nettlestock comprised one hundred and forty-two souls, all of them resistant to change. This was despite the fact that the village had been exposed to much in the past decades, with the coming, first of the Kennet and Avon Canal, and then the railway. Perhaps it was the village being in the vanguard of modern transportation that had caused the inhabitants to arm their defences against any other form of change, as they battled to keep things *"the way they've always been done round here"* in a last-ditch attempt to keep the twentieth century at bay. It was not that difficult. Canal traffic passed through the locks, some of the product from the whiting factory was loaded at the dock, but otherwise these days the canal left the village untouched. The passenger trains mostly passed through without stopping and when they did stop, it was for gentry from the large houses of the surrounding hinterland, rather than for villagers, who rarely ventured beyond the bounds of Nettlestock, except for the odd trip to the nearby market town at Michaelmas and Candlemas for the agricultural hiring fairs.

Merritt Nightingale was a new incumbent at St Cuthbert's, his predecessor, who had served the parish for more than thirty years, having fallen victim to influenza eighteen months earlier. The clergyman's youth and lack of history with the parish meant that he was viewed with deep suspicion by his flock, who believed no outsider capable of fitting in with the customs and practices of Nettlestock and no man of such tender years – he was twenty-four – capable of understanding them or ministering to their needs. This lack of faith in their spiritual guardian manifested itself in passive resistance. They attended church services, but neglected to include the Reverend Nightingale in any social activities and went out of their way to avoid bumping into him around the parish and thus being obliged to pass the time of day. Merritt knew his parishioners avoided him but he hadn't a clue how to go about winning their trust. He had raised the subject with his bishop, who brushed Merritt's doubts aside and told him the parishioners would accept him, given time. How much time, Merritt wondered?

He had not planned to enter the clergy, but inherited the living from his predecessor, who was a distant cousin several times removed. As Merritt had no particular thoughts about what profession to pursue, it appeared to be as good an option as any, affording him a comfortable place to live, a modest income and plenty of time to pursue his passions for classical literature and long country walks.

Merritt had first set eyes on Hephzibah Wildman a few years earlier, when attending tutorials with her father, the Dean of his Oxford college. She couldn't have been more than fifteen then, but the young undergraduate had noticed her. One early summer afternoon he had watched her through the window of her father's study while she was reading in the garden and he was translating Ovid for Professor Prendergast, who always looked distracted and rarely gave the impression he was listening to his students. Hephzibah was sitting on a bench under an elm tree, eating an apple. As Merritt spoke the words he was translating from *Metamorphoses*, he imagined the girl in the garden with her apple was Proserpina eating the seeds of the pomegranate. Caught up in the moment, he had paused, losing his place in the Latin text and causing his tutor to rap the desk impatiently. Every tutorial after that, he had looked through the window hoping to catch a glimpse of the girl, but she was never there. He wondered whether Professor Prendergast was not so absent as he appeared.

After coming down from Oxford and accepting the living in Nettlestock, Merritt occasionally thought of the young woman to whom he had never even spoken and had never expected to see again. When he heard about the tragic demise of both her parents he felt compelled to write to offer his condolences. He had included the suggestion of the position at Ingleton Hall without any real expectation that Hephzibah would take it up. When she did, he was surprised and strangely joyful. He told himself it was because he would no longer be the only outsider in the village and that Miss Wildman and he would be kindred spirits ranged against the hostile Nettlestock natives. He didn't want to admit to himself that he might have more romantic reasons, as he feared that, seeing her again after three years, he might be disappointed. He also feared that were he not to be disappointed in her, there was every likelihood that she would find little to commend in him.

When Hephzibah Wildman descended from the train

in the pouring rain, Merritt ran towards her then was overcome with embarrassment that, in his hurry to meet her, he had neglected to fetch his umbrella. He decided to offer her his coat to cover her head but realised he couldn't expect her to hold it over her own head, as she had a cloth bag in one hand, and he could not hold the coat for her without pressing up close against her. He stood in front of her, nonplussed, coat in his hand, dripping wet.

Hephzibah said, 'Why don't we each take a side of your coat and hold it between us so that we are both under cover.'

He looked at her gratefully, took her cloth bag from her and they raised the coat above both their heads like a canopy and stumbled their way, half running, the few hundred yards to the parsonage.

As they went through the village, Merritt could sense, but not see, the eyes upon them from behind the windows of the cottages that lined the muddy street. Give them all something to think about.

They arrived at the parsonage and stepped into the stone-flagged hallway. He showed her into the drawing room where, as always, there was a roaring fire. Miss Wildman unpinned her hat and looked around, and Merritt realised she was wondering where she might deposit it. Every surface was piled with books, even the chairs. He cursed inwardly. Why was he so incapable of thinking ahead? He was blind to his own surroundings, unable to picture them as others might – until it was too late. Covered in confusion and embarrassment, he rushed about the room, moving books from one pile to another. One of the resulting edifices toppled to the ground, covering the carpet and blocking Miss Wildman's passage. Merritt rubbed the back of his neck, conscious that his ears were probably red. They'd always teased him about that at school – radish-coloured ears on a carrot-coloured head.

He bent to pick up the scattered books and looked up at

Miss Wildman, who was struggling to control her laughter. Merritt wanted to kneel at her feet with gratitude and relief that she was amused rather than irritated. 'I'm frightfully sorry, Miss Wildman. Mrs Muggeridge, my housekeeper, is always berating me for failing to confine my books to the study, but there isn't room for any more in there.'

She raised her eyebrows. 'You mean there are more?' She looked around her and raised her hands in mock amazement.

He rolled his eyes. 'Every room in the house. But you must be used to that. Your late father had... I'm sorry... I didn't mean...'

She laid a hand on his sleeve. 'Don't worry, Reverend Nightingale. Don't be afraid to mention my father. It is worse when people try to avoid mentioning him or Mama. A surfeit of books is an impossibility as far as I am concerned and yes, Papa had hundreds of them. Hoarding books is a vice to which I am accustomed and would happily do penance for. Sadly, I no longer have any, save my mother's copy of *Shakespeare's Sonnets*.'

Merritt seized on the opportunity with the eagerness of a small child. 'Then I hope you will treat my books as your own personal library. Come here to the parsonage whenever you wish. I would be delighted.'

Hephzibah looked uncomfortable for a moment then said, 'That is most kind, Mr Nightingale.'

There followed a silence between them, broken only by the patter of rain on the windowpanes and the ticking of the clock. Hephzibah was still standing as the parson rushed around trying to liberate a seat for her.

The door opened and a small, rosy-cheeked woman bustled into the room. 'There you are, Reverend. What are you doing in here when I've already set up your tea in the back parlour? There's a nice fire and somewhere for the lady to sit,' she said pointedly, raising her chin in an effort at hauteur that somehow didn't match her portly shape. She led them to the rear of the house into a sparsely-furnished room. There was a fire in the narrow grate and a group of upright wooden chairs, where the parson was accustomed to receiving parishioners. Mrs Muggeridge pointed to the tray of tea and arrowroot biscuits she had laid out in readiness on a small side table, nodded, then left the room.

Merritt felt the blood rush to his ears again and instinctively his hand went up to rub the back of his neck. 'I'm sorry, Miss Wildman. I'm not used to receiving guests, just people here on parish business and I didn't explain to Mrs Muggeridge to ready the drawing room to receive you. Please forgive me. I hope you won't take this as a slight.' He motioned her to sit down.

Hephzibah, still clutching her bedraggled wet hat, edged into one of the upright wooden chairs, close to the fire. Compared to the roaring conflagration in the drawing room hearth, this was a miserly affair and she shivered, gathering her coat around her.

Merritt sat in a chair opposite. There was another long silence, then Hephzibah, evidently realising her host was not about to serve the tea, set about doing so herself, pouring him a cup and taking one herself.

'I'm so terribly sorry, Miss Wildman. I am failing every test of hospitality. What you must think of me.'

She looked at him quizzically. 'I don't think I have ever received so many apologies in such a short space of time and for so little reason, sir.' She gave him a shy smile.

Merritt picked up his teacup and looking at her seated opposite him, her hair damp where her hat and his coat had failed to protect it, he was overcome by embarrassment again and slopped his tea over the white linen tray-cloth as he returned the cup to the saucer. 'Sorry,' he said.

Hephzibah shook her head, smiled, then asked, 'But with all those books in your drawing room where do you sit yourself?'

Merritt looked down. 'Mostly on the floor in front of the fire.'

'I used to love to do that,' she said, her voice dreamy. 'Mama was always telling me off. My favourite thing was to lie on my stomach in front of the fire with a good book.'

He looked at her and saw this time it was she who was blushing.

'I mean not recently of course. When I was a girl. I didn't mean to imply I would still behave in such a manner.'

Merritt smiled and swallowed. Proserpina was not the lovely creature he remembered when she had sat in her father's garden – but a woman far lovelier. As she parted her lips to eat a biscuit he felt another rush of blood to his head and a desperate desire to kiss her. He'd never felt a compulsion to kiss a woman before. He didn't even know her. And yet he felt he did. It was as if he had always known her. Now that she was sitting here opposite him he knew he wanted her always to be sitting close to him like that. He watched as she brushed a biscuit crumb from the corner of her mouth and felt another inexplicable rush of desire for her. He had to marry her. He would die if he didn't. He wanted to spend the rest of his days looking into those beautiful blue-grey eyes and listening to the sound of her voice.

While they sipped their tea in silence, Merritt let his mind run away with him. He was walking hand-in-hand with Hephzibah by the water meadows and along the tow-path of the canal. He was turning sheet music and adding his tenor voice to her soprano as they sang Brahms duets together. He was kneeling at her feet and offering a posy of wild flowers to her. His fantasies were interrupted when she began to cough.

'You have taken a chill?' he asked, fear gripping his stomach.

'No. A biscuit crumb went down the wrong way. I'm sorry,' she said.

Merritt smiled. 'Who's apologising now?' Then, feeling he might have over-presumed upon their short acquaintance, added, 'I meant to say I am greatly relieved the wet reception you've received in Nettlestock has not affected your health.'

'I'm hale and hearty, Reverend Nightingale. I've hardly had a day's illness in my life and I've no plans to start now.'

As she looked at him he was overcome with shyness and self-doubt. How could such a beautiful creature ever be interested in him?

Hephzibah broke the ensuing silence. 'I was wondering, did we meet when you were up at Oxford?'

'No,' he said quickly, then added before he could stop himself, 'but I did see you once. A few years ago. You were in the garden. I was struggling with my Latin translation. I saw you from the window of your father's study.' He wondered if he had given away his interest and the fear of rejection gripped him again.

'Fancy you remembering that,' she said, sounding amused. 'I hope I wasn't climbing the tree. Mama was always cross when I did that.'

'No, no. You were behaving with perfect decorum, eating an apple and reading a book. I remember it because I was translating from Ovid. We had reached the story of Proserpina and you eating the apple made me think of Prosperina with the pomegranate. That must be why I remember it.'

Hephzibah smiled then looked down at her hands, shivering. 'I was so happy then. I wonder will I ever be able to feel that way again?' She gave a little choked cry, then just as quickly pushed her shoulders back and took a deep breath. 'Some mornings I wake up and for a moment I have forgotten that Mama and Papa are no longer here. One tiny little moment when everything is as it always was and then I remember it will never be that way again.' She looked up at him, her face blushing. 'I don't know why I am telling you this, I barely know you.'

Merritt leaned forward, longing to move across the gap between them, kneel at her feet and gather her into his arms. Hephzibah looked up at him and he felt light-headed.

Then she spoke again. 'I suppose it's because you are a parson. I imagine many people must open their hearts to you and tell you their innermost secrets. That's one of the things clergymen are for, isn't it?'

He felt a stab of hurt inside. But what did he expect? She saw the office not the man. If this was love it was the most painful thing he had ever experienced. But how could it be love when he had seen her once at a distance through a window and now had been in her presence barely half an hour? Yet he felt certain that it was.

He put down his teacup and said, 'Alas, Miss Wildman, that is far from the case. I have become something of a pariah since I moved to Nettlestock. My parishioners almost never confide in me.' His face flushed again and he closed his eyes. She would think him a failure now.

'Then I shall go out of my way to confide in you and set them an example. I am sure you are the most kind and caring of parsons. They should be grateful to have you. I do hope we can be friends.' She hesitated, looking embarrassed, as though wondering if she had stepped beyond the bounds of propriety and Merritt remembered how very young she was. She went on, 'You are the only person here who knew my dear papa and so that makes a connection between us, don't you think?'

Merritt felt himself melting. 'Miss Wildman, nothing would give me greater pleasure than for us to be friends. As I said before, consider my books to be your books, my home open to you always. And next time you do me the honour of calling upon me I will have rearranged the drawing room so you will have a comfortable seat before the fire.'

He looked at his fob watch and rose to his feet. '*Tempus fugit*,' he said. 'Time certainly has wings when one is in congenial company, but I don't mind confessing that I am a little in awe of your new employer and I would not like you to be late and hence get off to a less than perfect start. The carter should be waiting at the door.'

Hephzibah stood and moved towards him. She stretched her hands out in front of her and clasped them around his. 'Thank you for your kindness and hospitality, Reverend Nightingale.'

When she had gone and he had shut the front door, Merritt leaned against it, his body shaking and his pulse racing.

CHAPTER THREE

"You shall no more be termed Forsaken, and your land shall no more be termed Desolate, but you shall be called Hephzibah, and your land Beulah; for the Lord delights in you, and your land shall be married."

(Isaiah 62. iv)

Hephzibah had never travelled with a carter before. Nettlestock was proving to be very different from Oxford. The carter, who was wearing a yellowing smock covered with darning, had a large brimmed felt hat pulled low on his head so that most of his face was hidden from her view.

She felt uncomfortable, perched above the bed of the cart beside this clay pipe-smoking stranger. As the parson waved goodbye, she was grateful that at least it had stopped raining. Any worries as to how she would make conversation with George Baverstock, the carter, soon proved needless, as he puffed on his pipe in silence and acted as though she wasn't there.

The driveway to Ingleton Hall was long and lined with lime trees. As they turned a bend she saw the Hall in front of her, a large brick-built structure with a classical stone portico in front and a flight of steps up to the door.

Hephzibah swallowed, suddenly nervous. She looked up at the arched windows above the portico and felt herself shrink, her mouth dry. A wave of loneliness washed over her and she wished she could ask Mr Baverstock to turn around and take her back to the village and the next train to Oxford. Running away was a tempting thought. The Hall looked so grand. Terrifying.

The driver flicked his whip lightly at the carthorse and the wagon made a turn into a roadway that led along the side of the Hall and round to the rear, into a large area with stables and outbuildings.

'End of the line,' he said.

Hephzibah realised he expected her to get down from her perch without assistance. 'Where do I go?'

He shrugged and pointed at a doorway. 'Kitchens are through there.'

She gathered her skirt about her, fought her irritation and threw her cloth bag down onto the flagstones. Sliding off the seat, she landed in the yard, hoping that no one was looking and able to see the expanse of calf she must have revealed. Without another word, Baverstock flicked his whip, turned the cart around and drove back towards the main drive.

Hephzibah made her way to the back door and knocked timidly. After about a minute during which she felt a rising panic, the door opened and a tall, thin, middle-aged woman looked her up and down.

'Who are you?' the woman said, her tone conveying a mixture of suspicion and disdain. Her expression was severe, accentuated by hair scraped tightly from her forehead into a small grey bun.

'I'm Miss Wildman, the new governess for Miss Egdon.'

The woman's expression relaxed. 'Good gracious! What are you doing at the kitchen door? How did you get here? I was about to send Evans down to the parsonage to fetch you in the carriage.'

'I came with Mr Baverstock on his cart. The Reverend Nightingale arranged for him to come back to the parsonage to collect me after he brought my luggage here.'

The woman shook her head. 'That young man is clueless. Heavens above! Expecting a lady to travel with the carter. Bags are one thing, a governess is another. Whatever was he thinking! Dear, oh dear. Better not let Sir Richard know. He has little enough time for Reverend Nightingale as it is.'

Hephzibah imagined how the clergyman would be blushing to the roots of his hair if only he could hear what was being said about him. She felt a sudden urge to defend him. 'It was rather an adventure. I've never travelled that way before. I'm sure Reverend Nightingale meant no harm.'

The woman went on. 'Leaving you at the back door! It won't do at all. Anyway, come in, Miss Wildman. You look as though you've had quite a soaking. Thank heavens it wasn't raining when you were on that old cart. Come in. Give me your coat and hat and we'll get them dry for you. Your bags are already upstairs in your bedroom, but I'll take you up there later. The squire hates to be kept waiting. Come with me.'

Hephzibah followed the woman through the kitchen and into a long corridor which led to the front of the house. They arrived in a double-height hall with a marble floor and a collection of busts of ancient Roman dignitaries on columns around the perimeter.

'By the way,' the woman said, 'I'm the housekeeper, Mrs Andrews, but we'll have time for all that later. In here.' Then she added in a whisper as she knocked on the door, 'His bark's worse than his bite, but you'd do well not to be alone with him if you can help it.'

Before Hephzibah could ask the woman what she meant, a voice boomed out from inside the room, 'Enter!' Mrs Andrews nodded then disappeared back into the depths of the house, leaving Hephzibah to push open the door.

At first she couldn't see her host. The room was vast, with marbled columns, gilded mirrors and portraits, and tall windows looking out onto rolling rain-soaked parkland. Then his voice again, impatient, commanding, disembodied. 'Come over here and let me see you.'

She looked around the enormous room and realised the squire was concealed from view by the back of the sofa on which he was reclining. She moved forward. Sir Richard Egdon was wearing a silk dressing gown, with a woollen rug over his legs. His naked feet stuck out from under the rug, one of them angrily red and swollen. Hephzibah looked away, embarrassed.

He winced in pain. 'Gout. Damned painful. Too much roast beef. Have to stay off the shellfish too. Life's not worth living if a man can't eat what he wants. Damned doctors. Come over here and let me look at you.'

She lowered her eyes and took a tentative step forward.

'Don't be shy. I don't bite,' he said.

Squire Egdon might possibly have been handsome in his prime but now was puffy and florid in the face. He was almost completely bald and his eyes were large, like black grapes, hooded and with dark circles underneath. His full wet lips would have looked well on a woman but made him appear lascivious. The dark eyes stared at her as if trying to see inside her. She shivered.

He gestured at a nearby chair and she sat down.

'Tell me your name again. I've forgotten.'

'Hephzibah Wildman.'

He snorted in response. 'Hephzibah! What kind of name is that?'

She looked down. 'I was named for my late grandmother. My father's mother.'

He frowned. 'That's not what I meant. Where does it come from?'

'It is biblical, sir.'

'Biblical? What does it mean?'

'I understand the name appears in both the Book of Kings and in Isaiah.'

'What does it signify? Who was Hephzibah? I am expecting you to know about such things if you are to be trusted with the care and education of my only daughter.'

She felt a rush of impatience at his rudeness. 'Hephzibah was the wife of King Hezekiah, and according to Isaiah chapter sixty-two verse four it is also a name given to the promised land. *"You shall no more be termed Forsaken, and your land shall no more be termed Desolate, but you shall be called Hephzibah, and your land Beulah; for the Lord delights in you, and your land shall be married."* The name in Hebrew means my delight is in her.'

'Most impressive, Miss Wilding. My delight is in her.' He looked her up and down, letting his eyes linger over her bosom. 'Most appropriate. Well then, do you think you can knock some knowledge into my daughter? Not just the Bible, mind. We get enough of that on a Sunday. No need to overdo it. I am sure a woman of your evident talents has a lot more to offer.' Again, he fixed his eyes on her chest.

She decided she already loathed the man. 'I will do my best, as I am sure will she.'

He snorted again. 'I want her to play the pianoforte and speak French. If you manage that you'll be doing well. The child prefers to run around the estate like a wild thing. I've a mind to take her pony from her. I'll never get her married off if she doesn't learn a few graces.'

'Married? But I thought she was a child?'

'She is a child. Ten years old. But you can't start thinking about these things soon enough. Sit down. Sit down, Miss Wilding.'

'It's Wild*man*,' she said, conscious that her voice was barely more than a whisper.

'No matter. Whatever. You'll meet the child shortly.

She's been like an unbridled filly since her poor mother died.'

'I'm sorry, sir. When did that happen?'

'Four years ago.'

'And has she been without a governess all that time?'

The squire laughed. 'She must have got through half a dozen.'

Hephzibah was alarmed. What kind of wild child could scare away so many governesses in such a short time? 'Is she very naughty?'

'Naughty? No! Good as gold. Too much so. Needs a bit more spirit. I like a woman to have spirit. Do you have spirit, Miss Wildman?'

'I don't understand.' Hephzibah felt more nervous the longer the interview went on. 'You implied she was running wild?'

'Spends all her time mooning around the estate with nothing to do. A girl like her should be painting, sewing, singing, doing the things women are supposed to do. The things I hope you are going to teach her.'

'I see… but…' She took a deep breath. Better to ask questions now than find out later. 'Why then did so many governesses leave?'

He leaned over to a side table and poured himself a sherry from a decanter. The top of his head was as pale and shiny as a hard-boiled egg. He didn't offer a drink to Hephzibah. He sipped the wine slowly, licked his plump lips and said, 'Because they didn't give satisfaction, Miss Wildman. I hope you will be different.' His big blackcurrant eyes bore into her again, until she looked away, uneasy under his gaze, then his eyes settled upon her breasts and stayed there. She shivered again.

He looked up and fixed her with his stare. 'I have a feeling you will suit very well. Nightingale tells me you're an orphan?'

'Yes, sir. My parents died just over two months ago.'

'How did that happen?'

She swallowed and bit her lip. 'They were killed in a tram accident.'

'What? Both of them?'

She nodded.

'How?' The man had no sensitivity.

'I don't know exactly as I wasn't there.' Her voice was shaky. 'I understand that they were deep in conversation and probably didn't see the tram and stepped in front of it.'

'Killed instantly?' Was he deliberately trying to be cruel?

'My mother was. My stepfather died on the way to the hospital.'

He grunted. 'Streets get more dangerous every day. Stepfather? What happened to your own father? He die too?'

She bit her lip again. 'When I was four. He was a botanist and died in Africa of cholera, while he was doing research there. My mother married Edwin Prendergast, my stepfather, when I was seven. He was an academic too. Professor of Classics.' Hephzibah decided it was better to lay it all out rather than allow him to fire questions at her as though it were an interrogation.

The squire closed his eyes and winced in pain as he leaned sideways, grasped a bell-pull and rang it vigorously. He turned his attention back to her but said nothing, just stared at her, his focus again on her bosom, his finger rotating inside his ear. Hephzibah resisted the temptation to raise her arms and place them across her chest protectively and tried unsuccessfully to convince herself that it was only her imagination. A few minutes passed until the door opened and Mrs Andrews entered, ushering a young girl into the room.

Ottilie Egdon was small and pretty, her head crowned with a mass of heavy brown curls. Her features were delicate: a small retroussé nose and bright eyes under silky brows, with a porcelain complexion. It was hard to imagine that the slug laid out on the sofa had fathered this elfin creature. The girl approached Hephzibah and bounced into a curtsey, chanting, 'Pleased to meet you, Miss Wildman. I do hope you will stay.'

Squire Egdon jerked his head towards his daughter and on cue she skipped over to him, wrapped her arms around his neck and planted a kiss on his cheek. In return he patted her on the bottom. 'Right. That's enough. You can take her away now, Miss Wildman. And remember, I am of the school of thought that children should be seen and not heard.' He waved a hand in dismissal and Hephzibah left the room, her new charge following close behind.

Mrs Andrews was waiting for them in the hallway. 'Sir Richard will be dining alone this evening. A supper will be ready for you and Ottilie in the nursery in half an hour. That leaves a little time for me to show you your room.'

Ottilie looked as though she was overcome with joy. 'Can I stay up late afterwards?'

'Calm down, young lady. You certainly can't stay up. As soon as you've finished your supper you're off to bed.' Mrs Andrews looked at Hephzibah. 'Sorry Miss Wildman, I've no wish to trespass on your responsibilities, but I'd hate you to get off on the wrong foot with the squire by allowing madam here to take advantage. Not before you've had a chance to see how things work.'

The room to which she had been assigned was on the second floor, opposite Ottilie's. There was a bathroom next door, which the housekeeper told her was exclusively for her use and Ottilie's. Hephzibah's new bedroom was comfortable rather than grand; the rug on the floor looked rather threadbare and the curtains, while made of damask, had linings that had frayed and torn from their exposure to the sunlight. Someone had placed a small pottery jug with a few dahlias on the side table. There was a fire burning in the grate.

'Don't expect a fire every night, Miss Wildman. But as you got caught in the rain I thought just this once,' said Mrs Andrews. 'You'll be expected to take all your meals with Miss Ottilie. That is unless the squire asks you to dine with him... which he might do from time to time.' The housekeeper frowned and looked as though she had been about to say something else but had thought better of it. She pulled herself up to her full height and smoothed the surface of her apron. 'My advice to you, Miss Wildman, is to keep out of Sir Richard's way as much as possible. You're here to take care of Ottilie, not to get acquainted with him.' Seeing Hephzibah's shocked expression, Mrs Andrews added, 'Not that I think you'd try to do that, but one or two of your predecessors were a little over-friendly with the squire, if you follow my meaning.'

Struggling to hide her indignation, Hephzibah said, 'I am here to teach Ottilie. That is all I will be doing.'

Over the next few days Hephzibah discovered that Ottilie was as charming as her father was boorish. The child was clearly desperate for affection and attention. Her father saw her just once a day, expecting her to attend him in the drawing room before her supper, where he would ask her what she had done that day, receive a kiss on the cheek then send her on her way.

Joining her charge for an early supper in the nursery was preferable to being interrogated by her employer and she was relieved that he had not extended an invitation to join him for dinner, as Mrs Andrews had indicated was possible. As a result she had no adult company, apart from the odd brief exchange with Mrs Andrews. She would have liked to join the other staff in the servants' hall, but it appeared that her status as governess meant she fell into a strange no man's land that was neither above nor below stairs.

Ottilie was shy at first but soon revealed a mischievous spark and an affectionate nature. Ottilie began to confide in her, telling her how much she missed her mama. When she told the little girl that she too had lost her mother, Ottilie flung her arms around Hephzibah's waist and said, 'I wish you were my big sister. We can look after each other as we don't have our mamas.'

Touched and surprised, Hephzibah stroked the little girl's hair. 'I've never had any sisters or brothers and now I have no one at all.'

'No cousins?'

She shook her head.

'No aunts or uncles?'

Hephzibah drew her mouth into a mirthless smile.

'No one at all?'

'No one.'

'Then you must definitely have me. Even if it's just pretend.'

Hephzibah had been at Ingleton Hall for a week when she woke in the middle of the night. Lying motionless in bed, she listened intently, convinced a noise had broken her sleep. The room had been pitch dark when she went to bed but now there was a soft glow. She blinked, trying to adjust her eyes and orientate herself to the still unfamiliar surroundings.

Overwhelmed by an intense certainty that there was someone in the room, her chest tightened and her heart was hammering so hard she thought it must be audible. Slowly she turned her head on the pillow to face the doorway and saw that it was open and a woman was standing, silhouetted on the threshold. It was too dark to make out more than her shape but Hephzibah was certain it was not Mrs Andrews. She tried to summon up the courage to call out, but there was a click and the door closed behind the intruder. Someone had been watching her as she slept. Who had been in the room?

Hephzibah's fear turned to anger. She might only be the governess but she was entitled to an undisturbed night and the privacy of her own bedroom. She slipped out of bed, grabbed her shawl and went out of the room. The long corridor was lit only by a couple of night-lights outside Ottilie's room, opposite her own. Hephzibah listened for a moment at the child's door but heard only the gentle breathing of her charge. She moved on up the corridor. There was no sign of her mystery visitor and the house was quiet. Through the window at the end of the gallery she heard the screech of an owl.

She was about to go back to bed, telling herself she must have been dreaming, when she heard the sound of laughter. Shivering from the cold, she clutched her shawl tightly and put her ear against one of the doors. There were two voices: a man's and a woman's. It was impossible to make out the words. The speaking stopped, replaced by female laughter and Hephzibah realised that she was eavesdropping at what must be her employer's door. She felt the blood rushing to her face. Turning to go back to her bedroom, embarrassed and guilty, she bumped into Mrs Andrews. The housekeeper was wearing a woollen dressing gown and a cotton bed-cap, under which curling papers were visible.

Her face was stony. 'Those who listen at doors always hear more than they'd like to hear,' she said.

The blush on Hephzibah's face deepened and she started to stammer. 'I'm sorry, Mrs Andrews. I didn't intend to eavesdrop. It's just that I'm sure someone came into my bedroom just now. I heard voices. I had no idea. I didn't realise this was the squire's bedroom.'

Mrs Andrews raised her eyebrows and gave a little sniff. 'The squire? And why on earth would the squire go into your bedroom?'

'Not the squire!' Hephzibah's voice was horrified. 'No. It was a woman. It was dark but I am certain it was a woman.'

'Well, it wasn't me. And I can't for the life of me imagine why anyone would go into your bedroom in the middle of the night. The servants all sleep on the top floor and none of them would venture onto this floor at night-time and it certainly wasn't Ottilie. There's no one else in the house.'

'But...' Hephzibah turned to look at the door again, about to point out that there was a man and woman inside, but then thought better of it. Mrs Andrews must know what was going on as well as she did and pointing out the indiscretions of her employer would do her no good at all. Better to stay silent.

'I'm sorry, Mrs Andrews. I must have been dreaming and I was disorientated when I woke up.'

'No harm done. Now go to bed before you wake up Miss Ottilie. Goodnight, Miss Wildman.'

Hephzibah scuttled back to bed and jumped beneath the covers, rubbing her arms to warm herself. So Squire Egdon had a mistress. Who was she? And why had she come into Hephzibah's bedroom?

The following day was Sunday and Hephzibah put on her best clothes and sat down at the dressing table to dress her hair. As she tied a length of grey ribbon around the knot of hair at the back of her head she thought of the new green ribbons her mother had gifted her. She liked to pick them up and hold them to her hair and think about how she might have worn them in Rome and wonder if maybe a day would come when she would at last have reason to wear them. She reached out to the mantelpiece where she had placed them when she had unpacked that first night, but there was nothing there. She hunted round the room but there was no sign of the ribbons. Annoyed, she finished pinning her hair in place. She frowned at her reflection in the mirror. Every inch the governess. Perhaps one of the maids had tidied the ribbons away – or maybe Ottilie had taken them to dress up one of her china dolls.

On her way down to breakfast she diverted past the stairs and went along the passage to the room where she had heard the laughter the previous night. It was clearly not the squire's bedroom. He would of course have a room on the first floor. The door was open and all that was inside was an empty bedstead, springs bare and blankets piled untidily on top. A tallboy and linen chest stood against one wall and there was a faded carpet on the floor. Otherwise the room was empty. Mystified, she went downstairs to join Ottilie in the dining room. She asked the girl if she had happened to see her ribbons but was met with a shake of the head.

She decided to walk into the village for the Sunday service at Nettlestock church, politely refusing the offer to accompany Mrs Andrews and Ottilie in the horse and trap. Sir Richard went on horseback. Presumably his gout was giving him less pain. Hephzibah was a few yards from the end of the long driveway when the squire rode up behind her. He slowed his horse and looked down at her from the saddle.

'You enjoy walking, Miss Wildman?'

'I do, sir. This is my first opportunity to see something of the estate and the village without torrential rain.'

'Nothing worth seeing.' With a flick of his crop he signalled his mount into action and they trotted off ahead of her. What an odd man he was.

Although regular attendance at the village church had been impacted by the lure of the new Nonconformist chapel, the little stone church was packed and the only available seat left for Hephzibah was near the back, on the aisle a long way from the contingent of servants from Ingleton Hall, who all sat towards the front of the church. The squire and, presumably, Ottilie, were out of sight, in the enclosed seats reserved for members of the Egdon family.

There was a cluster of musicians in a cramped wooden gallery at the back of the church: a pair of violins, a bugle, clarinet, bass viol and a serpent. The singing was led by an elderly woman who was seated a few rows in front of Hephzibah and who sang with a lusty contralto but was none too particular about the accuracy of her notes. While Hephzibah waited for the Reverend Nightingale to emerge from the vestry and begin the service, she looked around her. From every corner of the building she was conscious of eyes upon her, studying her, appraising her, unashamed in their curiosity. She felt herself blushing, more from annoyance than embarrassment. She hated being the centre of attention.

Just as the parson appeared and took up his position in front of his congregation, Hephzibah spotted what she was absolutely certain were her missing green ribbons. They were gracing the back of the head of a young woman several rows in front of her on the other side of the aisle. The girl in question had a cascade of chestnut curls worthy of a Titian portrait and Hephzibah had to admit that her green ribbons set off the colour of her hair perfectly. The plush velvet was a marked contrast to the coarse linen of the woman's dress. As the parson began to deliver the order of service, the young woman turned around in her seat and looked straight at Hephzibah as if challenging her outright to reclaim her property, then turned back and joined in the service as though innocent of any misdemeanour. Her audacity shocked Hephzibah. She was brazen, defiant, unrepentant. So the girl with the chestnut hair was the intruder in her bedroom the previous night. That must also mean that she was the mistress of Squire Egdon.

Hephzibah studied the girl over the top of her prayer book. She had never come across a woman of easy virtue before. She appeared to be in her early twenties and was undeniably pretty. How could someone like her fall prey to the advances of the squire? Hephzibah thought of his swollen red foot, his penetrating eyes with the dark circles beneath and that shiny bald head. She found him repulsive and could not imagine why a young woman would choose to visit him in an empty bedroom, doubtless let him touch her in the way only a husband should touch his wife. She had even been laughing. Hephzibah shuddered involuntarily. It was too horrible to think about. If the girl was prepared to go through all that, then she was welcome to her stolen ribbons. Then she asked herself why Sir Richard would have a tryst in an empty room, close to the accommodations of his daughter, the governess and the housekeeper. It must mean that someone else was in that unused bedroom. Perhaps one of the servants?

When the service was over, Hephzibah lingered in her seat while the congregation filed past. Mrs Andrews was one of the last to leave and she stopped at the end of Hephzibah's pew.

'Are you walking back to the Hall, Miss Wildman, or would you like to travel with Ottilie and me in the trap?'

'If you don't mind, I'll walk. It's such a beautiful day.'

'Luncheon is at one-thirty. The squire expects you and Ottilie to join him.' Then with a slight twitch of her lips, conveying unspoken disapproval, she went on her way.

The Reverend Nightingale was stationed in the church doorway when Hephzibah emerged. Seeing her, he said goodbye to the couple he had been talking to and turned to greet her. 'Miss Wildman, what a pleasure to see you.'

Hephzibah smiled, noticing the spread of a blush from his ears onto his cheeks.

'I do hope my sermon met with your approval?'

Hephzibah realised she had been entirely oblivious to the content of the homily and sent up a silent prayer that he would not expect her to discuss it further. 'Most thought-provoking,' she said. 'Inspiring, in fact.'

He laughed. 'I fear you are overstating the case.'

When he laughed, his face appeared less ordinary. She decided she liked him.

'I'm afraid the carriage for Ingleton Hall has already left. You will have a long walk back.'

'I chose to walk. I've been shut up indoors for days while it poured with rain. I have a full three hours before I'm expected at luncheon so I intend to explore the village and maybe the grounds of the Hall.'

Nightingale's blush deepened. 'Then perhaps you will allow me to accompany you as your guide?'

She was taken aback and hesitated a moment.

The parson went on, his words tumbling out of his mouth. 'No, of course not. You will have had enough of listening to me after that sermon! Not right to inflict more of my presence upon you. I'm sorry. It was thoughtless and intrusive.' He looked down at his feet and twitched the hem of his cassock between his fingers.

The man was clearly a bag of nerves. She wondered if he was always this way. It might explain what he had said about his parishioners avoiding him. But she liked him. He was kind, warm and intelligent. And he had a nice smile. 'I would be delighted if you would accompany me, Reverend Nightingale. You can show me the local landmarks.'

'Really?' he asked. 'If you're quite sure I won't spoil your morning?'

CHAPTER FOUR

By the margin, willow-veil'd,
Slide the heavy barges trail'd
By slow horses;

(from The Lady of Shalott, Alfred, Lord Tennyson)

Merritt left Hephzibah to wait in the drawing room of the parsonage while he rushed upstairs to fling off his vestments and change into a sturdier pair of shoes. The drawing room had been transformed in the days since she had last visited. He had enlisted the grudging help of his mystified housekeeper to move most of his books into the study, where they were now piled high on the floor and overflowing from the many bookshelves. He and Mrs Muggeridge had carried the rest upstairs to his own bedroom and the two guest rooms, where they were piled on top of the unused beds. No one came to visit anyway.

If Mrs Muggeridge attributed the parson's sudden change of heart about restoring order in the drawing room to Miss Wildman, she did not let on. Merritt was relieved as he would not have known what to say if the housekeeper had confronted him about his desire to make a good impression on the new arrival in Nettlestock.

Mrs Muggeridge had often muttered audibly about how it wasn't right to have a parson who was unmarried – his predecessor had been married with two daughters. If she began dropping hints about Hephzibah Wildman, he didn't think he would be able to conceal his feelings. Fortunately, Hephzibah's presence in the parsonage this morning would not be remarked, Mrs Muggeridge having gone to visit her sister in the next village, as was her custom every Sunday after the church service.

When Merritt returned, Hephzibah was standing by the window, looking out at the garden, which was awash with swathes of pink and purple phlox, with pink and white roses growing against the flint stone wall.

She turned to face him. 'You have a very pretty house and garden, Reverend Nightingale.' She stretched her arm out to sweep the room. 'But I think the room would look all the better for some books. I always feel a room to be unfurnished without them.'

Merritt stopped dead, his mouth open.

'I am teasing you, sir,' she said. 'I have a terrible habit of using irony. Pay no attention.'

He grinned at her, relief flooding over him. 'Yes, Miss Wildman, as you can see, your visit was the spur I needed to take some drastic action. There is now at least one room in the house that is devoid of books. I have to thank you for that and I must admit that I am greatly enjoying the unusual pleasure of sitting in an empty chair in front of the fire with the single book that I'm reading in my hand. When I am done, I return it to join its fellows in what has now become the most cluttered and disorderly library in the world.'

'How then can you find what you are looking for?' she asked.

'I usually don't. When I seek out a particular title I am always diverted by the tempting sight of another, so it doesn't make a lot of difference. Those books that I need to prepare my sermons I now keep in that cold little parlour I subjected you to on your last visit, so they're always to hand. One day I shall find the time to organise all my books properly and permanently.'

'By then you'll need a larger house as your collection will undoubtedly have grown.'

'Ah,' he sighed. 'You already have the measure of me. Shall we go for that walk?'

They left the parsonage and walked through the village, with Merritt pointing out the stern facade of the Wesleyan chapel, the two inns, the blacksmith's forge and the village school. It was a pretty village, many of the houses being very old, but cared for, with roses trailing over their walls and thatches well-groomed. Hephzibah appeared to be listening but asked no questions and Merritt lapsed into silence, worried that he had bored her.

'I have always lived in Oxford,' she said eventually. 'I know nothing of village life. Don't you find it dull?'

'I do miss conversation... the opportunity to debate with others, the stimulation of life at the university. But there are many compensations in Nettlestock. I love the countryside, the quiet, the opportunity to study without interruption. I sometimes fear I'm at risk of becoming something of a hermit. But then my duties do require me to interact with my flock from time to time, so there's no real danger of that.'

'You don't seem to me to be a person who shuns the company of others,' she said. 'You're far too nice for that.'

Merritt coughed. Did she really like him? Did he dare hope that one day she might come to feel for him a little of what he felt for her?

'Growing up,' she went on, 'I had lots of friends, but since Mama and Papa died, it has felt as though they have abandoned me. As if my loss might somehow contaminate them, or bring them misfortune. Oh, they were terribly kind and friendly when they saw me, but they stopped inviting me to their homes and went out of their way to avoid meeting me. But nothing is as hard as knowing I will never again see Mama and Papa. Even as time passes it is no easier.'

Her words filled him with sorrow for her. She looked so small and frail and he wished he could fling his arms around her and press her close against his chest.

Before he could find the right words to say, she continued. 'Are your parents alive, Reverend Nightingale? Are you close to them?'

'Yes and no,' he said. 'They live near Birmingham and I see them rarely. My father is a doctor and both my brothers followed him into general practice. He was disappointed that I didn't share their talent for the natural sciences, but preferred literature and studying the classics. He tried to push me to work harder and ready myself to study medicine, but I had neither the aptitude nor the desire. We quarrelled often. He told me once that I had let him down. I swore then that if I am ever blessed with children I will let them find their own paths and not expect them to follow mine.'

'And your mother?'

'An obedient wife.' He shook his head and looked away.

'What did they think about you becoming a clergyman?'

'I think Father thought it was the best possible outcome under the circumstances. His cousin was the former incumbent here and the living was passed to our family so Father urged me to take it.'

'You didn't set out to become a parson?'

'No. I never gave a lot of thought to religion. I went to church of course but that was as far as it went. I am not what one might call a man with a mission. I see it as a job. The duties are light. Just the regular services, the odd funeral, my sermon to write and, once a week, a Bible class at the village school.'

She smiled. 'I'm rather glad to hear that. I don't think I've ever got on with people who are very pious. I had hoped religion would have been more of a comfort to me when my parents died, that my faith would deepen, but instead their death has stretched it to the limits.'

As they turned off the village street and skirted around a large expanse of common-land, Merritt laid a hand on her arm. 'I can understand that. Sometimes I struggle to comprehend why God places such a heavy burden on some individuals and allows others to lead a charmed life. Every time I visit the workhouse in Mudford and see the wretched state of decent, honest people, or if I have to bury a small child, it feels so wrong. Last week I conducted the funeral for a young man whom I had married just six months earlier. He's left a widow expecting a child and with no one to provide for them. God can be very cruel.'

'You don't doubt your faith though?' she asked.

'To be honest I don't let myself think too deeply about it. I am afraid that if I did I might lose it altogether.' He stopped and turned to look at her. 'Have I shocked you, Miss Wildman?'

She shook her head and looked at him with interest.

'Only, I think if any of my parishioners or the bishop ever heard me speak like this I'd be run out of Nettlestock.'

'Your secret is safe with me.'

They were walking past a large red brick building that Merritt, in an effort to steer the conversation onto safer ground, told her was a water mill. 'There used to be a silk factory next to the mill, but now it's just used to grind corn. It's cheaper to import silk from abroad. I'm afraid a lot of the village's industries have suffered in recent years. There are chalk quarries nearby and there is a factory making whiting from the chalk. It's still going, but it produces a fraction of what it once did. It's hard here in the south. Industry is all about the north. We depend on agriculture here and with cheap imports of foodstuffs even that's dwindling every year. Nettlestock has become a backwater. Speaking of which…'

They were at a bend in the road and in front of them was the canal. A lock was on one side of the road bridge and an empty loading dock on the other. They went to stand on the bridge.

'Even the canal has seen better days. Built less than a century and already hardly used. All the whiting used to go by barge to Bristol, but now most of it's sent by train. There's the railway goods yard over there.' He pointed further down the lane. 'Poor old canal. The towpath's getting overgrown and I doubt the lock here opens more than once or twice a week.'

'What do the villagers do for work?' she asked.

'Mostly agricultural work. There are some still employed with the chalk pits and the whiting works. Not a lot else. Many left and went up north to work in the big mills and factories. The villagers tend to keep their distance from newcomers. They don't take to strangers. I think a lot of it stems from the riots back in 1830. Made everyone suspicious of everyone else.' He looked at Hephzibah sideways to reassure himself that he wasn't boring her. He was all too aware of his tendency to get carried away with his own enthusiasm.

She was frowning, her head on one side but her eyes reflected her interest. 'Riots? Here in Nettlestock?'

'Yes, here in this sleepy old village. Machine breakers. They went around smashing agricultural machinery and burning hayricks. It was all done out of fear. They were scared that the newfangled farm machinery would do them out of their jobs. They only wanted to protect their livelihoods. Feed their families. But the authorities had little sympathy. One night the ringleaders were meeting in the local ale house to plan their next raid when the doors opened and

Sir Rupert – Sir Richard's father, some of the other local magistrates, Lord Rochester-Palmer from Heddon Hall, and a troop of constables burst into the room. One of the so-called conspirators swung for it, poor devil, and the rest were all transported to Tasmania.'

'How dreadful. What happened to their families?'

'Who knows? Some will have struggled on. Most probably ended up in the workhouse. Hard to get by when the breadwinner's gone.'

'So their protests were self-defeating then?' She looked thoughtful.

'Aren't these things always that way?' he said. 'But it doesn't stop men hoping and wanting to make things better. I suppose they thought it was better to try than to do nothing. But we can't stop progress. It's seventy years ago but memories are long around here.'

They walked on along the towpath. The morning was warm with just a gentle breeze stirring the weeping willows on the banks. Merritt touched her arm and silently signalled to her to look across to the opposite bank where, in a flash of emerald green and blue, a kingfisher skimmed low across the water and then stopped motionless in the air before plunging down into the water after a fish. The bird burst up carrying its prey in its beak and disappeared into the foliage of the trees.

Hephzibah's face lit up and she squeezed his arm. 'I've never seen a kingfisher. What a thing of beauty it is. Thank you, Mr Nightingale, for showing me.'

They walked on, Merritt helping her around any obstacles – part of the path was waterlogged after the heavy rains. After a while the towpath almost disappeared, it was so overgrown. There were a couple of barges moored and covered over with waterlogged tarpaulins. There was no sign of any barges actually still plying the waterways.

They turned and took a path that led to the churchyard.

Hephzibah saw the clock on the tower showed a quarter to one. 'I'm going to be late,' she said. 'The squire won't like that.'

'I'm sorry,' Merritt said. 'My fault for talking too much. I'll walk with you back to the Hall. I promise to walk faster than I talk.'

He was rewarded with a beaming grin and a squeeze of the arm.

'Thank you, Reverend Nightingale. I'm so enjoying our conversation that I'd hate to cut it short. But won't I be keeping you from your own luncheon?'

He explained that he ate in the evening on Sundays to allow Mrs Muggeridge to spend the day at her sister's. 'I would be spending my time walking anyway and it is so much more pleasant to do so with you than alone.'

As they headed in the direction of Ingleton Hall, Merritt asked Hephzibah for her first impressions of the squire.

Hephzibah wrinkled her nose and then gave him a rueful smile. 'According to the housekeeper his bark is worse than his bite, but I've never been very fond of barking. I dare say I'll get used to him. I don't want to let you down after you have secured me the position, sir.'

'You won't do that,' Merritt said. 'I have faith in you. I know what you mean about Sir Richard though. I'm a bit afraid of him myself. He invites me to dinner occasionally and I find it something of an ordeal.'

A few minutes passed, then Merritt swallowed, took a deep breath and blurted, 'As we're both outsiders in Nettlestock and I feel we're already becoming friends, I wonder if you'd do me the honour of using my Christian name. Reverend Nightingale is such a mouthful. Please call me Merritt.' He wanted the ground to open up and swallow him as he waited for her response. Why had he wrecked things when they were going so well? Why did he try to rush her?

'Very well, Merritt, but you must do the same – I'm afraid though that my own name is even more of a mouthful. It's Hephzibah,' she said.

'Ah, Hephzibah, *my delight is in thee.*'

'You know your scriptures!'

'It would be unfortunate for me if I didn't. Although I must confess my knowledge of the Greek and Roman gods surpasses that of the Old Testament.' He paused for a few seconds then, conscious that his ears were turning their customary red, added, 'To tell you the truth, I already knew your name and I consulted my Bible the other day to find the source. It is indeed a most fitting name.' He looked at her intently.

To his relief, she laughed. 'My late father – my real father – was extremely fond of reading the Bible. He chose my name. My mother protested, saying it was old-fashioned, but he was determined to have his way.' She frowned. 'I had the impression, though I barely remember him, that my father was a man who always got his way.'

'I dislike my own name intensely,' he said.

'Why?' She gave him a puzzled look. 'I rather like it. It's unusual. And it has the benefit of having a mere two syllables.'

He shrugged. 'Unlike Nightingale.'

'Now I will not have you complain about that. To share a surname with a songbird is the most romantic thing.' She sighed. 'I'd swap you for Wildman!'

His heart hammered as he said the words in his head that he was too fearful to say out loud. *Take my surname. It's yours if you'll have it. If you'll have me.*

The moment passed. She appeared to be unaware of the ambiguity of her words. She turned to face him. 'Here we are. With ten minutes to spare.' She pointed to the clock on the tower of the stable block. 'Thank you so much, Merritt. I've had the most lovely time, since… well, you know… it has been very hard for me to feel the slightest lightness of spirit and this morning I have been... happy. Yes, happy! We must do this again.' She stretched out her hand to him.

He took her hand in his, feeling her thin fingers through the fabric of her gloves. Before he could stop himself he bent over it and brushed the back of her gloved hand with his lips.

'Goodbye, Hephzibah, and thank you. Perhaps we can do this again next Sunday?' Then before she could answer or he could give himself away, he turned on his heels and headed down the drive.

He walked briskly, fuelled by excitement. For the first time since setting eyes on Hephzibah he allowed himself to hope that, given time, she might consent to marry him. Walking the two miles back to the parsonage he indulged himself by imagining her sitting across the dining table from him or sitting at the other side of the fireplace in the drawing room, both of them reading, looking up every now and again from the pages to exchange a glance, a smile, or share something they had read. He pictured her brushing out her long brown hair at the end of the day in what would then be their bedroom.

He gave a little gasp. Dare he hope? She had seemed to enjoy his company. Hadn't she told him she'd been happy today? She was probably as lonely as he was. She'd given him some encouragement so now he must seize it.

CHAPTER FIVE

And the sunlight clasps the earth
And the moonbeams kiss the sea:
What are all these kissings worth
If thou kiss not me?

(from Love's Philosophy, Percy Bysshe Shelley)

Hephzibah entered the drawing room, where Sir Richard was sitting beside his daughter on a sofa. The little girl was reading aloud to him from a storybook and, judging by the expression on his face, the squire was becoming impatient. As Hephzibah walked over to join them he took out his fob watch and said, 'Cutting it fine, Miss Wildman.'

She decided to ignore him. She wasn't actually late.

When she failed to rise to his bait, the squire changed tack. 'Ottilie appears to be making some progress already under your tutelage, judging by her reading. Keep it up, Miss Wildman and you may even make a lady out of my little savage.'

Indignant, Ottilie slapped her father on the arm. 'I'm not a savage, Papa.'

He rose to his feet and Hephzibah was relieved to see that he was wearing shoes.

'Time for luncheon. Don't be a bore, child, or next Sunday I'll have you and Miss Wildman eat in the nursery and you don't want that, do you?'

'No, Papa,' she said, looking down, her big eyes welling with tears.

'Here. Take this.' He thrust the book into the girl's hands. 'Now where is that idiot? His timekeeping is worse than yours, Miss Wildman.'

'That idiot is here. I've been here for the last thirty minutes.' A disembodied voice spoke from behind a Chinese lacquer screen that stood in the corner of the room.

Hephzibah jumped. She was unaware of any guests joining them for lunch. Mrs Andrews had said nothing.

The man who stepped out from behind the screen caused her heart to skip a beat. He was older than her, perhaps about thirty, tall with long legs encased in riding breeches and leather boots. His blue eyes fixed upon Hephzibah.

'So you're the new governess,' he said. His voice was lazy, patrician, indulged, but the sound of it made Hephzibah feel weak-kneed. He moved towards her, those blue eyes appraising her from head to foot and coming back to rest on her face again. His mouth formed a smile which seemed to reach out and wrap around her. 'Miss Wildman.' He rolled the syllables of her name in his mouth as though he were tasting fine wine. 'I've heard a lot about you.'

Hephzibah felt herself blushing. 'I'm afraid you have the better of me, sir.'

The squire drained the contents of his wine glass. 'This is my son, Thomas. Now let's go and eat.' He ushered Hephzibah into the dining room, placing her on his left with Ottilie beside her, while Thomas Egdon sat on his right.

Trying to conceal her nerves, Hephzibah said, 'When did you arrive, Mr Egdon, and have you travelled far?'

'Late last night. I've been up in town for a week.'

The squire glared at his son. 'He spends his life in

London. And spends my money there too. It's long past time for him to choose a wife and settle down and give me some grandchildren. There have been Egdons in Nettlestock for five centuries and he seems determined to be the end of the line.' He slammed his hand down on the table, splashing red wine from the glass he had refilled. 'Damn it all, Thomas, I'll take another wife myself if you don't – and disinherit you.' He glanced at Hephzibah. 'Yes, I've a mind to do just that. A mother for Ottilie too. That'd stop you from gambling away what little's left in the estate.'

The conversation and language were hardly suitable for a ten-year-old child and Hephzibah, embarrassed by the outburst, said, 'Perhaps you would like to discuss this in private with your son, sir? I could ask Mrs Andrews to arrange for Ottilie and me to eat in the nursery so you can speak frankly.'

The squire put his hand on her arm. The pressure was hard, as though he were exerting control over her. 'You'll go nowhere. Ottilie's heard worse before and I daresay she will again. I expect you to make sure she understands the difference between the words that are acceptable for her to use and the words her long-suffering father says when he's severely provoked.' He glared at his son who was leaning back in his chair, staring at the ceiling.

One of the maids came in, bearing a tureen of soup, and there was silence until everyone had been served and she exited the room. Hephzibah took the opportunity to examine Thomas Egdon more closely. He was undeniably handsome, with a shock of thick, dark, almost-black hair and those limpid sapphire eyes. She was surprised that he had not seen fit to change out of his riding clothes before sitting down to eat. Perhaps that's how the landed gentry behaved. It was outside any canon of civilised behaviour known to her. She wondered if he had done it just to provoke his father. There was no disguising the hostility between them. As she looked at Thomas he glanced up and caught her watching him. She felt the blush suffusing her face. He smiled at her and she felt a shiver of pleasure.

'Yes, I've a mind to marry again,' said the father, his soup spoon suspended just below his blubbery lips. 'Someone to keep me young and take care of me in my old age. Someone to give me another son, one who won't be a wastrel and a gambler.' He slurped his soup and gave a chesty laugh.

Hephzibah wondered what sort of woman of child-bearing age would contemplate marriage to him, then remembered the mystery woman of the night before. The girl in church with the auburn hair. Was she the object of his plans? Then, with a sinking feeling, she realised that Thomas Egdon had arrived late last night. It was more likely that the ribbon thief had been visiting him than his father. She put down her spoon, her appetite gone. She wanted to make her excuses and get up from the table but she knew that she couldn't.

The squire was still talking. 'What do you have to say? Is it entirely up to me to safeguard the Egdon name?'

He turned his attention to Hephzibah, who was now rigid with shock. 'According to village gossip he's bedded half the young women in Nettlestock and not managed to get a single one of them in trouble, so even if he does take a wife I doubt I can rely on him to produce the goods.'

She looked across the table at Thomas Egdon, who must have been used to this kind of talk from his father, as he carried on eating his soup and appeared not to be listening. Ottilie also ate in silence. What kind of family was this?

It was then that a hand landed on her right thigh. Her leg jerked in reaction and she tried to edge away from his touch, but the squire's grip was firm. He ran his hand proprietorially up and down her thigh then rested it on her knee and squeezed her leg before taking his hand away. 'Yes. I've a mind to marry again.'

Hephzibah didn't know how she endured the rest of that wretched luncheon. She tried to steer the conversation onto safer ground, first encouraging Ottilie to tell her father and brother about the book she was reading and getting her to recite a poem she had learned the day before. That occupied but a few minutes. Valiantly, she tried to ask questions about the village and the history of the house, but Thomas Egdon remained silent and his father yawned and told her to ask Mrs Andrews. He drank steadily throughout the rest of the meal, leaving a growing pattern of red wine stains on the tablecloth.

When she was finally reprieved, Hephzibah left Ottilie playing with her dolls and went to walk alone in the gardens. There was a wooden seat under an oak tree where she would be out of sight from the house. As she sat down she realised she was still shaking with anger and fear. It was humiliating. Squire Egdon had treated her as though she were his to do with as he wished. Hephzibah was ashamed that she had not cried out when his hand pawed her leg – and asked herself why she hadn't. It had been so embarrassing that she had scarcely believed it was happening. She'd also been conscious of Ottilie sitting beside her and Thomas Egdon seated opposite. Her face burned at the thought that he had witnessed her humiliation. Then she reminded herself that the son and heir had been more publicly humiliated than she had. At least the squire's wandering hands were concealed beneath the tablecloth whereas the aspersions he had cast upon his own son's manhood were not.

The sun was weak and watery and there was a slight chill in the air. Autumn would soon be coming. Hephzibah inwardly cursed that she had not thought to bring her shawl with her, but was not inclined to go back into the house and risk another encounter with her employer. Instead she decided to go for another walk. Being on the move would warm her up and at least she was getting plenty of exercise.

She followed a path that led in the opposite direction to the village and soon found herself close to a small tributary that fed into the canal. There was no clearly defined towpath here, just a well-worn track, muddy in places from the recent rain. On the other side was an expanse of water meadows, grazed by a few sheep. It was quiet and she stopped, standing still, listening to the sounds of the birds. She would have to get to know them – a project for her to undertake with Ottilie perhaps? There was a large illustrated book of British birds on a side table in the drawing room and she made a mental note to build a lesson around it tomorrow. She wandered along beside the stream, heedless of the mud sticking to her boots, lifting her skirt clear of any puddles.

Hephzibah forced herself to focus on the dilemma that faced her. Here she was with a position that she enjoyed, teaching a child she was already growing fond of, in a part of the country she found attractive and, most important of all, with a modest income and a roof over her head. Until today she had thought of Sir Richard Egdon as an eccentric, a boor, a bit of a bully perhaps but – using Mrs Andrews' words – with a bark worse than his bite. Now she felt contaminated, dirtied by his insistent hand upon her leg and, worse still, by the words that had accompanied his action. Did he seriously expect that she would marry him? Doubtless he thought of himself as a good catch: a wealthy man with a substantial property. The thought of his swollen red foot, his thick wet lips and those piercing dark eyes with the deep shadows underneath them, made her shiver. He had said he wanted to marry in order to father more children. She felt sick at the thought of him touching her. What was she to do? If he asked and she refused him, she would jeopardise her employment, risk being made homeless. Had this been the fate of all those other governesses? In anger, she kicked at a rotten tree stump by the side of the path, sending up a small shower of damp wood chips.

Being a woman was hard enough, but being a woman alone was worse. Men thought of women as mere commodities to be bargained over. Would this be her fate, pressured to accept the advances of an old, gout-ridden lecher in preference to being cast out on the streets?

As Hephzibah walked along, her mind churning over her lack of choices, she worked hard to convince herself that the squire's behaviour was down to the fact that he was drunk and just posturing in front of his son. He had already started drinking before luncheon and had gone on to consume an enormous quantity of wine during the meal. People did behave out of character when they drank too much – the students at Oxford had often demonstrated that. Somewhat mollified, she turned back towards Ingleton Hall. She decided to vary her route, taking another path that skirted the edge of a copse of trees.

As she moved towards the copse she saw there was someone there. A man and a woman were leaning against the trunk of a tree, locked in an embrace. Embarrassed, she stopped dead, looking around her for another pathway that would avoid passing close by the couple. As she hesitated, they drew apart and the man ran his hands through the woman's chestnut hair. She lifted her face up to his. The ribbon thief. The man bent down and dropped a kiss on the top of her head and then she disappeared into the trees. Hephzibah was frozen to the spot.

Thomas Egdon leaned down and picked up his jacket from the ground, brushing off the leaves that had clung to it. He didn't appear to have seen her and Hephzibah tried to calculate whether she could get out of sight before he noticed her. She looked about but there was nowhere to hide. Going back the way she had come risked that if he spotted her he would think she had walked past him while he was kissing the woman. Hephzibah decided to walk on and hope that he would think she had been too far away to see anything, wondering why his behaviour was making her feel guilty, as though she had done something wrong.

Hephzibah moved slowly along the pathway, looking at the sky and bending now and then to inspect a flower – a piece of theatre designed to convey that she was too preoccupied to have noticed anyone else.

'Miss Wildman!' He came over the grass in a half-run. 'Taking a walk?'

She felt herself blushing again. Damn the man. Why did he have this effect on her? She knew it was because she was imagining herself being pushed up against the trunk of that tree and kissed passionately.

He fell into step beside her. 'I apologise for my father's behaviour today. He's always at his worst when he's in his cups.'

'It's not up to you to apologise for him. I think he owes an apology to you, sir,' she said.

'Water off a duck's back. He never varies his routine. It's such a bore. I'm just sorry you had to listen to it.'

She wondered whether the squire knew about his son's relationship with the Ribbon Thief, as she had taken to thinking of her. Did Thomas Egdon plan to marry the woman? She supposed he must since he had kissed her so openly. He had done more probably, as the woman had been with him in that bedroom. Did the squire know? If he did, he would be unlikely to regard it a suitable match.

Hephzibah shook her head and tried to change the conversation. 'The Hall grounds and the area around Nettlestock is very pretty. I've been walking beside the stream over there.'

He shrugged. 'I hate it here. Petty-minded people. Nothing of interest to do. I stay up in town as often as I can. The old man keeps me on short rations, so I have to come back whenever I need a top-up of funds.'

Hephzibah frowned. He did indeed sound like the

wastrel his father had called him. 'How do you spend your time? Are you occupied in some way with the running of the estate?'

He raised his eyebrows. 'Running the estate? Not much of it left to run and what's left is mostly handled by the bailiff. Between him and my father, there's no room left for me. Ingleton Hall saw its best days long ago.'

'I'm sorry to hear that.'

'Mishandled by my father who has about as much grasp of land management and modern agricultural methods as Mrs Andrews does.'

Hephzibah glanced sideways at him. He was impossibly handsome. In profile his nose had a slight hook and his chin was strong. His moustache was the same dark silk as his hair and eyebrows. His mouth had a slightly cruel look that made her feel vulnerable and excited and she shivered as she walked beside him.

He noticed, and slipped the jacket he was carrying over her shoulders. 'I suppose you get along with all your relatives?' he said.

'I have none left to get along with. My parents died two months ago.'

Egdon looked away. 'I'm sorry,' he said, eventually. 'Did you get along with them when they were alive?'

'Yes,' she said. 'And I miss them both every single day.'

He was silent for a few moments then said, 'I missed my mother when she died. I still miss her. Badly. That's why I hate my father so much. I hold him responsible for her death.' His voice took on a quiet, angry tone. 'He left it too late to summon the doctor. By the time he did, she was too far gone. He's always been a miser. Unless it's to keep his wine cellar stocked.'

'I'm sorry about your mother. Apart from Ottilie, do you have any brothers and sisters?'

He sighed. 'I had two brothers. One older and one younger. The younger one, Roddy, was killed last year at

Magersfontein. Samuel died six years ago. Sam was my father's favourite.' He looked at her, his eyes narrowing and his expression closed. 'Shot himself. Father has never got over it. Every time he looks at me it's as if he's wishing me gone and Sam or Roddy here in my place.' He picked up a twig from the path and snapped it, casting the two pieces into the grassy meadow.

'And your sister?' she asked.

'Ottilie's not my real sister. She's my cousin. Father adopted her after her mother died. My mother and my aunt both contracted tuberculosis. My aunt soon after Ottilie was born, my mother a few years later, just before Sam killed himself. It was Mother's dying wish that Father take Ottilie in. She's like you – an orphan.'

'How terribly sad. I had no idea Ottilie wasn't Sir Richard's daughter.'

'Why would you?' He bent down and picked up another twig to snap apart. 'Father has always treated her as though she were his own daughter. I wouldn't even be surprised if she were. He's always been a womaniser. I doubt the fact that Ottilie's mother was the sister of his wife would have held him back.' He turned to look at her. 'You're shocked, aren't you, Miss Wildman?'

She didn't know how to respond. What kind of place was Ingleton Hall? What kind of morality did the occupants live by? It was very different from her own.

'And your uncle? Didn't he object to the squire adopting Ottilie when his wife died?'

'You ask a lot of questions, don't you, Miss Wildman?' He smiled at her and she felt herself blushing again.

'I'm sorry,' she said. 'It's none of my business.'

'He was in the army. He wasn't around. Barely saw Ottilie. Then he was killed at Magersfontein too. He was the damned fool who persuaded Roddy to join up. Same regiment.'

'Does Ottilie know all this?'

Egdon shrugged. 'I doubt it. She was only a baby when her mother died and four when my mother passed away. The squire is the only parent she remembers. She was very close to Roddy though. Cried for days when she found out he wouldn't be coming home.'

Before Hephzibah could ask anything else, Thomas Egdon stepped in front of her, blocking her way. 'You are an uncommonly pretty woman, Miss Wildman.' He reached a hand out and tucked a stray curl behind her ear. 'Yes, uncommonly pretty.' He tilted her chin up and examined her face. Running a finger down her cheek, he said, 'I know my father tried to touch you at lunch today.'

Hephzibah felt her face burning. Thomas looked into her eyes. 'I know him of old and I could see the expression on your face. You showed remarkable self-control not to cry out.'

'I was in shock. I didn't know what to do.'

'Yes, that's what he relies on. Tell me if he tries to touch you again – and I'll kill the bastard.'

Thomas set off without another word, walking briskly away from the path, cutting across the long grassy meadow towards the distant Hall, leaving Hephzibah in a state of confusion.

When she got back to the house, she found Mrs Andrews placing an arrangement of flowers in the hallway. Hephzibah realised she was still wearing Thomas Egdon's jacket.

'I hope you enjoyed your walk, Miss Wildman?'

Hephzibah was relieved at the absence of sarcasm in the woman's tone. 'I did. The countryside around here is beautiful.'

'You think so? A bit too flat for my taste, but then I come from the West Riding of Yorkshire. I like a few rugged hills to look at. Look at only, mind. You won't catch me traipsing around the countryside in all weathers.' The older woman paused as though weighing something up, then said, 'Would you care to join me for a cup of tea in my parlour, Miss Wildman?'

Surprised but pleased, Hephzibah mumbled her thanks and followed Mrs Andrews back to the rear of the building, where the housekeeper's parlour was next to the kitchen. As they entered the room Mrs Andrews stretched out her hand in the direction of the jacket and said, 'I'll take that, shall I? I'll give it a brushing and see Master Thomas gets it back.'

Hephzibah felt herself blushing but handed over the garment without a word.

Once they were seated with cups of tea in a pair of uncomfortable chairs either side of the small unlit fireplace, Hephzibah took the opportunity to satisfy her curiosity. 'There was a woman at church this morning whom I've seen about the estate. She has copper-coloured hair and I was wondering who she might be, as I've not seen her among the servants here.'

The housekeeper nodded her head slowly. 'Abigail Cake. The daughter of Ned Cake, the squire's bailiff.' Mrs Andrews pursed her lips. 'Why are you asking?'

Hephzibah hesitated, then decided not to tell her about the missing hair ribbons. Instead she said, 'I noticed her in church this morning. Her hair is such a pretty colour and with those curls she looks like a girl in a painting by Titian.'

Mrs Andrews sniffed. 'I wouldn't know about that. I can't say as I've ever seen a painting by Tish… whoever you said. But she is a pretty girl, I'll grant you that. Too pretty for her own good, if you ask me. Too handy with her favours. Down to the lack of a mother, I suppose. Hers died ten years ago and the lass has had to be mother to her brothers and sisters. Eight of them there are.' She sipped at her tea, dabbing at her mouth with a napkin. 'Abi comes up to the Hall once a week to polish the silver. She's been doing that since she was a little girl.'

The housekeeper looked thoughtful and shook her

head slowly. 'Ned Cake is a hard man. Can't be easy for Abi. I may not approve of her behaviour but I can't criticise her hard work. She also works as a seamstress – takes in mending, as well as looking after her father and those wild children. And still finds time to help others who need it in the village. No, I'll not be one to judge the girl.'

Sipping her tea, Hephzibah was glad she'd refrained from mentioning the ribbons, but she couldn't help thinking about how Thomas Egdon had kissed the girl with such passion. Was that what Mrs Andrews meant about her being too generous with her favours? Or did that mean Thomas was one of many of Abigail's admirers? And was she one of many of his?

Lying in bed that night, Hephzibah tossed and turned, unable to sleep, her brain in a turmoil. In just a few months her whole world had changed and she felt ill-equipped to deal with this new reality. She thought of the three men she had met since coming here: the kindly parson, the lecherous squire and the handsome troubled Thomas. The vicar had extended the hand of friendship and his company was not uncongenial. He knew a lot about the parish and was undoubtedly intelligent and well-read, but Hephzibah suspected she might find him dull with further acquaintance. The squire was definitely a man to be avoided – especially when he was drinking. She shuddered to think of that hand on her thigh and the ominous tone he had used when expressing his intent to marry again. She told herself it was said just to annoy his son: he couldn't possibly have had her in mind.

And then there was Thomas, handsome Thomas, who made her both afraid and excited. She had never felt that way about a man before – when she had first seen him it was as though moths were fluttering in her stomach. At the thought of him kissing that Cake woman she was riven with jealousy. She wondered what it would feel like to be crushed against the trunk of a tree, to feel his body pressing against hers, to have his hands tangled up in her hair, to feel his mouth on hers, to have those icy blue eyes looking into hers. *Stop it! He loves someone else.* The way he had been kissing the woman, wrapping his hands in her hair, sent a signal that he must care for Abigail Cake. On the other hand, Sir Richard had said that Thomas had seduced half the women in Nettlestock. The red-haired woman had been in one of the bedrooms with him. Perhaps he didn't love her but was using her? Either way, he was not a man of honour. And not the man for her. As she said this to herself she groaned. She wanted him. Wanted him in a way she had never wanted anything in her life before. It was a desperate, all-consuming desire. She wanted him to be lying here beside her now.

She asked herself how she would have felt if the hand on her thigh under the table had been Thomas's. She moved her own hand there and gave a little gasp as she ran it up her leg and touched herself. Hephzibah had no knowledge of men, had never held a man's hand or been kissed. She turned onto her front and buried her head in the pillow as her fingers moved between her legs. She tried to imagine the fingers touching her were Thomas's and began to moan softly. It felt strange, thrilling, as little ripples of pleasure ran through her body. Excited, but ashamed, she abruptly pulled her hand away, shocked at herself and her lack of control.

Her last thought as she fell into a deep sleep was of Thomas Egdon, his blue eyes locked onto hers, his hard mouth moving towards hers, his arms crushing her against him.

The next morning at breakfast she discovered he had already returned to London.

CHAPTER SIX

I dare not gaze upon her face
But left her memory in each place;
Where'er I saw a wild flower lie
I kissed and bade my love good-bye.

(from I Hid My Love, John Clare)

October 1900

The autumn sun reflected off the water and the wind rustled through the branches of the willow trees that lined the banks of the canal beyond the towpath. There was a sharp chill in the air. The summer was now a distant memory.

Merritt walked briskly, trying to keep warm. He was still smarting from the standoffish reception he had received from most of the parishioners he had called on that morning. No matter how hard he tried, they were willing enough to seek help for financial problems, to arrange for their babies to be baptised, for the banns to be called or their dead to be shepherded into the next world, but inviting him to cross their threshold was still a step too far. Was he destined always to be an outsider, a cuckoo in the Nettlestock nest?

The parson's heart lifted when he saw a distant figure sitting on a style. Hephzibah was motionless, staring out over the fields watching a gang of agricultural workers, mostly women, digging turnips.

Merritt came up beside her and asked if he might join her, suddenly heedless of the cold. She motioned for him to sit beside her. 'I stopped to watch the workers. It's bitterly cold and the ground looks hard as stone. What a miserable way to make a living.'

The clergyman nodded. 'It's unpleasant work, but at least it's dry today and the sun is shining. It's must be much worse in the rain. And they have to get the turnips in before the frosts.'

Hephzibah looked at the gang as they worked, a frown creasing her brow. 'Some of them are still children. They should be at school, not standing bent double in a freezing field picking turnips. The accident of birth is a cruel thing. I have never had to lift a finger in labour but have been privileged to be taught, to study, to read. Those girls probably know nothing of the world, of the magical places they can visit through books. I can't begin to imagine what it would be like to do what they are doing, day after day, no matter what the weather.'

'Many of them would disagree with you. They would see a classroom as akin to a prison and long to be out in the fields. It's a matter of what one's used to.' Merritt shivered, less from the cold than from her proximity. It would be so easy to stretch out and touch her cheek or stroke her hair, but he kept his hands clamped tightly to his knees. 'At least now and in winter, though the weather is cold, the daylight hours are shorter. In summer they are in the field from dawn until dusk.'

'Would you care to walk a while with me?' she asked, her voice hesitant. 'Unless you are about your parish business?'

In response, Merritt jumped to the ground and held out

a steadying hand to help her down from the style. 'It would give me great pleasure.'

They skirted the turnip field and took a stony track down to a stream that fed the water meadows. For a while they walked in companionable silence, until Hephzibah broke it with a question. 'Last time we went for a walk you told me you never planned to become a clergyman. What did you want to be when you were a boy?'

He looked at her, surprised but flattered by her interest. 'A bargee,' he said.

Hephzibah raised her eyebrows.

Merritt told her of his childhood near Birmingham and how he had loved watching the bargemen taking their craft through the locks. 'I'd spend many a happy hour helping to open the gates and never got tired of seeing the locks fill up and empty. So many times I wished I could jump on board and sail down the canal on one of those barges – floating away to wherever it carried us. What about you? Did you always want to be a governess?'

Hephzibah looked at him, her eyes sad. 'You must know I didn't. The thought didn't enter my head until you wrote to me and suggested the position at Ingleton Hall.'

Merritt felt his face reddening. He muttered an apology. What an idiot he was to so tactlessly remind her of her parents' deaths and how that tragedy had radically changed her life and her expectations.

'When I was a child I wanted to be an explorer,' she said. 'My father was a botanist and spent a lot of time in Africa.'

'Dr Prendergast?' Merritt asked in surprise.

'Dr Prendergast was my mother's second husband. My real father died when I was a small child. I don't remember him at all but I used to look at all the maps and books in his study. I thought that might make me feel closer to him, since I never knew him. I would dream of visiting all those faraway places, like Mungo Park or Livingstone and Stanley.'

Her eyes looked up, as though trying to conjure up the memory of her childhood self. Merritt studied her profile as they walked along. She turned to face him. 'If you could go anywhere in the world, Merritt, where would you go?'

He smiled. 'That's an easy choice. It has to be Italy. Rome. I would dearly love to walk the remains of the streets where Ovid once walked. To stroll along the Appian Way. To stand on the Capitoline Hill. To watch the sun setting behind silhouetted cypress trees and know that I was gazing at the same vista that the emperors looked upon.' He blushed again and rubbed at the back of his neck. 'One day, Hephzibah, I will do it.' He paused a moment then said tentatively, 'I suppose you would choose Africa?'

She shook her head. 'Certainly not. Now that I'm older and wiser I know I wouldn't like Africa at all. Like you, I wanted to visit Rome. In fact I would have been there now had my parents not died.'

She paused and Merritt felt a surge of joy – they had so much in common. Then she spoke again and his heart sank. 'I will never go now – I wouldn't want to – not without Mama and Papa. It would be unbearably sad. I'd spend the whole time feeling lonely without them and imagining how different it would be with them there. No. I will never go to Rome. It's ruined for me.'

A horse whinnied and they heard the clopping of hooves behind them on the hard track. They moved apart, off the centre of the footpath to allow the horse room to pass them. Instead the rider pulled his horse up and jumped off. It was Thomas Egdon.

Merritt raised his hat in greeting, but Egdon ignored him, turning to Hephzibah, whom he greeted effusively. 'Miss Wildman, what an unexpected pleasure. Please allow me to accompany you back to the Hall.'

Hephzibah gave the briefest of glances towards Merritt and the slightest of hesitations, before replying that, yes, she would be delighted if he would walk back with her as the afternoon was growing late and it would save Reverend Nightingale having to make a diversion. She turned then to Merritt. 'Thank you so much for accompanying me this afternoon, Reverend Nightingale. It is always a pleasure to have a companion when walking and you know so much about the area. We must do this again.'

Egdon gave her a beaming smile. He wished a good day to Merritt and set off on foot, leading his horse, with Hephzibah walking beside him. A despondent Merritt headed back to the village in the opposite direction, seething at the way Egdon had treated Hephzibah as though she were his personal property and Merritt himself as if he were invisible and inconsequential.

CHAPTER SEVEN

Say what strange Motive, Goddess! cou'd compel
A well-bred Lord t'assault a gentle Belle?
Oh say what stranger Cause, yet unexplor'd,
Cou'd make a gentle Belle reject a Lord?
And dwells such Rage in softest Bosoms then?
And lodge such daring Souls in Little Men?

(from The Rape of the Lock, Alexander Pope)

Three months after Hephzibah had arrived at Ingleton Hall, she and Ottilie were in the small drawing room that they used for daily lessons. The nursery was cold and sparsely furnished and Mrs Andrews had suggested that they make use of the little room that overlooked the formal gardens at the side of the house. While referred to as the "small drawing room" it was far from small, except in comparison to the much grander rooms on the front elevation. There was a pianoforte, a mahogany table where they could work on lessons, and a comfortable sofa where they sat for the last hour of study every day, so Hephzibah could hear Ottilie read.

The child was bright, although behind in her studies. The frequent changes of governesses had disrupted her education and her reading was slow and hesitant. She preferred to spend time in the saddle rather than with her head in a book. Hephzibah tried to instil confidence in the little girl by praising and encouraging her and Ottilie began to show a gradual improvement. Her piano playing and singing became more confident – she had a strong but sweet voice and loved to use it. The pair sat side-by-side at the piano for an hour every morning, and again in the afternoon while the governess first heard her scales. After practising her pieces, the child would play duets with Hephzibah and sing.

As they finished the music lesson that afternoon, Ottilie turned on the piano stool and looked up at her teacher, her eyes anxious. 'You won't leave me like the other ladies did, will you, Miss Wildman? Please don't go. I like you better than any of them.'

Hephzibah laid a hand on the child's arm. 'What do you mean? What other ladies?'

'The other governesses. They all went away. One of them after only a week.'

'Why did they leave?'

'I don't know. I thought at first it was because they didn't like me, but Miss Walters cried when she said goodbye to me and told me she would miss me, so that can't be true, can it?'

'Did your father ask them to leave? Perhaps he wasn't happy with how they were teaching you.'

'He did ask Miss Baxter to go, but I think the others just decided to leave. Two of them went without saying goodbye to me. Mrs Andrews had chosen Miss Baxter while Papa was away and when he came back he didn't think she was suitable. I was pleased because I didn't really like Miss Baxter. She was very old and had whiskers growing out of a big mole on her face and when she talked bits of spit flew out of her mouth.'

Hephzibah smiled. She could imagine why Miss Baxter would have found no favour with Sir Richard.

'My favourite governess was Miss Gordon. She was pretty, like you. Papa used to spend a lot of time with her. He always asked her to read to him in the library when I went to bed, but then one evening I looked out of the bedroom window and saw her crying in the garden and the next morning when I got up she'd already gone.'

'I see.' Hephzibah remembered the wandering hands under the table. Was she about to suffer the same fate as her predecessors?

Hephzibah saw Ottilie to bed and heard her prayers. She came back downstairs to the small drawing room, where she intended to read for a while before going to bed herself. The hall was in semi-darkness apart from a welcoming sliver of light under the drawing room door. Mrs Andrews had instructed the maids to light the lamps for her. She was turning the door knob when someone came up behind her and placed his hands either side of her waist. Hephzibah almost burst out of her skin. She cried out and jerked forward as she felt the squire's breath on her neck. His body pressed against hers, pushing her against the door. She turned the handle and they lurched into the room.

Sir Richard lost his footing and landed on his knees at her feet. 'Goddammit! What the hell?'

She seized the advantage to back out of the door and race up the stairs as fast as her legs would carry her. She burst into her bedroom, turned the key in the lock and leaned against the door, panting as she tried to regain her breath and her composure.

How could she possibly stay any longer in this house? The man was insufferable. She was in danger, scared he would stop at nothing and might even try to take her by force. Was it her own fault? Was she to blame for having lustful thoughts about Thomas? Was God punishing her?

She flung herself on the bed and felt the tears pricking her eyes. Why was she alone like this with no one to turn to? Mama, why did you leave me? What should I do? What would you advise if you were here?

There was no response from her mother. Just the hooting of an owl. If she were to sort out this situation she must do it alone.

By the next morning she had made her decision. She went to seek out Mrs Andrews and, finding her in the kitchen supervising the breakfast preparations, asked if she might have a word in private.

The housekeeper frowned but led her into her parlour.

'I'll get straight to the point, Mrs Andrews. Last night the squire acted in an inappropriate way towards me. It's not the first time. He put his hand on my leg under the table while we were at luncheon the first Sunday I was here.'

Mrs Andrews sighed and motioned Hephzibah to sit. 'I wondered how long it would take. I did warn you.'

'But I had no idea. Not that he would go so far. And I got the impression from Ottilie that none of the governesses lasted long here. I think you need to tell me the truth.'

Mrs Andrews leaned back in her chair and folded her arms. 'I don't know whether you've noticed, Miss Wildman, but the maids who work here are not exactly endowed with youth and beauty. I'm responsible for hiring them so I choose those who are unlikely to attract the attention of his lordship. I have no say over governesses. I hoped that you, having been found by Reverend Nightingale, might be… how shall I say? …plainer than the squire himself would have chosen.' She pursed her lips. 'But you have turned out to be anything but.'

Hephzibah ignored the back-handed compliment. 'I need you to tell me everything.'

The woman sighed, then unfolded her arms, placed them on her knees and leaned forward. 'It's not really my place to say this, but say it I will. The squire is lonely. I don't think he means real harm. He's a man without a wife. And he does have a sense of… how shall I put it? …entitlement. He seems to think everyone in his employ is fair game. The trouble is most of those governesses had ideas above their station. Thought when he showed them a bit of attention they'd soon be mistress of Ingleton. Too daft for their own good.' She shook her head.

Hephzibah stared at her with horror. What had she let herself in for coming here to Ingleton Hall?

The woman went on. 'He'd drop hints about taking a new wife and they were flattered. When they realised he had no intention of marrying them they were out of here, full of indignation and hurt pride. The only one he managed to take to his bed was Emily Gordon. She was dafter than the others. Sir Richard was engaged to be married to Lady Catherine Roderick but that girl thought she'd win him over. Maybe he promised her and she was soft-headed enough to believe him.'

Mrs Andrews let out another long-suffering sigh. 'The lass was young and pretty and thought she'd see off Lady Catherine. But men like Sir Richard don't marry pretty young girls. They marry to bolster their fortunes. Lady Catherine's a widow. Her husband was a Member of Parliament, a friend of the squire's. It would have been a marriage of convenience. But then Lady Catherine got wind of what that girl had got up to with her intended and forced him to send her packing. And then she jilted him herself.' She tutted, shaking her head again. 'And the truth is, the one who really suffers from all this is Ottilie. She was very fond of Miss Gordon, whatever the woman's faults were. And the others. Just as she gets used to a new governess her father causes them to leave.'

'How dreadful,' said Hephzibah. 'The man must be a monster.'

'Don't let him drive you away, Miss Wildman. I can tell Ottilie really likes you and the girl deserves better. Only the other day the squire told me how well she's doing with you.'

'But I can't put up with him trying to molest me – creeping up on me and pouncing. I can't live like that.'

'Tell him then. Now I have to get on.' Mrs Andrews rose and held open the door for Hephzibah to leave.

She took a few deep breaths and marched straight into the dining room where the squire was accustomed to taking his breakfast alone each morning. He was there behind a copy of the *Berkshire Chronicle*.

He lowered the newspaper in irritation. 'Oh, it's you,' he said. 'What do you want?'

Hephzibah pulled out a chair and sat down. 'I want to talk about what happened last night.'

'Don't know what you're talking about.' He picked up the newspaper again and shook the pages into place.

'I think we need to get a few things clear,' said Hephzibah. 'I am here as your daughter's governess and expect to be treated as such. I am not a common prostitute or a milkmaid looking for a tumble in the hay with the master in exchange for an extra loaf of bread.'

She could hear the trembling in her voice but forced herself to go on. 'I understand you've already worked through a long procession of governesses and Ottilie's education has suffered as a result. She is doing very well at the moment. Her reading and writing and piano playing are improving. She likes me and I like her. She needs continuity and not the sudden changes that have been inflicted on her as a result of your behaviour. I want you to think of your daughter, not just of yourself.'

His eyes were hooded and narrowed but she fancied he looked ashamed as well as angry. He put his newspaper down on the table.

She continued. 'Here's what I propose. We will forget

about what happened last night. We will forget about what you did and said during that Sunday luncheon when your son was here. I will continue to teach your little girl and you will afford me the respect that I deserve. But if you ever lay a hand on me again I will go straight to the Reverend Nightingale and tell him exactly what kind of man you are so he can shame you from the pulpit if he chooses. And I will be on the next train back to Oxford. I will explain to Ottilie that my departure is due to the predatory behaviour of her father. I will explain to her that you did the same thing to all the other governesses. The choice is yours.'

Hephzibah got up from the chair and clutched the back of it to steady herself, hoping he would not realise how much her hands were shaking.

The squire picked up his paper again and made a show of folding it back into its previous neat sections. He turned to her and looked at her in silence for a moment, then said, 'Feisty little filly you are, aren't you? And you drive a hard bargain. I like that. Very well. We will forget about it and it won't happen again. Now get out of here and let me enjoy my kippers in peace.'

CHAPTER EIGHT

Oh! the pain of pains,
Is when the fair one, whom our soul is fond of,
Gives transport, and receives it from another

(from Busiris, Edward Young)

The squire was entertaining guests – a rare occurrence these days according to Mrs Andrews. The excuse for the dinner was the early December victory of the Conservatives over the Liberals in the general election, on the wave of Boer War sentiment. His dinner guests were the parson, the local doctor and his wife, the village schoolmistress, the local postmistress, Hephzibah and Thomas Egdon, who had returned from London that afternoon for the occasion.

Hephzibah was nervous – the prospect of seeing Thomas again, after what had turned into a lengthy absence from the Hall, both excited and terrified her. And it would be her first meeting with the other guests – indeed the first time she had been formally introduced to any of the people of Nettlestock, apart from Merritt Nightingale. Her nerves were made no calmer by Mrs Andrews letting her know that the invitees were, in her opinion, while perfectly respectable pillars of village life, definitely not "out of the top drawer".

The implication was that Hephzibah wasn't either.

'You must have made a good impression on Sir Richard,' Mrs Andrews said. 'He's made an effort to invite guests of a similar status and background to your own. He doesn't always bother.'

Hephzibah tried to conceal her irritation at Mrs Andrews' poorly concealed belittlement.

The housekeeper raised one eyebrow and turned her head slightly, assessing Hephzibah through narrowed eyes. 'I presume you've had no more trouble from Sir Richard since you talked to him?'

'I think he and I understand each other now, Mrs Andrews.'

Hephzibah wore a simple black gown, cinched tightly at the waist, with embroidery above the hem, adding her mother's locket and a pair of pearl earrings. She hoped the evening would not be too much of an ordeal. The only dinner parties she had ever attended had been Oxford college ones, with dons and their wives, where the conversation focused on her stepfather's passions for classical culture and architecture, university politics, art and music. Occasionally, she had been asked to play the piano and she had always felt relaxed and in her element. She wondered what topics the good people of Nettlestock would talk about and whether she would feel out of her depth – she hoped it would not be all Boer War and politics. She decided her best approach was to smile, look interested and volunteer nothing.

The first to arrive were Dr and Mrs Desmond. He was a thin, bespectacled man who had little to say. His portly wife was like a roly-poly toy and had one of those unfortunate faces that, when resting, appeared to be permanently scowling, but she proved to be friendly enough when drawn into conversation.

The parson arrived soon after, along with the schoolmistress and postmistress, all in the carriage the squire had sent for them. Miss Pickering, the teacher, was painfully shy and looked as though she wanted to flee. Small and slender, she had a pale face and fine, wispy hair that resembled a dandelion clock that would blow away in the slightest breeze. Her lips looked raw and bitten and when she removed her gloves, Hephzibah saw that she chewed her nails.

Mrs Bellamy, the postmistress, was a tall widow with a mop of white curls, a walking stick and a booming voice. She appeared to brook no opinion but her own and had a tendency to talk over the top of the other guests, ignoring anything they had to say. If someone mentioned the wet weather, she took it as a cue to speak of her own experience during the wettest-ever winter. When Miss Pickering mentioned that her mother came from Ireland, Mrs Bellamy immediately launched into a lengthy diatribe about Irish history and Irish people she had known. When the conversation inevitably took in the victory of Lord Salisbury in the election she took that as a cue to speak about a recent visit to the town of Salisbury.

The last to enter the room was Thomas Egdon, who ignored the guests, sat down, slumping indolently in his chair, then appeared to notice Hephzibah was in the company. He adjusted his position and smiled at her across the drawing room as she sipped her glass of sherry. He scowled at the parson, who had assumed a position between Hephzibah and the doctor's wife and was speaking to them both animatedly.

Merritt Nightingale was recounting the story of Cephalus and Procris, the subject of his Ovid translation that day. As he told the tragic tale of the couple who were desperately in love yet each misled into believing the other's adultery, he used his hands in extravagant gestures. Hephzibah and Mrs Gordon were enthralled, less by the story than by the passion with which it was recounted. Hephzibah reflected that the parson was a gifted and expressive storyteller. A good quality for a minister.

Merritt ended the tale with Cephalus mistaking his wife for a stag, when she spied on him from the undergrowth, and spearing her to death. The story over, Hephzibah glanced in Thomas's direction but he had disappeared. The gong was sounded to summon the company into the dining room and she felt a little stab of disappointment that he was not to join them at dinner after all.

On entering the dining room, to her chagrin on the arm of the squire, she saw Thomas was waiting in position, holding her chair for her before slipping into the seat beside hers at the opposite end of the table to the squire whose face resembled an angry dog's. As they all took their places Thomas whispered to her that he had moved the place cards.

'Where was I meant to sit?' she asked him, smiling, taking advantage of the murmur around the table as everyone greeted the people next to them.

'Beside my father, of course. I felt duty-bound to rescue you.'

Postponing the continuation of their conversation, Hephzibah turned to greet her other neighbour and found that it was Merritt Nightingale. The squire, at the head of the table, was flanked by the rotund Mrs Desmond and the imperious Mrs Bellamy. He looked as though he had been forced to suck a lemon. Miss Pickering sat on Thomas's left, beside Dr Desmond.

For the first ten minutes or so Thomas monopolised Hephzibah, asking her what she thought of life in Nettlestock, whether she had explored the extensive grounds and what she thought of Ottilie. He appeared to be fond of his adopted sister and praised the little girl's advanced riding skills.

'She's a natural horsewoman, that girl. Mind you, my father gave her her first lesson in the saddle before she knew how to walk. If it were up to her, she'd spend all day riding.

Do you find it hard to keep her attention on her lessons?'

'Not at all. Ottilie is an intelligent girl and takes a lot of interest in her lessons. She's full of curiosity and is a joy to teach. She's perhaps not so keen on practising her pianoforte scales, but otherwise she is an exemplary pupil.'

Merritt interjected from the other side of Hephzibah. 'That is because she has an exemplary teacher.'

Hephzibah thought she saw a flash of irritation in Thomas's eyes and rather than respond to the clergyman or include him in the conversation, he changed tack, still addressing his attention to Hephzibah.

'Do you ride, Miss Wildman?'

When she told him she did not, Thomas immediately offered to teach her. Hephzibah felt herself blushing and said, 'I couldn't possibly presume upon your time, Mr Egdon. And my own time is dedicated to preparing for and giving Ottilie her lessons.'

'As the parson has pointed out, you are an exemplary teacher and as such I am sure a little space can be found in your timetable for some riding lessons. Ottilie will be delighted and, once you are proficient, you and she can ride together. You'll be able to see more of the estate and the countryside around the village. You don't want to be stuck here in the house all day.'

Merritt inserted himself into the conversation again. 'Miss Wildman is certainly not to be accused of being stuck in the house. She is out and about in all weathers and I am sure already has become familiar with many of the most interesting sights in walking distance. She has been kind enough to accompany me on several of my regular walks.'

'Yes, Reverend Nightingale has been a most informative guide. He has already taught me so much about the history of the area. Did you know that Nettlestock was once a Roman settlement?' She turned to direct the question at Thomas, including Miss Pickering.

Thomas narrowed his eyes slightly, then laughed. 'I think I have heard that, but I find that history is a bit of a bore. I'm more interested in the here and now.' He smiled at Hephzibah and his face was illuminated by the smile.

Hephzibah looked at him, again feeling herself beginning to blush. His blue eyes locked upon hers and forced her to hold his gaze. She opened her mouth to speak but the words wouldn't come out. Meanwhile, Miss Pickering's quiet and slightly squeaky voice responded to the parson, engaging him in a discussion of the Roman occupation of the area and the various examples of evidence of it.

Thomas eased his chair back and to the side, moving it slightly closer to Hephzibah's, leaning towards her and away from Miss Pickering, thus drawing Hephzibah into a more intimate pairing and separating them from the discussion of Roman Nettlestock.

'I mean it, you know. I would love to teach you to ride.'

'I have never been near a horse, sir, and I intend to keep it that way.'

He looked at her intently. 'You can't live in the countryside and not ride. We'll soon have you jumping tree trunks and streams. And hunting next season. Ottilie will be very happy at that. Father won't allow her to ride out with the hunt, but with you to accompany her I think he'd have to relent. And she'll be eleven by then. I started hunting when I was seven.'

Hephzibah had never felt the slightest desire to ride a horse, much less ride out behind a bunch of baying hounds, chasing foxes across the countryside. But the thought of riding beside Thomas Egdon was not a distasteful prospect.

Merritt was still deep in discourse with Miss Pickering. Hephzibah heard him mention Roman pottery shards and mosaics. She glanced in his direction and immediately the parson switched his attention back to her and said, 'I will take you to the ruins of the Roman bathhouse, Miss

Wildman. It's just five miles away from here. On a fine day, perhaps in the spring, we might walk over there together.'

Thomas spoke over him, 'By the spring Miss Wildman will be a horsewoman. No need for her to tramp all the way there. I can ride over with her and show her the ruins.'

Merritt frowned. 'But you have no interest in history, Mr Egdon. And Miss Wildman would, I am sure, like to understand about the Roman settlements in the area, wouldn't you?'

Hephzibah looked from one to the other, then said to Thomas Egdon, 'Perhaps we could all make an expedition of it, in the spring or summer, with Ottilie, Reverend Merritt and I hope you too, Miss Pickering?'

The schoolmistress clasped her hands together, her face a mixture of delight and anguish. 'That would be so wonderful, but I'm afraid I don't ride and I have a fear of horses. What a pity as I would have loved to join you.'

Thomas leaned past Hephzibah and said to Merritt, 'You could accompany Miss Pickering on foot and meet us there. That way you two can tell each other all about the Romans.' He smiled at Merritt, his head tilted on one side.

'Then it's settled!' said Hephzibah. 'Now we all have something to look forward to – assuming Mr Egdon can manage to teach me how to stay on the back of a horse.' She realised Merritt was frowning. Had she put her foot in it? Was he uncomfortable at the idea of accompanying Miss Pickering? She looked across at the young woman, who was still beaming and clasping her hands together. It dawned on Hephzibah that Miss Pickering was probably in love with the parson. A good match, she thought – both of them educated lovers of history and books. They were of a similar age – perhaps Miss Pickering was slightly older. Hephzibah made a mental note to find out more about the teacher and to sound out Merritt on whether he might like her. Yes, it would make a most suitable match.

Merritt was speaking again, this time addressing Thomas Egdon. 'Tell me, Mr Egdon, is it true that you are spending most of your time in London these days? If so you will be hard pressed to find time to teach Miss Wildman to ride.'

Egdon smiled and said, 'I plan to be here more frequently. I have a pair of colts stabled nearby and will be spending a lot of time watching their progress on the gallops.' He turned his attention to Hephzibah. 'Did I tell you, Miss Wildman, that I own racehorses? It's my passion. I will bring you to watch them in training – Ottilie too – if you can tear yourselves away from your lessons.' He glanced at the Reverend Merritt, before adding, 'Have you ever seen racehorses training, Miss Wildman?'

Hephzibah told him she hadn't and that she would like nothing better.

The rest of the meal continued with Thomas Egdon doing his best to engage her exclusively in conversation. Hephzibah was too delighted to notice the growing cold-ness between him and the parson, who did his best to draw them both into a wider discussion but was compelled to settle with Miss Pickering or Mrs Desmond. At the other end of the table Sir Richard was holding forth about poli-tics and the ludicrous idea that the two seats Keir Hardie's Labour Representation Committee had won in the election were anything but a temporary blip.

When Hephzibah went to bed that night she felt she was walking on air. Thomas Egdon had offered to teach her to ride and to take her on some trips – he had added the suggestion of a trip with her and Ottilie to the horse fair in a nearby town. Surely, if he was suggesting spending so much time with her he must like her a little. Then she remembered the sight of him kissing Abigail Cake and told herself it was pointless to hope.

CHAPTER NINE

The Gypsy Woman
Lives on the moor,
She sleeps in a tent
With a curtained door.

(from Songs of Dreams, Ethel Clifford)

Thomas Egdon was leaning against the stable door, one booted leg bent back behind him. He pushed himself off when he saw Hephzibah approaching. 'I thought you'd backed out, Miss Wildman. I was about to give up on you.'

Hephzibah didn't want to confess that her lateness was caused by her trying on everything in her wardrobe to find a garment that would avoid restricting her, while still preserving her modesty. She'd finally settled on a white cotton blouse, a black skirt and a pair of laced leather boots.

He looked her up and down. 'You need a proper habit and the right boots.'

Hephzibah stopped. 'I'm sorry. I have no suitable clothes.' She felt a wave of relief that this venture was likely not to proceed and she would postpone the embarrassment of Thomas Egdon discovering the clumsiness in the saddle she knew she was going to exhibit.

'You'll do for now while you're on the lunge rein, but you'll need a proper habit when you ride out.'

A saddle was resting on the stable door. Thomas opened the door, led out a small bay horse, which he had already bridled, and lifted the saddle on to the horse's back.

'This was my mother's saddle,' he said. 'I gave it a good cleaning and polishing this morning. The little horse is very quiet. Ottilie learned on her. You'll be safe and secure with her.'

Hephzibah looked up at Thomas and once again was hypnotised by the sight of him. He fastened the horse's girth, loosely first, then tightened it. 'Have you been on a horse before?' he asked, his voice quiet.

She mumbled that she hadn't and he took her hand and led her towards her mount. 'Her name is Dandelion. But we call her Dandie.' He led her up to the pony and encouraged her to lay her hands against the silky hair on its neck. 'Let her get used to you.'

Hephzibah stroked the beast, feeling the softness of her coat and the rougher texture of the mane.

'Right. I'll give you a leg up,' Thomas said and before she knew what was happening he had placed his hands about her waist and lifted her up and into the saddle.

When he held her, she felt light and inconsequential, weightless, as though she might float away. His hands stayed around her waist a moment too long. She shivered.

'Here's how to sit,' he said as he lifted her right leg over the higher pommel and tucked her left under the other pommel and placed her foot in the stirrup.

Hephzibah felt his hands on her legs through her skirt, moving her limbs into position as though she were a doll. The blood rushed to her face. As soon as she was in the saddle she realised why her skirt was unsuitable – there wasn't enough fullness and she was conscious of the way it rode up, revealing her calves over the top of her ankle boots.

Nothing to be done about it now. When she was arranged in position, Egdon ran a hand down her left leg to make sure that she was securely positioned and her foot correctly in the stirrup. He rearranged the skirt, easing it down to cover more of her leg. A rush of adrenaline went through her and she felt excited and also slightly afraid.

'Sit up straight,' he said. 'Don't hang onto the mane like that. And leave the reins alone. I want you to concentrate on balancing. Leave the rest to me.'

Thomas led her into a fenced-off paddock behind the stable block and paid out the lunge, standing in the middle as the horse, with Hephzibah on board, walked slowly around in a circle.

Hephzibah was terrified – insecure and vulnerable. She wanted to do well, to please Thomas Egdon, but she felt displaced, out of her natural element. She knew she had to trust the horse and trust Thomas but there was something inside her that resented this surrender of control. Perched in the side saddle, the ground felt very far away. She wanted to get down, but was terrified that she would disappoint him. Part of her wanted the lesson to end, to be over quickly, for her to be back on terra firma – and yet another part of her wanted it to go on and on. Thomas's eyes were fixed on her and he called out reassurance and encouragement and continually told her to sit up tall in the saddle and stop hunching forward.

After a while, Egdon cracked the long whip he was holding in his left hand and Dandie broke into a trot. Hephzibah instinctively leaned forward and grasped at the horse's mane, only for Thomas to call out to her to sit up and look ahead. Rising panic overtook her and then with another crack of the whip her horse was cantering and she felt a mixture of exhilaration and abject terror. Her legs tightened around the pommels and she leaned forward and held onto the front of the saddle, her balance out of control.

After a few more minutes of careening around the paddock in alternating directions, Thomas slowed the horse down to a trot and then a walk and, looping in the lunge, walked over towards her.

'You have to sit up. Let the horse do the work. Stop trying to fight it.'

'I've had enough now. I don't think horses and I are meant to be together. I like to have my feet on the ground.'

She thought she saw a small frown of irritation, though he said, 'We'll try again another day.'

The following day, Hephzibah was sitting at the table in the small drawing room, going through some arithmetic with Ottilie when Thomas Egdon burst in unannounced. He moved across to them and placed his hands over the top of the text book they were working from, then snapped it shut with a flourish.

'That's enough schooling for today, ladies.'

He was greeted with a squeal of delight from Ottilie. Hephzibah was unsure whether it was for the promised reprieve or for his calling her a lady – probably both.

'I'm taking you to the horse fair.'

'I'm sorry, Mr Egdon, but Ottilie and I have work to do.'

'Nonsense,' he said and bent down and picked Ottilie up by the waist and swung her around as the girl giggled wildly.

When he put her down, she turned to Hephzibah, her hands clasped together in supplication, 'Please, Miss Wildman. I've never been to the horse fair. It will be so exciting. Please, please. I promise I'll work extra hard tomorrow to make up for it.'

Egdon tousled the little girl's curls and turned his attention to Hephzibah. 'I'll hear no excuses, Miss Wildman. The fair happens only once a year and it would be a crime to miss it.'

'But the squire…'

'Is in Reading at a meeting. He won't be back until late tonight or even tomorrow.' He tilted his head on one side and gave Hephzibah a look of mock pleading before directing his winning smile at her.

She was powerless to refuse.

The winter horse fair at Mudford was a lively event. The small country town was thronged with people and horses. The latter lined both sides of the street, staring each other down across the roadway as the people passed between them and behind them. The air was thick with the scent of roasting chestnuts, the sickly sweetness of spun sugar and the competing smell of horse manure. The farmers and horse traders moved up and down the lines, stopping to inspect a fetlock or squeeze a knee, arguing animatedly as they discussed the merits and demerits of each beast.

Hephzibah was fascinated but unsure why they were here. Thomas made it clear he was not in the market for any horses, turning his nose up at what he described as old nags.

'You won't find racehorses here. That's what I'm interested in. I have to know the full pedigree. The fair here is for working horses, riding horses, hunters and ponies. We're well supplied with all of these at Ingleton Hall.' He paused and then ruffled Ottilie's hair again. 'But I'm going to keep my eyes open for a nice new ride for Ottilie here, now that she's ceded Dandie to you. I think she's ready for something with a bit more spirit, don't you think, Ottilie?'

'But does Sir Richard know?' asked Hephzibah.

'Not yet.'

'But shouldn't he decide whether Ottilie should have a new pony?'

Ottilie put her hands on her hips, shook her head and rolled her eyes at Hephzibah. 'Papa's a spoilsport. He's sure to say I'll have to wait for my birthday. But that's not until June and the horse fair only happens once a year.'

'She's right.' Thomas Egdon took his sister's hand and placed a hand momentarily on Hephzibah's shoulder. 'We have to strike while the iron's hot. Come on, ladies.'

He led them through the crowd of dealers, men standing, pipes in mouth and hands in pockets, until they came to a black mare with a white blaze on her forehead. The horse was bigger than Dandie and Hephzibah felt immediately uncomfortable. It was frisking about as though unhappy to be so tightly confined, tethered here on the street. It swished its tail constantly and hopped about from one foot to the other.

'What about this one, Ottilie?' Egdon said. 'She looks as though she'll be a lively ride. A bit more fun than old Dandelion, eh?'

Ottilie was already in love. She placed her head against the horse's neck and began to talk to the animal, introducing herself. She fumbled in her pocket and produced an apple which she fed to the horse, which devoured it hungrily.

'Please, please, Tom. I love her. Please may I have her?'

Egdon turned to the dealer and began to bargain with him. He inspected the horse with what appeared to Hephzibah to be great care and finally counted out some notes into the hands of the trader.

'Done,' he said. 'Now all you have to do is find a name for her.'

'I know already. She's going to be called Bess, like Dick Turpin's horse.'

Hephzibah said, 'But is that wise, Ottilie? Poor Bess died of exhaustion. Do you really want to name your horse after such a sad story?'

'She only died after galloping all the way from London to York. I won't be doing that to my Bess. And if Dick Turpin hadn't had to do that she would have lived for lots longer, wouldn't she?'

'I suppose so,' Hephzibah conceded.

'Bess it is then,' said Thomas Egdon. 'Now we have one more important task and then it's time to try our luck on the coconut shies.'

He steered them away along the main street until they came to a ladies' dressmakers. 'Here we are. Time to get you kitted out,' he said to an astonished Hephzibah as he pushed open the door.

Hephzibah was embarrassed. Why had he brought her here? She was about to ask him but he was studying himself in a mirror.

It was a few moments after they entered the gloomy interior before a woman rushed from the back of the shop to serve them.

'This lady needs a full riding habit. Hacking not hunting. I'll leave you to sort her out,' said Thomas.

He addressed Hephzibah. 'I'll take Ottilie to knock over a few coconuts and will be back to collect you in half an hour. Then we'll get you a topper, boots and a crop.' Before she could protest the door shut behind him, leaving her with the shopkeeper and the sound of the jangling bell.

The woman showed her a book of patterns and some fabric samples, advising her to stick to a dark wool serge and to choose a safety skirt. She explained how the buttoned seams allowed the skirt to detach in the unfortunate event of her being dragged by a runaway horse. Hephzibah felt sick at the thought. They selected a short tailored jacket and a cream shirt with a cravat.

As they completed the selection the door jangled again and a happy-faced Ottilie entered the store, still chewing her way through a stick of spun sugar, with Thomas behind her.

'Send the account to Ingleton Hall,' he told the dressmaker when she said it would be ready for delivery within a week.

He shepherded Hephzibah through the door and steered

her across the road to a saddlery, ignoring her protests.

'I can't afford all this, Mr Egdon. My only means is the stipend your father pays me and that's not sufficient to pay for a riding habit.'

'Don't be foolish. You'll risk your neck if you ride with the wrong clothing and equipment. I'll pay for it.'

'Then I won't ride at all.'

'Nonsense. I intend to make you a good horsewoman.' He fixed his blue eyes upon her. There was something about Thomas Egdon that dissolved any possibility of dissent.

After he had added a bowler hat and a riding crop to their purchases, Egdon suggested they take a last turn around the fair, to Ottilie's evident delight. The crowds in the street were thinning, most of the people moving now to the common land where a funfair was doing a brisk trade. There was an even larger crowd there as the horse dealers and buyers were joined now by agricultural workers, their day at work done, treating their sweethearts to a ride on the merry-go-round, a piece of gingerbread or a bag of hot chestnuts. The sound of music filled the cold winter evening – fiddles, flutes and drums to keep the beat. They walked through the throng, pausing to watch some folk dancers and a troupe of morris men. Many of the stall holders were gipsies and the common land was edged with brightly coloured wooden caravans.

Hephzibah was conscious of the advancing hour and suggested they think about getting back to Nettlestock as it would soon be past Ottilie's bedtime.

Thomas looked at her and laughed. 'You have no sense of adventure, Miss Wildman. We need to encourage your governess to let her hair down, don't we, Ottilie?'

A sudden feeling of annoyance gripped her. She didn't like the way he was trying to use her pupil to influence her. He was undermining her authority. Just as she was about to tell him as much, he seemed to read her thoughts and said, 'You're quite right, Miss Wildman. You've had enough excitement for one day, little sister. Time to go home.'

They moved back in the direction of the town when, out of the darkness, a gipsy woman stepped into their path. She grabbed Hephzibah's hand and said, 'Read your palm, miss? Tell you your fortune?'

Hephzibah jerked her hand away but the old woman grasped hold again, her bony hands squeezing tightly and looked towards Egdon. 'Let me read the young lady's fortune, sir. She won't regret it.'

Thomas Egdon laughed. 'Go on then.' He pressed a florin into the gipsy's hand.

Hephzibah felt as though her day had been stolen from her. This man thought he could do as he wished and she would happily go along with it. Then he looked at her, his blue eyes filled with concern.

'Don't be annoyed, Hephzibah. It's just a bit of fun. You don't have to take it seriously.' He made a face at her, like a naughty boy and she couldn't help but laugh.

She turned back to the old woman. 'Very well but you need to be quick. We have to get home.'

Hephzibah knew it was ridiculous. Apart from the fact that she didn't believe in fortune-tellers, the words the gipsy spoke were so ludicrous they couldn't possibly be true. The gipsy led her inside a tent, which was so dark that Hephzibah could barely see the old woman. The fortune-telling was brief. The Romany traced the lines on Hephzibah's palm as though she knew where they were without looking.

'You'll be wed before the summer comes.'

'That's not possible.'

'But it's true.'

Hephzibah withdrew her hand, then the woman added, 'Two men will love you. Both will pay the price for it.'

Hephzibah laughed. 'That's ridiculous. There's no one.'

'You're wrong about that, miss. And you'll be wrong

about a lot more afore you're done. Mark my words. Two men will be destroyed by loving you.'

Hephzibah turned away and began to walk towards Thomas and Ottilie when the old lady caught hold of her arm. 'Your parents met a violent death. But they're at peace now.'

She gasped in surprise, then pulled her arm away.

The old lady snatched Hephzibah's hand back and pressed something scratchy into it. 'Take this. It will protect you. It's lucky for brides. Carry it in your posy when you wed.'

In her hand was a little sprig of white heather. Hephzibah stuffed it into her pocket and ran over the grass to join Egdon and his sister.

Later that night when she was in bed, she couldn't stop thinking about what the woman had told her. All the way home Thomas and Ottilie had pestered her to reveal the fortune, but there was something that made her hold back. There was something about the quiet but insistent voice in which the old gipsy conveyed her message. And how could she have possibly known about the tram accident? Back in her bedroom Hephzibah put the sprig of heather at the bottom of her drawer.

The following morning, Hephzibah's thoughts of the gipsy's prophecy vanished in the face of the uproar she encountered at the breakfast table. Ottilie was in floods of tears while Sir Richard paced up and down, hands behind his back and an expression of righteous indignation on his face.

'Were you a party to this foolish purchase?' he asked. 'My son is a blessed idiot. Ottilie's just shown me the horse he bought for her. Utter waste of money. He's fallen for the oldest trick in the book. That old nag is probably already long past her twilight years and is halfway to horse heaven.'

Ottilie was sobbing, so Hephzibah put a comforting

hand on her shoulder. 'The horse appeared very lively yesterday when Mr Egdon purchased her. In fact I was worried she might be too much of a handful for Ottilie. She was hopping about as though ready to break free of her halter and race away. She certainly didn't seem to be half dead, quite the contrary.'

'Ginger.' The squire's response was almost a grunt. Seeing Hephzibah's puzzled expression he added, 'Ginger under the tail. Works every time. Has a horse hopping about like a damned kangaroo. Anyone with half a brain would know that. Especially at a horse fair. All kinds of villains and tricksters there. Must have seen my fool of a son coming a mile off.'

The squire pulled out his chair and sat down at the table. 'Besides, he's no business buying Ottilie a horse. That's my responsibility. No wonder the man's run up so much debt.'

Hephzibah picked up a piece of toast then put it down again, her appetite deserting her. Why had she allowed Thomas Egdon to buy her the riding habit? Should she tell the squire about that too and risk an escalation of his anger? She would offer to pay Egdon back. It would take her many months, maybe as much as a year, but she must do it. She swallowed and cursed her own stupidity. She didn't even like riding. How would she explain to Sir Richard that she had felt powerless to stop his son? Thomas had brooked no opposition. And she had been mesmerised by him.

The squire was acting in a particularly callous manner that morning. 'Only thing that nag is good for is feeding my dogs. I'll have to send her to the slaughterhouse.'

Ottilie wailed.

Hephzibah again felt obliged to mediate. 'Is the horse so bad that she can't be ridden? Isn't it better for Ottilie to have a mount that's quiet than one that's too frisky? She is only ten after all. And she does love Bess, don't you Ottilie?'

The little girl nodded. 'Please, Papa. Don't kill her. I

promise to be good. Let me take care of her. I love her. I really do.'

The squire leaned back in his chair and frowned, but Hephzibah could see that his anger had already dissipated.

'No complaining that's she too dull a ride for you.'

Ottilie nodded, but Hephzibah knew that the child's relief at the horse's reprieve was mixed with disappointment that her new mount was not the lively creature she had thought her to be.

CHAPTER TEN

Christ leads me through no darker rooms
Than He went through before;
And he that in God's kingdom comes
Must enter by this door.

(Traditional Hymn – words by Richard Baxter)

Merritt couldn't concentrate. The words kept dissolving on the page as he tried to read them. He kept going over the same piece of text, unable to take it in or make sense of it, his mind drifting away to conjure images of Hephzibah.

He was relieved when Mrs Muggeridge appeared at the door of his study and told him it was time to deal with enquiries from parishioners. He put aside the work he was doing to come up with a sermon for the following Sunday and made his way to the back parlour.

The number of needy parishioners who queued up to seek his help each day was increasing. These visits were not what he'd expected before he took on the parish. Yes, there was the odd request for marriage banns, christenings or funeral arrangements, but lately for the most part his audiences were with the poor and needy. It depressed him to know how little he could do to help them.

Times were hard throughout the whole country and getting harder. The price of grain and produce had plummeted, the tenant farmers were facing higher rents and in consequence were paying lower wages and so more people were turning to the parish for help.

The first person he saw was a widow, twenty-eight years old, whose husband had drowned when he fell into the canal after a binge on the cider.

'I've not a penny to put food in the mouths of my little ones and I'm weak myself from lack of eating. My eldest is just twelve and works in the whiting mill. I have to send her off to work a twelve hour day with nothing in her stomach but a crust of bread. What am I to do, sir? What am I to do?'

Merritt avoided her gaze and studied the cracks on the tiled floor as he struggled to find some words of consolation. The trouble was there was nothing he could do, short of advising her to throw herself on the mercy of the guardians at the poorhouse. He had already taken up her case with the Charitable Aid Society the previous week, but they had questioned her respectability. Mrs Bellamy, the postmistress and a vocal member of the society, had claimed that she entertained men in her house when her children were in bed. He tried to break the news to the widow as tactfully as possible.

'Mrs Budd, the society has reviewed your circumstances and questions have been raised regarding your... character. Under the circumstances–'

'My character? My character? What about my character?'

'I'm sorry but my enquiries raised questions about your respectability. The Charitable Aid Society will not sanction payments to anyone whom they believe to be of less than unimpeachable morals.'

'Talk proper will you. I don't know what you're on about.'

Merritt coughed and asked himself how he had ever

thought the profession of clergyman would prove a worthwhile occupation. 'There has been talk that you… that you may have other sources of income. That you have visitors who may be contributing to your household income for services that the parish cannot condone.'

'What you trying to say? What you accusing me of? I'm a decent, hard-working woman and anyone who says otherwise is lying.'

'It's not up to me, Mrs Budd,' he said. 'I'm only the messenger.'

'They're just saying that so they don't have to pay out. I'm a respectable widow. I'd never go with another man, even now my Malcolm's gone.'

Merritt shook his head and avoided her eyes. He didn't know whether to believe her or not, but even if she were entertaining men for a few extra crusts to eat, the odd log for the fire and a bit of warmth in bed at night, who was he to judge or blame her? Then he reminded himself that as a parson he was expected to do just that. Another reason why he was sure he was in the wrong job.

'So what am I to do?'

'Can you find some work?'

'Work!' Her voice was sardonic and bitter. 'I've a child that's still crawling. How can I work?'

'Could you take in a lodger?'

'I already have two lodgers. Why else do you think there's all the tittle tattle? And how else do you think I have what little we have got? One of them has been laid off so I've told him he has to go and the other barely brings in anything since he's had his hours cut.' She gave a little strangled sob. 'What will I do, sir? What will become of us?'

He swallowed and averted his eyes from her evident pain. 'Then I can only suggest you find another lodger – or enter the workhouse. At least you and your children would have food and shelter there.'

'I'm not going up there. I'd never see my older children. I'm not breaking up our home. Please help me.'

In the end he agreed to take up her case with the society again, but held out little hope.

Mrs Budd was replaced by a woman in an advanced state of pregnancy, clutching the hands of two small children. She told him her husband had broken his ankle and was unable to work for another three weeks. The family income was now entirely based on the few pennies she made from mending, so she was seeking a referral to fund her care during her forthcoming confinement. Merritt was relieved to be able to write the required reference and hoped that the Charitable Aid Society guardians would be willing to grant her the assistance of a midwife.

The rest of his visitors consisted of an elderly widower who had been evicted from his home by his daughter and son-in-law, a desperate young mother unable to care for her child with rickets, and an elderly woman who wished to arrange for the funeral of her husband who had died after three years' confinement in the mad house and whom she didn't want consigned to a pauper's grave.

When they had all gone and Merritt was served with a hearty stew by Mrs Muggeridge, he found his appetite had deserted him. He would gladly offer his own food to some of these needy parishioners but he knew it would be scratching the surface of the growing levels of deprivation, destitution and despair.

Back in his office, Merritt tried to pick up where he had left off in his preparations for writing his sermon. His intended theme had been the darkness of winter and the need to have hope for the eventual arrival of spring. What was the point? What did they have to give thanks for? The harvest had been a disaster last year and the majority of his parishioners wanted nothing but food in their bellies, a roof over their heads and some wood for the fire. It was bitterly cold and signs of spring were months away. One of the old fellows who had visited the parsonage that morning told him he'd known it was going to be a long harsh winter as his onions had all had thick skins. When he mentioned it to Mrs Muggeridge she had muttered, 'There were plenty of acorns on the ground too. I'll not be holding my breath for spring this year.'

When the Reverend Nightingale climbed into his pulpit the following day, the first person he saw in his congregation was Hephzibah. A shaft of winter sunlight came through the east window and the rays landed on her head, giving her an angelic aspect. Her hair spilled out from under her bonnet and the light caught her eyes. He was confused, staring open-mouthed at her, watching the dust motes dancing around her head like a halo. Someone in the back of the church coughed and Merritt grasped at the sheaf of papers on which he had scribbled his sermon. In his confusion, he knocked them off the lectern, forcing himself to scramble around on the floor of the pulpit to retrieve them. As he struggled to reorder the pages he was conscious of murmuring and suppressed giggles spreading around the church. He cleared his throat and was rewarded with silence. He glanced towards Hephzibah who was looking straight back at him, her beautiful face, expectant and open. *Don't look at her. Address the sermon to someone else.* He looked around the church in rising panic, spotting Mrs Budd and her children. This is for Mrs Budd, he told himself. Speak to her. No, that wouldn't be right. She would think he was criticising her when all he wanted to do was offer some comfort. He took a big gulp of breath. *Now. Slowly. Look around. Look at everyone except Hephzibah.*

'My sermon today is about temptation,' he began.

He spoke of Adam and Eve's failure to withstand the

guile of the snake and how all mankind suffered from the same weakness from time to time. There was a murmuring of assent in the little church and, his confidence growing, he went on. 'As a man, even Jesus was vulnerable to temptation. He was made human by his father and sent to save us and so it was inevitable that he too must suffer from that terrible affliction. When he fasted in the desert for forty days and forty nights, as Moses had done before him, the devil taunted that starving man to use his heavenly powers to turn a stone into a loaf of bread. Imagine how easy it would have been for Christ to do just that. Imagine his hunger. The pain of not eating for a full forty days.' He stressed the words forty days.

'How easy would it have been for Jesus to fill his belly and sate his hunger?' Merritt flicked his fingers and saw the congregation jump in their seats in unison. 'As easy as that.' He paused for effect. 'But he didn't do it. And God, his own father, could have stepped in to help him. But he didn't. He sent no miracle to help his only son. So why then would he send one to us?'

He looked around the church, his gaze met by a sea of faces, hanging on his next words. 'We must follow the example of Christ and remember his words: "*Man does not live by bread alone, but by every word that proceedeth from the mouth of God*".

'We must remember that where we suffer, Christ has already suffered before us and he shares our suffering with us now. So when temptation comes our way, whether it be to set a trap for a rabbit, steal a loaf from a neighbour or succumb to other temptations to earn an extra crust' – *don't look at Mrs Budd* – 'we must neither blame God nor doubt him, but instead trust in him and follow the example of Jesus Christ. Now let us all sing the hymn, "Christ leads me through no darker rooms than he went through before".'

The sermon over and the singing hearty, Merritt allowed

himself some satisfaction that his homily had struck home. But as he looked around the congregation he felt a growing unease. These people were genuinely suffering. Christ had also fed the five thousand with miraculous loaves and fishes. Who would feed these people here? Christ's fasting had lasted forty days and forty nights whereas some of these people went hungry month after month with no sign of any improvement in their fate. And Christ suffered alone. Mrs Budd's hunger was not just her own, but that of her children. He looked towards her and saw the skinny twelve-year-old daughter who slaved away for long hours in the whiting mill on an empty stomach. Hadn't Christ also said, 'Suffer the little children to come unto me'? Before the winter was out many of the members of the congregation in front of him now would doubtless be returned to join Christ – victims of hunger, cold and disease. He felt ashamed, hypocritical. Who was he to lecture these people? He who would eat a hearty meal this evening, who had never known what it was to go hungry. Then he told himself that even if today he had given them a few minutes of false comfort it was better than nothing at all. He was powerless to change the conditions these people lived in, so what was wrong with offering them some small salve, however slight or temporary?

Merritt waited outside, greeting his parishioners as they left the church.

Squire Egdon took his hand and pumped it enthusiastically. 'Thank you, Nightingale. Excellent sermon. That's what they need to hear. Encourage the vagrants and idlers to work harder and keep their thieving hands off others' property. I particularly liked the way you spoke out against poaching. It needs to be stamped out and the perpetrators punished properly. Otherwise there'll be no game left to hunt.' He slapped the parson on the back. 'Keep it up, Nightingale. Good work.' The squire limped through the churchyard and heaved himself up onto his waiting horse.

Merritt stared after him, astonished, angry and ashamed. He also felt powerless. He had no real attachment to the religion he stood for, but he had genuinely begun to care for the plight of his flock. What was the point if landowners such as Egdon saw him as their stooge, their mouthpiece, twisting his words to their own ends? He turned to go into the vestry to remove his vestments and saw Hephzibah waiting for him, her back against the stone archway into the church.

'Your sermon was well received this morning, Reverend Nightingale,' she said.

Merritt wondered whether she was being sarcastic, whether she had overheard the words of the squire. He shook his head. 'It seems that Squire Egdon took it as an endorsement for the game laws.'

'People hear what they want to hear.'

'You think so?'

'I do. Most of the people here will have taken comfort from knowing that they are not alone in suffering and that God is with them. Even if it's only for a few hours, you have given them a little strength.'

'I wish that were true, but somehow I doubt it. I feel guilty that I'm telling people to put up with things they shouldn't have to put up with. These people don't need words and prayers. They need a fair wage – enough to feed, house and clothe themselves and their families. Is it right that they should resist the temptation to steal a rabbit running wild on the squire's lands only to watch their children go hungry? Does God really think the squire's right to hunt every last creature that happens to cross his fields is more important than their right to feed their families?'

Hephzibah stared at him. 'You appear very disillusioned this morning. What's brought this on?' She gestured towards the last of the parishioners walking away down the lane. 'You can't right all the wrongs of the country. You can only try to help people to bear them.'

Instinctively he reached forward and took her hands between his. 'Thank you.' He dropped her hands and felt the blood rush into his face.

Hephzibah smiled. 'I was rather hoping we might take another walk this morning. That is if you've nothing more pressing?'

Merritt was gratified to see that her cheeks appeared slightly suffused with a blush. He was already pulling his cassock over his head. 'Give me one minute.' He disappeared inside into the vestry, his heart pumping.

They headed through the churchyard and down to the canal. It was a cold day, with traces of frost still clinging to the hedgerows and the puddles on the path frozen over, but the sun was shining and the sky a deep blue. They walked in silence and he kept glancing sideways at Hephzibah as though afraid she might disappear. Their silence was a companionable one and as they walked on, Merritt felt himself relax.

'Tell me what made you feel so discouraged this morning,' she said. 'Your sermon went down well with the whole congregation. Everyone was paying attention and I didn't see anyone nodding off at all.'

'Thank you – I suppose that's a comfort. Not to bore one's parishioners to sleep.' His smile was rueful.

'You preach very well, Merritt. Everyone can hear you. You have a voice that commands attention. You speak with authority and confidence. It makes people sit up and listen.'

'You're too kind.'

'Not at all. I don't believe in flattery. If I didn't think it I wouldn't say it.' Hephzibah reached out and plucked a stray brown leaf off a tree and as she walked, she scraped off the surface of the leaf with her fingers leaving only the skeleton. 'Why then were you feeling bad?'

'There's so much poverty in the village and no sign of things getting better. Before I came to Nettlestock I had no idea that people suffered so much.' He told her about the visit of Mrs Budd, without naming the woman, and how he was powerless to do anything to help her when he was up against the collective judgment of the parish council and the Charitable Aid Society.

'Can't you convince them otherwise?'

'I have no more influence in Nettlestock than the King of Siam. They see me as an outsider and resent my interference. Besides, they may be right about the woman and if I'm being honest I can't say I'd blame her if she was sharing her bed with her lodger. If it helps her put bread on the table and stay a bit warmer at night... and she must be lonely losing her husband. Now I've shocked you, haven't I?'

Hephzibah tilted her head on one side. 'Not at all. I don't believe in judging people. Particularly those whose circumstances are harder than our own. It must be desperate having to live like that, worrying where the next meal will come from. What will happen to her?'

'She has a twelve-year-old daughter who works at the whiting mill. No doubt the eight-year-old will join her there next. When I raised that with the board they accused the mother of being lazy and suggested she take in washing and mending. She has a ten-month-old baby. How can she manage doing laundry? It must be hard enough getting her own washing done.' He kicked at a clump of grass. 'I wish I could help people like her more. I go every week to visit the workhouse up the hill in Mudford. Some of the stories I hear there are shocking.'

'Perhaps you could take me with you one day?' She touched his arm.

'You'd visit the workhouse?'

'Yes. I'd like to see for myself what it's like. Once a month I have a Wednesday afternoon free. Might you be able to take me then?'

Merritt was taken aback. 'Are you sure? You must have

better ways to spend your free afternoon than going there.' He wanted to say riding lessons with the squire's son but decided against it. 'And I warn you, some of the poor souls there are desperate cases.'

Her expression was serious. 'I want to go. And it might make me feel more grateful for my own lot. There may even be something I could do to help.'

'Very well,' the parson said, trying to control the delight in his voice. 'I will have to seek permission from the guardians. I'll tell them you're new to the parish and interested in finding out about the good work done there.'

They walked on, the low winter sun making the frost on the ploughed fields sparkle. Eventually, he summoned up the courage to ask her if she had begun her riding lessons.

'Mr Egdon kindly gave me a lesson. I think I was a disappointment to him as a pupil. I lack the natural gift of horsemanship. It would require a lot of practise to bring me to a level approaching competency.'

Merritt swallowed, wishing he hadn't asked, as he imagined Egdon spending hours with her to help her improve.

'Besides,' she added, 'Mr Egdon spends very little time in Nettlestock. If he is kind enough to give me another lesson when he next returns, I am likely in the meantime to have forgotten everything he has so far taught me.'

Merritt looked away so she would not see the smile on his face. He suggested they take a path through a copse of trees that bordered the grounds of Ingleton Hall. As they entered the wood, they passed a fenced section with signs warning off trespassers. A faint groaning sound was coming from the other side of the barrier. They stopped to listen.

'Over there,' said Hephzibah, pointing towards a thicket. 'Someone must be hurt.'

The fence was rotten in one place and had collapsed so there was a way through. Merritt pulled aside the overhanging branches and they stepped across the broken fence and went deeper into the woods. Under a large elm tree a man lay writhing in pain on the ground, his arms grasping the trunk of the tree and one leg twisted underneath him. A pair of dead rabbits lay beside him. As they approached, his expression changed from agony to terror.

'Please don't tell Squire Egdon. I've five children at home and a sick wife. I had no choice. They're all hungry. Please help me.'

Nightingale dropped to his knees in front of the man and eased his leg out from under him. It was stuck in a rusting gin trap. Merritt examined it as the man screamed in pain.

The parson turned to Hephzibah. 'Can you hold onto his shoulders and try to keep him steady while I see if I can get him out of this?'

Addressing the man, he said, 'This is going to hurt badly for a moment, but I'll soon have you free. What's your name?'

'Peter Goody.' The man's voice was barely a whisper, then he gave another agonised groan.

'Take deep breaths, Mr Goody, and try to count to ten. It will soon be over.'

Hephzibah knelt behind the trapped man and gripped his bony shoulders as he shivered in fear and shock. Merritt wondered how long he'd been trapped. The parson stood up and carefully edged the trap upright. The man let out a blood-curdling scream as the angle of the bar twisted his trapped ankle. Merritt found the spring and stepped on it, releasing the jaws of the trap from the man's leg.

Visibly relieved but still in terrible pain, the poacher said, 'Don't tell the squire. Please don't tell him. He'll send me to jail. We'll lose the cottage. What'll happen to my family? I beg you. Don't tell him.'

'It's not you who should be jailed, Mr Goody. It's the squire himself – or his gamekeeper. Setting traps for men has been illegal for years – maybe this one has been lying here forgotten –but that doesn't mean the gamekeeper didn't have a responsibility to find and remove it. He must have known where the traps were set. I've a mind to report this to the magistrates.'

'Don't do that, sir. Please. I beg you. They're all in it together. They'll have me up before the assizes for poaching.'

'Stealing a few rabbits is nothing compared to maiming a man.'

'They don't see it that way, vicar.'

Hephzibah moved around to kneel in front of the man and rolled up the bottom of his torn trousers. His leg was a bloodied mess. She reached under her skirt and tore a strip off her petticoat and mopped at the blood. 'I don't think the trap has penetrated the bone but his ankle could still be broken.' She looked up at the parson who nodded.

'All right, Mr Goody,' he said. 'Let's get you upright and see how bad the damage is.'

With Merritt on one side and Hephzibah on the other, they helped him to his feet, but his left leg immediately buckled under him.

'You won't get far on one leg. You can't hop all the way back to the village. We need to get some help.'

'Can you fetch Dan Flowers? He and his son will help me get home. He lives in the cottage next to the forge. He'll not let on to anyone what's happened.'

Merritt looked at Hephzibah. 'I'll go,' she said. 'You can't risk being involved. Better that you stay here with Mr Goody.' And before he could object she was running back towards the towpath.

CHAPTER ELEVEN

Lucy Locket lost her pocket
Kitty Fisher found it;
Not a penny was there in it,
Only ribbon round it.

(traditional nursery rhyme)

Peter Goody was weak and exhausted when Hephzibah arrived back at the scene with the smithy, Dan Flowers, and his son, a lad of about eighteen who looked as sturdy and strong as his father. The pain was etched into the poacher's face. Hephzibah stood beside Merritt, watching the two men half-carrying Goody, his arms draped around their shoulders and his feet dragging along the ground.

'He'll be lucky if that ankle isn't broken, but either way the flesh is cut so deeply that he won't be working again before the summer, poor devil,' Merritt said, shaking his head. 'And the rust on that gin trap could poison his blood.'

The diversion back into Nettlestock to fetch Dan Flowers, caused Hephzibah to be fifteen minutes late for luncheon. Her fears of the squire's displeasure were unfounded, as when she arrived at the house she discovered Richard Egdon was out – lunching at the home of his friend, Lord Maltravers.

It was fortunate that the squire hadn't been at home that afternoon, as Hephzibah knew she would have found it hard not to rage at him for his inhumanity and neglect in leaving mantraps lying around the estate. She made a mental note to keep to the paths and the open meadows and avoid the woods and she would tell Ottilie to do the same.

It had been hard for Hephzibah to concentrate lately, her thoughts returning always to the continuing absence of Thomas Egdon from the Hall. There had been no more riding lessons and the smart new habit hung untouched in her wardrobe like a silent reproach. The visits to the ruins, and to view Thomas's racehorses training on the gallops, had not materialised and Hephzibah forced herself to acknowledge that his attention had been fleeting and she had been forgotten by him as soon as he was away from Nettlestock.

All these thoughts receded into the background when the news of the Queen's death at Osborne House reached Nettlestock a few days later. Victoria had been monarch for longer than any of the occupants of Ingleton Hall had been alive. At eighty-one, with sixty-three years on the throne and having been in ill health since December, it was not surprising that Victoria should have died, but so durable had her reign been that people found it hard to believe that this was indeed the end of an era. Her death, and the accession of her son Edward to the crown, made little real impact on the residents of Nettlestock, who, after observing the day of mourning on 2nd February, went on with their lives as usual.

The spring of 1901 arrived more quickly than Hephzibah had expected. It was hard to believe that she had now been at Ingleton Hall for almost nine months and it would not be long to the anniversary of her parents' death. Since she had laid the law down to the squire, his behaviour had been exemplary. He was as crotchety as usual, showed no inclination to moderate his drinking or his aggressive stance to his son, but to Hephzibah he was courteous if distant. While she was relieved at his remoteness, she did not feel the same about Thomas's. He was absent more than he was present at Ingleton Hall and she found herself thinking of him all the time he was away. The riding lessons resumed whenever he was home and Hephzibah's abiding fear of horses was outweighed by her excitement at being tutored by him. She had graduated from the lunge and was riding in the parkland around the Hall with Ottilie. She found herself grateful to poor worn-out Bess, whose advancing age meant she moved in a slow and stately manner while Dandie trotted along happily beside her. Hephzibah wondered if she and Ottilie should swap mounts but realised that her greater weight would be an added strain to the old mare. Ottilie, for her part, never complained, evidently still fearful that her father might change his mind about her horse's fate.

Hephzibah's newfound interest in horse-riding, and bad weather over the winter, meant that her request to accompany Mr Nightingale on one of his monthly visits to the workhouse had not yet taken place. It could wait until the weather improved. The workhouse wasn't going to disappear.

One day in April, Hephzibah sat in the small drawing room, reading and planning Ottilie's lessons for the rest of the week. Ottilie was in bed with a slight cold. The parkland had been shrouded in mist earlier but as she finished, Hephzibah noticed the sun had burnt off the fog and the grounds around the house shone in the sunlight. The temptation to go outdoors was irresistible. She picked up the book she was reading and went to fetch her coat – she would find a spot to sit and read outdoors.

She followed a path that ran behind the house, running behind the back of the stables and outbuildings. She had never been this way before. Someone had been burning cleared undergrowth and there was a pile of still smouldering ash. The smell of the embers was in the air, mixed with a peaty smell where someone had been turning the soil over for spring planting. The path went past a row of compost heaps and a collection of near-collapsed old wooden sheds, then petered out as the ground sloped away. There was a collection of dense trees at the top of the incline. Hephzibah was about to turn back when, on a whim she moved through the clump of trees. She had expected that this would be one of the boundaries of the estate but instead found a grassy slope in front of her, stretching down towards meadows on the other side of a ha-ha. Just before the ha-ha she saw a small, domed building resembling a Grecian temple. It was bathed in sunshine and she decided it would make a good sheltered spot to sit and read.

The building, some kind of eighteenth century folly, was screened by the trees from the pathway and the house, so she had not noticed it before. Her approach was angled towards the back of the structure, which was closed in, and she could just make out that the front was open and supported by a row of columns, looking out towards the water meadows.

As she drew near, Hephzibah heard a noise coming from inside the structure and thought at first it was a wounded animal. She rounded the corner and recoiled in shock. Sir Richard Egdon was naked from the waist down, his trousers around his swollen ankles and his fat white buttocks pumping backwards and forwards as he grunted like a pig. Wrapped around the squire's girth was a pair of legs, clothed in woollen stockings. Hephzibah took less than a second to take this in, before retreating and running as fast as her legs could carry her, back the way she had come. When she reached the safety of the stable yard she leaned, panting against the wall, struggling for breath and overcome by shock.

Eventually she went back into the house and sought sanctuary in her bedroom, trying to blot out what she had seen. Hephzibah had been unable to see the face of the woman but it had been impossible to miss the tumble of chestnut hair.

She picked up her book and tried to concentrate, but the image of those pumping buttocks, the woman's moans and the squire's grunts would not leave her.

Abigail Cake was disporting herself with the father as well as the son.

Hephzibah knelt on the floor, surrounded by the contents of her trinket box. She had sorted through everything three times already and there was no sign of her mother's locket. She was certain she had taken it off the previous evening when she went to bed, carefully stowing it inside the trinket box with her few other items of jewellery. Her door had been locked during the night – as was now her custom since the unwelcome visitation from Abigail Cake – then this morning she had gone down to breakfast in a hurry and, when she put her hand up to her neck, she had realised she had forgotten to put the locket on. The bedroom had been unlocked for the half hour she was breakfasting. Opening all the drawers, she pulled out the contents then refolded everything and returned it, before moving on to check the small side tables, one in front of the window and the other beside the bed. Finally, she lay on the floor on her stomach and looked underneath the bed. Nothing. The Ribbon Thief had struck again.

Was the girl a kleptomaniac – a magpie, unable to control her actions? The defiant look Abigail had given her in church when she was wearing the ribbons indicated that her thefts were deliberate acts. Had she seen Hephzibah the previous day when she was engaged in sexual intercourse with the squire? Was this punishment for Hephzibah discovering her secret? Thinking about what she had witnessed made Hephzibah feel nauseous. It was impossible to get the memory of those huge white buttocks pounding against the body of the woman and the woollen-stockinged legs wrapped around the squire's pale flabby flesh. Did the bailiff, Ned Cake, know that his daughter was servicing the squire? Did he condone it?

She had to get her mother's locket back. Letting that woman keep it was unthinkable. The locket meant too much to her. It was the only possession she had that came from her real father. It had been a gift from him to her mother and thence to her. Tears of grief and anger rose up inside her. She wouldn't let Abigail Cake get away with it. She couldn't. That locket meant nothing to the bailiff's daughter. She pondered her options. She could go to Mrs Andrews, but the housekeeper would inevitably launch a full investigation of all members of the household, risking that the servants would henceforth treat her with contempt for mistrusting them. And what was the point? Abigail Cake didn't live in the Hall and had no reason to be there so would not even be included in the enquiries.

The only solution was for Hephzibah to confront the woman directly. She ran downstairs and sought out Mrs Andrews. She told her she needed a dress to be altered and wanted to know where she might find Miss Cake.

The bailiff's cottage was on the edge of the estate, close to the village. It was a brick-built dwelling, surrounded by trees which shielded it from the driveway, so Hephzibah almost walked past it. She had never noticed the narrow track despite passing by so many times before.

The place looked scruffy – green moss covering half the thatch, piles of rusty farm implements stacked against the wall and a pair of pigs truffling around in front, eating food scraps from a pail they had knocked over. A dog on a long chain began barking as Hephzibah approached the door.

Wisps of smoke were coming from the chimney so someone must be at home. Hephzibah prayed she would find Abigail Cake alone. She picked her way through the scattered potato peelings and bits of bone and knocked on the door, her heart thumping as loudly as the knocker. After a few moments, the door swung open and Abigail Cake was standing there, hands on hips.

'I was expecting you,' she said. 'Better come in.'

Hephzibah was so surprised she was lost for words, but followed the young woman inside the cottage. The interior was gloomy but clean. A large cooking range stood in the fireplace, the wall above it blackened with smoke and hung with pots and pans. The furniture was sparse – just a pair of wooden chairs and a wooden settle, a cradle in the corner and some rush matting on the floor in front of the range. The cradle held no baby but appeared to be used for storing clothing.

Abigail pointed to one of the chairs and Hephzibah sat down. She was about to speak when Abigail came towards her with her hand outstretched. In her open palm was the missing locket.

'I only took it so as you'd come and find me. I knew you'd know it was me as you saw me wearing your ribbons. I haven't stolen your locket. But I am keeping the ribbons.' Her voice was sly. 'They suit my hair colour better than they would yours.' Her expression was defiant.

Hephzibah put the locket around her neck and nodded at her. 'It was my late mother's. She died recently. She gave it to me when I was twelve.' As she said the words she wondered why she was explaining herself to this woman. 'I was devastated when I thought I'd lost it.'

The girl gave a sarcastic snort. 'You didn't think you'd lost it. You knew I had it. Same as the ribbons.' She sat down in the chair opposite, dragging it closer over the stone-flagged floor until she was sitting with her knees almost touching Hephzibah's.

Abigail leaned forward, her hands on her hips. 'So, Miss Wildman, has the squire asked you to marry him yet?'

Hephzibah gave a little gasp of surprise.

'Don't look so shocked. He asks them all. Maybe not the old ones. But all the others. You are one of a long line of governesses. One of them actually said yes to him. That put the fear of God in the old buffer. He just says it to get their hopes up. Make them think they're about to be lady of the manor. But it's just to soften them up so he can have his way with them. As soon as he made a move they ran a mile. Those bookish women don't like the idea of a fat old man pawing them and sticking his tongue down their throats and his hands up their skirts. Except for Anne Gordon. She actually shared a bed with him until his fiancée Lady Roderick found out, sent her packing and then dumped him.'

'How do you know all this?'

'Because he tried the same tricks with me. Well, he's never offered marriage. Doesn't need to in my case. And he knows I'd know it was too daft to be true.' She stared at Hephzibah defiantly. 'You saw us in the temple yesterday didn't you?'

Hephzibah nodded, increasingly puzzled by what Abigail wanted with her. Why was she telling her all this?

'I let him have his way with me because if I don't he'll dismiss my father and then we'll all be out of a home. I've the rest of my family to think about. I'd never let that old devil touch me otherwise.'

She gathered her apron up in her hands, squeezing the fabric into a ball, then smoothing it out again. Hephzibah realised that under her insolent exterior the girl was nervous.

'Look,' said Abigail, 'the reason I wanted to speak to you is I don't want you telling anybody about what you saw. My reputation is bad enough anyway and I don't want folk knowing I've been with the squire.' She paused for a moment. 'That is, I don't want my father to know. He'd kill the old devil, then they'd send him to the gallows and where would we be? And he's always looking for any excuse to take a strap to me.' She got up from her chair and carried it back across the room, then went over to the range and gave the contents of simmering pot a stir.

'But that's dreadful,' said Hephzibah. 'You shouldn't have to put up with that. Not with what the squire is doing and not with your father beating you either. Have you told the Reverend Nightingale? He might be able to intercede on your behalf.'

Abigail turned back to face Hephzibah. 'Mind your own business. I don't like you, Miss Wildman. I don't like what you stand for. You with your city ways and your fondness for the parson. They say you're going to marry him afore long.' She gave a dry laugh. 'As long as the squire doesn't get there first and spoil you for him.'

Hephzibah stood up. 'I don't know what you're talking about. I barely know the parson and as for the squire…'

The Ribbon Thief tilted her head on one side and curled her upper lip. 'No? Then how come you're always out walking with him. Can't blame folk for talking.' She sighed. 'You're all the same, you governesses. I've no time for any of you. You keep your mouth shut, Miss Wildman, or I'll be after more than your fancy gold locket next time. Now get out of here. I've work to do.' She held the cottage door open and Hephzibah went out.

Walking back to the Hall she was shaking with anger.

The woman had humiliated her. No one had ever spoken to her that way before. But then she had never before witnessed anyone behaving the way Abigail Cake behaved. The woman was clearly shameless.

CHAPTER TWELVE

Stitch – stitch – stitch,
In poverty, hunger and dirt,
Sewing at once, with a double thread,
A Shroud as well as a Shirt.

(from The Song of the Shirt, Thomas Hood)

Hephzibah was coming to the conclusion that Thomas Egdon had flirted with her just to pass the time – or possibly to annoy his father. She constantly revisited their conversations, the riding lessons and the way he had touched her on that first lesson when getting her to sit the horse correctly. How was it possible that he had lavished so much attention upon her only to withdraw completely? Why had he spent a fortune kitting her out with riding habit, then absented himself? His promises to take her around the county had not been fulfilled, apart from their visit to the horse fair. Forget him, she told herself. Why would he be interested in you anyway? You're only the governess. The man was a known philanderer and probably used women like her and Abigail Cake, before eventually marrying an aristocratic woman of fortune and connections. But whenever she thought about him – those intense blue eyes looking into hers, his thick silky black hair, strong nose, his cruel but beautiful mouth – she felt weak with longing.

The appointment to visit the workhouse in Mudford with Merritt Nightingale was made at last for late April. It was a pleasant two mile walk over open downland to the outskirts of the small market town of Mudford, where the workhouse was situated. As they walked, Merritt told her about the place.

'There used to be a small poorhouse in Nettlestock, but when the Poor Laws were introduced they shut it down and opened the Union Workhouse to serve the whole area. Apparently, it didn't go down well in the village. People liked having a local poorhouse. They used to come and go when times were hard and it was small and friendly. Now they have to be at their wits' end to agree to going "up the hill", as they call it.'

'Why is that?'

'The place is very regimented. If they're fit, they have to do what amounts to hard labour. Families are separated. Men in one section, and women and children under three in another. The older children don't get to see their parents while they're inside.'

Hephzibah stopped in her tracks, causing Merritt to look back at her. Her face was a mask of disbelief. 'Why on earth would they do that? It's cruel.'

'The belief is that everything needs to be done to discourage people from seeking assistance and encourage those who are able to find employment. The trouble is there isn't enough of that to go around.'

'But that's punishing children for their parents' failure to find work. How unjust.'

Merritt shook his head, his eyes sad. 'I know, Hephzibah. The assumption that all these unfortunate people, except the old and infirm, are idlers and layabouts is badly misguided. What man would not choose honest work in order to keep a home for his wife and children? But men can't make jobs that don't exist appear like a conjuring trick. All it takes is a bout of illness and they can fall behind with the rent and be thrown out of their home and cast on the mercy of the parish. In the old days they could claim poor relief while remaining in their own homes but the powers-that-be reckoned that too many of them were too comfortable living off the parish.'

'There was a workhouse in Oxford, but I never went near it. I am ashamed to say, Merritt, that I never even gave it a thought – apart from sending my late parents' clothes there, when the house was cleared. The kind of people who lived there never touched my life in any way. I suppose I was selfish and privileged and went about with blinkers on.'

He looked at her, resisting the desire to take her hands in his. 'Don't be so hard on yourself, Hephzibah. I had no idea what went on in these places either. Living in a small community like Nettlestock brings into sharp relief the problems that are all too easy to ignore in a city like Oxford.'

They walked on over the open downland, past rows of ancient oak trees that edged the road into the town. The spring had come late this year and there were still a few clusters of buttery daffodils as well as seas of bluebells in the woods they passed alongside.

The workhouse stood just outside Mudford at the top of a grassy bank. It was a forbidding building, of brick construction, with a grey slate roof and tall factory-like chimneys.

'It's grim. Like a prison. It seems wrong to make people live in a place like this when their only crime is poverty,' said Hephzibah.

They went through the gates, past the chapel and into the porter's lodge, from where they were shown to the guardians' boardroom to await the arrival of the master.

For twenty minutes or so the master discussed the

business of the workhouse with the parson, outlining the agenda for the next guardians' board meeting, then going through the numbers of admissions and departures. Hephzibah got up from the table and went across to the tall narrow windows that looked out onto the enclosed courtyards. Merritt glanced up at her. She was standing sideways to him and he studied her profile, trying to gauge what she might be thinking. She was frowning, thoughtful, worried. He shouldn't have brought her here. It was no place to bring a lady. And yet, he told himself, if she were to marry him he would want her to understand and share in all the elements of his life as a village parson. She turned round, caught his eye and smiled and he felt that same little surge of joy inside him that he experienced whenever she looked at him. The master coughed loudly and Merritt reluctantly returned his attention to the columns of figures.

Once the official business was out of the way, Merritt led Hephzibah downstairs and, accompanied by the matron, they undertook a tour of the facility. It being mid-afternoon, the inmates were hard at work and Merritt watched Hephzibah's reactions as she witnessed the men smashing rocks, crushing bones for bone-meal, and chopping timber; the women at work in the kitchens, laundry and tailoring shop, or picking oakum, their fingers raw from the rough fibres of the ropes they were pulling apart. Finally, they looked through the glass panel of the classroom door where about eighty children of different ages sat tightly packed on benches as their teacher instructed them. Hephzibah gave little away. Merritt had no idea what she was thinking.

He was relieved when the tour was complete and they left the institution. As they walked back towards Nettlestock it began to rain, a fine April drizzle that soon turned into a downpour. He grabbed hold of Hephzibah's arm and they ran towards a wooden shelter at the side of the road and flung themselves onto a bench fixed to the back wall, the front being open to the elements.

Settling on the bench, side-by-side, Hephzibah turned her face to him and said, 'I'm so grateful to you for taking me there today, Merritt.'

It was not the reaction he had expected. He had believed she had found the experience harrowing and he had been cursing his stupidity for dragging her there with him.

'You're not distressed by what you saw?' he asked.

'Of course I am. I had no conception of how people like that live. I'm grateful though, because it has made me thankful for my own good fortune. I've felt lonely and miserable since the loss of my parents, but today has made me realise how much I still have to be thankful for. I think I would die were I to be shut away in a place like that. So thank you for showing me.'

She took off her hat, held it arm's length and shook off the raindrops. 'What drives a person to accept living like that, Merritt? What makes them so desperate that they're prepared to dress in an ugly uniform and tear old ropes apart for hours until their fingers bleed? Did you see the tiny quantity of meat that went into the stew? A bit of tough old mutton gristle cut into tiny pieces and mixed in with a lot of turnips. It was turnip soup but the matron called it mutton stew!' She shook her head. 'How many people live there? More than one hundred and fifty the master said, didn't he? There was only enough meat going into that pot to feed about a dozen. If they could even get the gristle down their throats.' She squeezed her hands into fists.

Merritt placed his hand on her arm. 'I know. And the numbers are growing. Times are hard and getting harder. One of the farmers told me the other day that it's cheaper to ship a sack of grain all the way from the prairies of America than from here to London.'

'Are they all agricultural workers then?'

'Most of them. But there are unmarried mothers too. Widows with no means of support. Widowers who'd rather live in an institution than fend for themselves without a wife to care for them. And then there's the tramps and drunkards. Most of those only stay a few days.'

They stared out at the rain, silent for several moments. At last Merritt spoke. 'I imagine our friend Peter Goody will be joining them soon.'

Hephzibah twisted in her seat to look at him. 'The poacher? Oh no! Have you seen him again?'

'I called on him this morning. His wife is trying to care for him but he needs medical help and they have no money to pay for it. He'd had no work for weeks before what happened and the children look half-starved. I took them a basket of food, but he asked me not to come again. He's terrified of someone telling the squire about his poaching.'

'It's not right. Is there nothing else you can do for him? Isn't there anyone who can help the poor man? He must be distraught.'

'Oddly enough, he's not. He's resigned to it. I suppose he thinks anything's better than being thrown in jail. Even a spell in the workhouse. He'll be treated in the infirmary there and maybe by springtime summer he'll be fit enough to find paid employment.' He thought for a moment, then said, 'I threw the mantrap in the canal.'

She gave him a rueful smile. 'I'm glad. Do you think Sir Richard knew it was there?'

He pulled his mouth into a mirthless smile. 'Probably not. But his bailiff or the gamekeeper would have done. And they do what they think the squire wants without bothering to clarify. And the squire knows that as well as I do. All these landowners care about is a keeping plenty of game for shooting. Egdon's no different from hundreds of others up and down the land.'

'I wish we could do more to help Peter Goody and the others like him,' said Hephzibah. 'You must carry some influence, Merritt. People will listen to you.'

The parson looked away then turned back to look at her. 'I've been in this parish for almost three years and still no one trusts me. The squire puts up with me because it's the expected thing, but he doesn't really approve of me because I don't ride to hounds. He wasn't amused when he found out that I got the butcher to cut up the side of venison he sent me last month so I could give it away to those in need. Gave me a mouthful for being an ingrate. Told me I wouldn't be getting any more.'

Hephzibah smiled. 'I can picture him saying that!'

'The village shopkeepers are civil enough but I know they still see me as an interloper. The rest of the population view me with suspicion. My predecessor never darkened the doors of the cottage dwellers and when I called on a few of them I was kept standing in the doorway. They see me as some well-to-do stranger who gets to dine with the squire and so must be far too grand to be invited inside their humble abodes.' He gave a dry laugh. 'Unlike my Wesleyan colleague, Mr Leatherwood. They see him as one of their own and invite him in for tea.'

'You still manage to pull in the crowds on a Sunday.'

He sighed. 'It's a small church. They were standing three deep at the back when I first came, but every week a few more of them switch their allegiance to the chapel. And they don't like the fact that I am a single man.' As Merritt spoke the words he felt the blood rush to his face.

Hephzibah appeared not to notice his embarrassment and said, 'Couldn't you ask Mr Leatherwood to help?'

'He has less time for me than the rest of them. Sees me as the devil incarnate. Mrs Muggeridge, who is the fount of all knowledge in Nettlestock, told me she overheard him saying that I'm only in the job for the five hundred a year it pays whereas he has a true vocation and believes the words he preaches – all the fire and brimstone – I just go through the motions. And the awful thing, Hephzibah, is that he's right.'

'You may not be as devout as he is, but it's obvious that you care about your parishioners. I think it's more important to care for one's fellow man than for an invisible God. That's far more important than spouting scripture all over the place and scaring the daylights out of people. Besides, isn't one showing love for God by loving one's neighbour?' She sounded indignant.

Merritt laughed. Her eyes were shining as she spoke and he knew that what he felt for her was real, more than just a reaction to a pretty face and a fine figure. He loved her. He really loved her. This afternoon had cemented what he felt about her. He wanted her with a hunger that he felt powerless to control, but on top of that he felt she really understood him, cared about the same things as him and would be his perfect helpmate in life.

He turned towards her, knowing that there would never be a better time to ask her to marry him than now. Here they were, trapped in the rain, away from everyone, alone. It was early in their acquaintance, but what was the point in delaying when he was so sure, so certain, so absolutely convinced that they were meant to be together? It all made perfect sense. No point in delay. He cleared his throat and was about to speak, when she jumped up.

'Look, Merritt, the rain has stopped and there's a herd of deer over there. Look. Quickly! Let's try to get a bit closer before they run away.'

Before Merritt could respond, Hephzibah was moving across the grassy sward towards the large herd of grazing fallow deer. All his new-found courage deserted him and he cursed inwardly as he followed her.

A few days after her visit to the workhouse, Hephzibah walked into Nettlestock to the post office. Not that she expected to find any mail there – but she couldn't help hoping that one of her old friends might drop her a few lines. She longed for news of life in Oxford – it was hard to imagine things going on as usual there as she felt so divorced from it. It was another world. She realised she was lonely. Ottilie was a delight and she was building a cordial relationship with Mrs Andrews, but the housekeeper still maintained enough distance to signal that Hephzibah would never be able to regard her as a confidante. There was Merritt Nightingale of course, but he was a man and that automatically meant they could never be close friends.

Hephzibah left the post office, having been subjected to a ten minute monologue from Mrs Bellamy on the need for the village to find a way to memorialise the late queen and her personal view that six weeks of deep mourning and six of half mourning were utterly insufficient to mark her passing. Hephzibah wandered along the village street, stepping aside as the children poured out of the school. A large group were heading en masse for the common ground where they liked to play games. Others clustered around the village street, dodging any passing horses and traps and bouncing a ball against the schoolhouse wall.

As she passed by the school, Miss Pickering, the school teacher, emerged and called out her name.

'Miss Wildman, I am so pleased to see you. I had meant to catch you after church last Sunday but I must have missed you in the crowd. I was going to ask you if perhaps we might organise our expedition to the Roman ruin now the weather is at last improving.'

Saddened by this reminder of Thomas Egdon, Hephzibah gave the woman a weak smile. 'What a lovely idea, Miss Pickering. I'm afraid Mr Egdon has forgotten all about it but perhaps the parson might still accompany us and I know Ottilie would love to be part of such an excursion.'

The teacher clapped her hands together. 'I'm so pleased. Do you think the Reverend Nightingale would be willing to spare us the time? Maybe in May? The ruins aren't far. The only thing is I think you may be disappointed, Miss Wildman. There are only the faintest traces of what was once an old bathhouse and all the mosaics were removed many years ago. I'm afraid you might be bored when you must have seen so many treasures in the Ashmolean at Oxford. I visited there once myself when I was sixteen. Did I tell you my brother was an undergraduate at Balliol College?' Miss Pickering was breathless.

'I didn't know you had a brother, Miss Pickering.'

The woman stretched her lips and frowned. 'Not any more. Hector died.'

'I'm so sorry. He must have been very young.'

'He was. Just twenty-four. Engaged to be married and with a bright future as a lawyer. He had just been called to the Bar.' Miss Pickering shook her head and her lip trembled. 'I still miss him every day. It was a perforated appendix. They operated but the sepsis had already set in and he died shortly after.'

The schoolmistress brushed away a tear then squeezed Hephzibah's hand. 'Won't you come inside and take a cup of tea with Mama and me?'

Hephzibah hesitated for a moment then accepted.

The house adjoined the school and the interior smelled strongly of the sickly scent of potpourri in bowls in every room. Mrs Pickering was a small woman with an imperious manner. She persisted in banging her walking stick on the floor whenever she wanted to summon the maid. The old lady scrutinised Hephzibah with ill-concealed disapproval and after going through the formalities of greeting, lapsed into silence and before long was snoring away in her chair.

'Mama has never got over the loss of Hector and Papa. Some days she doesn't even leave her bedroom. You have found her on a good day.'

Hephzibah refrained from comment, trying not to

imagine what a bad day might comprise. Grateful that the old woman had nodded off, she adopted the same hushed tones that Miss Pickering was using, having decided that this would be a good opportunity for her to test out her theory that the teacher might be in love with the parson.

'Mr Nightingale is most agreeable, don't you think?'

The teacher's face broke into a beaming smile. 'He is indeed. And such a learned man.'

'Have you had an opportunity to spend some time with him?'

'Indeed. He attends the school each week to supervise a Bible class with the children. I do look forward to that so much as I always learn something new. Occasionally, he has graced this house to visit Mama and take tea with us.'

Hephzibah decided to coax along what she was already seeing as a budding romance. Whether Thomas Egdon accompanied them on the trip to the ruins or not, with Ottilie present she could easily find a way to engineer the teacher and the parson being together.

'Do you enjoy reading, Miss Pickering?'

'It is my greatest pleasure.'

'Then you must ask Mr Nightingale to show you his book collection. I am sure he would be willing to let you borrow any books that might interest you.'

The teacher nodded absently, then said, 'I am fortunate to have a large library here at home. My late father and Hector were both avid readers.'

'You and Mr Nightingale have so much in common.'

'I don't know him enough to know whether that is true or not.' Miss Pickering looked at her with an expression that was both a smile and a frown. 'But you too like reading, Miss Wildman?'

'Very much so,' said Hephzibah. 'Now, tell me, did you enjoy Mr Nightingale's sermon last Sunday? It was very inspiring, don't you think?'

'I'm not sure I can remember what he spoke of – I'm ashamed to say. How dreadful of me,' said Miss Pickering. 'He always speaks eloquently. What was the subject this time?'

Hephzibah found herself blushing as she couldn't remember. She hesitated then said, 'I believe he spoke of the importance of charitable deeds.'

Miss Pickering was looking at her with a puzzled expression. 'Really? I don't recall. But you must be right since you found the sermon such an inspiration.' She smiled at Hephzibah. 'Or is it rather Mr Nightingale himself who is the source of fascination?'

This wasn't going at all as Hephzibah planned it. It was clear that Miss Pickering was implying that Hephzibah herself was interested in the clergyman. She decided to try a different tack.

'I often take a walk after church on Sunday with the parson. Perhaps you would care to join us? I'm sure Mr Nightingale would welcome your company. He must get rather weary of mine.'

'I'm quite sure he doesn't. And much as I would love to, Mama always likes me to return from church promptly on Sunday. As I am in the schoolhouse so much she regards Sundays as her special time with me.'

'But surely she must realise that you need some social discourse outside the house?' Hephzibah lowered her voice remembering that the lady in question was snoozing in her chair across the room. 'After all, one day, you will marry and she will have to share you with your husband.'

Miss Pickering smiled and shook her head. 'Oh no, Miss Wildman. I don't think Mama needs to worry about that. Now, let me show you the library here.' She rose to her feet and indicated that Hephzibah should follow her into an adjoining room. 'You see we have a collection here with more than enough books to keep me occupied for the rest of my life.'

The conversation about Merritt Nightingale was closed. While Hephzibah knew better than to push her hostess, she left the house more convinced than ever that Miss Pickering was nurturing a secret passion for the parson. Her very reticence spoke volumes. She would have to try and encourage the romance from the other side by giving Merritt a nudge in the right direction.

CHAPTER THIRTEEN

A moment ago, she'd have struck even Pluto as sad,
but now she is glowing with radiant smiles,
like the sun which was formerly hidden
behind a blanket of rain clouds and then emerges victorious.

(from The Rape of Proserpina, Metamorphoses, Ovid)

Ottilie was upstairs in the old nursery, working on her times tables. Hephzibah had promised to find her a new book to read. She was alone in the library searching for something suitable for the girl, as Ottilie was making exceptional progress and devouring every book that Hephzibah put in front of her. She stood on the top step of the wooden ladder and stretched her hand towards a high shelf, where she could see a copy of *The Water Babies*. Why on earth were the books suited to children placed on the higher shelves, while there were well-thumbed copies of *The Romance of Lust* and *Fanny Hill* at eye level?

Absorbed in her search, she didn't hear the squire enter the room and she almost exploded with fright when his hand touched the bare skin of her inner thigh just above the knee. She screamed and nearly fell off the ladder. Egdon withdrew his hand, using it instead to steady her as she scrambled down from the stepladder. She pushed him away.

'Take your hands off me! I told you never to touch me again.'

Ignoring her protests, the squire pulled her towards him and pushed his face up against hers. She felt his fat whiskered cheek on hers and then his blubbery mouth was on her lips, like a damp slug, and he pushed his tongue insistently against her teeth.

She jerked her head back. 'Get off! I don't want you to do that. Stop it! Now!'

He gripped hold of her shoulders and his hooded eyes fixed on hers. 'I have to have you. You're driving me out of my mind, Hephzibah. I'll marry you. I'll do the right thing. But I have to have you. I can't go on like this. You're sending me mad with desire. Marry me! Whatever you want will be yours.'

His bloated face was close to hers and he kept a tight grip on her shoulders. Hephzibah could smell the whisky on his breath.

'You're young. You'll give me a son. That idiot Thomas will never marry and produce an heir. All he cares for are horses, gambling and spending money he hasn't got. I need to protect Ingleton Hall. Marry me and you'll want for nothing. Let me put a child in your belly.'

He took one of his hands off her shoulders and cupped it over her breast and squeezed. Hephzibah tried to scream but was so terrified she was unable to make a noise.

The squire tried to kiss her again, this time more roughly as he pushed her onto a chaise longue and lay on top of her. 'Hephzibah, Hephzibah, you have enchanted me. I'm in your thrall. I'll do anything to have you. Please say you'll marry me. I will make you Lady Egdon.'

He straddled her, his hands on her shoulders and his face close to hers. Hephzibah was paralysed with fear. Did he intend to rape her here in the library, with the servants in the kitchen and Ottilie upstairs?

Before she could say anything, he spoke; again, his voice hoarse with lust. 'Just say yes and I'll wait until we are married. I'll do the right thing. Just say you'll marry me. All I want now is a kiss and cuddle. I won't hurt you. I promise.'

He bent his head down and pressed his mouth against hers as she writhed beneath him, her mouth clamped shut and her head twisting from side to side. Her movement under him excited him more and one of his hands was under her skirt working its way up her bare leg again.

What could she do? His weight was heavy on her and she struggled to breathe. His breath was stale and tainted with whisky and cigars and she wanted to gag. She twisted sideways and said, 'The servants will hear. And Ottilie is expecting me. You don't want her to walk in and see this.'

He lifted his gaze and looked at her. 'No one's coming. I locked the door.' He lowered his head and moved his mouth onto her neck where he nuzzled at her like a puppy. 'You smell so fresh. Like a flower. You beautiful creature.' His wet tongue moved into her ear. He was astride her, knees planted either side of her.

Anger and revulsion surged through Hephzibah, giving her strength and courage. As he ran his hands over her breasts again, she jerked her head back and sunk her teeth into his cheek, biting as hard as she could.

The squire gave a howl of pain and rolled off her and onto the floor.

Hephzibah jumped to her feet, tasting blood in her mouth. She moved away from her assailant, backing into the library ladder and knocking it over. The squire's groans followed her as she opened the French windows and ran out onto the terrace.

Without stopping to get her breath back, Hephzibah ran, shocked as much by the way her instinct for self-preservation had caused her to bite her employer, as by his aggression towards her. The afternoon sun was moving low in the sky and there was a slight breeze. A faint smell of wood smoke was in the air. With no coat or shawl to protect her, she shivered. But she didn't want to go back inside. She couldn't risk running into Squire Egdon again. The man was a monster. He assumed that some kind of feudal system operated where, as lord of the manor, he was entitled to do as he willed with any member of his household.

Nothing in Hephzibah's life had prepared her for dealing with this. What was she to do? Where was she to go? One thing was certain – she couldn't possibly stay at Ingleton Hall. Hard as it would be to say goodbye to Ottilie and to go out alone into the world, she couldn't remain under the same roof as Sir Richard. Besides, after the way she had bitten him, it was unlikely he would be giving her the option anyway.

She went to find Mrs Andrews to tell her what had happened and ask her to help her pack without the squire intercepting her.

The housekeeper looked shocked when Hephzibah told her she had bitten Sir Richard in order to break free of him, and acknowledged that, indeed, Hephzibah had no choice but to leave immediately.

'I thought at last we'd got a governess who would stay. I'd begun to believe that you had managed to keep Sir Richard under control. You've lasted longer than any of the others and I'll be sorry to see you go, Miss Wildman.' She twitched at the hem of her apron, shook her head, then stretched out a hand to Hephzibah. 'I will miss you. As will Ottilie. Are you sure you won't reconsider? Once the squire has sobered up he'll realise what he's done and will regret it. Perhaps if you were just to go away for a night or so he'd come to his senses and might even apologise.' She looked at Hephzibah plaintively.

Hephzibah shook her head. 'I can't, Mrs Andrews. I made it clear last time. I have to leave.'

The housekeeper nodded. 'I understand, but I don't like it.' Then on an impulse, she pulled Hephzibah to her and gave her a quick squeeze. 'When you know where you'll be staying, send word and I'll arrange for your trunk to be sent on.'

The pain of leaving without saying goodbye to Ottilie was acute but Hephzibah couldn't risk the little girl causing a scene and alerting her father. Tears welled up as she thought of how the child would feel betrayed. Ottilie would be devastated to find out her favourite governess, like all the others, had abandoned her. It would be impossible for the girl to understand the reason for Hephzibah's hasty departure. She'd leave her a note – but she couldn't carry out the threat she had made to Egdon to tell his daughter what kind of man he was – Ottilie was too young to understand and too adoring of her father to be so cruelly disillusioned.

But where to go? She thought of Miss Pickering, but Hephzibah was uncomfortable presuming upon their brief acquaintance or the goodwill of the rather grumpy mother. Besides, she didn't want word of what had happened to spread around the village and possibly get back to Ottilie. There was only one option. The Reverend Nightingale had secured her the position at Ingleton Hall so he must take some responsibility for the consequences. He could help her find a lodging overnight and then she would take the train tomorrow to return to Oxford. She'd worry about what to do next when she got there. One step at a time.

It took less than half an hour to pack her holdall. She sat down in the housekeeper's sitting room to pen the brief note to Ottilie, who was upstairs learning French verbs and would be soon wondering where her governess had gone. Hephzibah wept as she wrote the short letter, telling the little girl that she had to leave on urgent personal business.

Hephzibah left the riding habit hanging in the wardrobe. She'd have no use for it now and she didn't consider it her property. As she emptied the drawers of her chest she saw the sprig of white heather the gipsy had given her. She didn't need that either.

When Mrs Andrews reported that the coast was clear and the squire was sleeping off his overindulgence with the whisky decanter in an armchair in the drawing room, she slipped away from the Hall.

Hurrying down the driveway towards the village, she heard the sound of hooves and was gripped in a momentary panic that Sir Richard Egdon was coming after her, but the sound was coming from the direction of the village. As she turned the curve of the driveway she saw Thomas Egdon riding towards her. He reined his horse in.

'Where are you heading, Miss Wildman?' He looked her up and down, saw her large carpet bag and jumped off his horse. 'What has he done to you? Has he hurt you?'

To her astonishment, he gathered her into his arms, holding her pressed hard against him. Hephzibah was so shocked she couldn't speak, feeling his body against hers and his hands on her back.

'Tell me,' he said. 'Tell me exactly what happened.'

Thomas took her by the hand and led her over to a fallen tree trunk and they sat down on it, side-by-side. Hephzibah hoped he couldn't hear the hammering of her heart.

'Your father tried to touch me.' She hesitated then added, 'In an intimate way. He even asked me to marry him. He told me he wanted me to…' She swallowed, revolted again by the thought of the squire's proposal. 'He said he wanted to have a baby with me. He said you will never produce an heir. He kissed me. He tried to force himself on me. It was horrible.'

Thomas Egdon reached for her hand again, turned it palm upwards, then bent his head over it and kissed the inside of her wrist. 'I am so sorry, Miss Wildman. I'm ashamed of my father. He's nothing but a beast. His conduct is unforgivable. I only hope that you don't let his behaviour influence your opinion of me. We are very different.' He looked at her, his eyes serious, fixed on hers.

Hephzibah gulped. How was it possible that this man was the squire's son? The same flesh and blood. How was it possible? She felt a desire for Thomas as strong as the repulsion she felt for his father. He was still holding her hand and she prayed that he wouldn't let it go. Ever.

They sat in silence for a few minutes. She could feel his body close against hers, then his left arm went around her waist, while his right hand still held hers, his skin warm against her own.

Eventually he spoke. 'What will you do?'

'I will go to the parsonage and ask the Reverend Nightingale to find a suitable lodging for me in the village tonight and then I will take the next train back to Oxford.'

'Then what?'

She shook her head. 'I don't know. I will find another position as a governess. I will seek help from friends of my parents. From my late father's college. Something will turn up. I trust in God.'

'Do you?' he asked, frowning.

'Well, I hope in God,' she added, 'and I trust in myself.'

He smiled at her then lifted his hand and tucked a stray lock of hair back under her hat. 'You are indeed a beautiful creature. No wonder you have driven my father mad with desire.' He laid his hand against her cheek. 'Not that I am condoning his behaviour.'

She looked down, wondering that she could feel such desire herself. She wanted him to kiss her. She wanted to know what his lips would feel like on hers. To know how it would feel to be held in his arms. She turned towards him, hoping that he might feel the same way about her, but he jumped up and moved round to crouch in front of her, taking both her hands in his.

'I have an idea. I want you to consider it seriously.' He looked at her, his eyes giving away nothing. 'Marry me instead.'

Hephzibah was so taken aback she nearly fell off the tree trunk. 'You are trifling with me, sir,' she whispered. 'That is too cruel.'

'I mean it. Now that I've said it, it makes perfect sense. It will serve the old dog right. It will solve all our problems in one stroke. Yes, marry me, Miss Wildman.'

'But you don't care for me. Why would you marry me?'

'Not care for you? Of course I care for you. How could I not? You are an exquisite creature, the most lovely I have ever laid eyes upon.'

'But you barely know me,' she said, her voice trembling.

'Don't we have a lifetime for that? How much does any man know a woman before he marries her? I will look forward to finding out. Do you think you might be able, after a little time, to feel something for me?'

Hephzibah swallowed, then said, 'Yes. Yes I think I might. In fact…' She swallowed again. 'I think perhaps I already do.'

Thomas leaned forward and kissed her lightly on the lips, then looked into her eyes. 'How was that? Better than my father?'

She responded by raising her mouth to his and, as he kissed her slowly, she felt a growing hunger for him. She reached her hands up behind his head, feeling the soft fullness of his hair, tangling her fingers in it and holding onto him, desperate for the kiss to go on, willing him not to stop.

After a while he pressed her shoulders gently and drew back, looking into her eyes. 'I think I have my answer, Miss Wildman – Hephzibah. No, I can't possibly call you that. Too much of a mouthful. I shall call you Zee. Let's waste no time. I don't want the old dog to know what we're doing until it's too late for him to stop us. Here's the plan.' He told her they would ride together to an inn in Newbury where they would take rooms for the night before taking a train to Scotland where they could marry at Gretna Green. 'Don't worry. I won't lay a hand on you, Zee, until I've put a ring on your finger.'

Hephzibah tried not to wish that he didn't mean that. All she wanted now was to be wrapped in his arms and to feel his mouth on hers, his body against hers. She felt a thrill inside at the thought of being alone with him, of doing things with him, with his body, in his bed. Her heart wouldn't stop pounding against her ribcage. She was almost grateful to the squire for his part in bringing about this miracle, for precipitating this magic, for bringing her Thomas. And she loved the way he called her Zee, just as her stepfather had done when she was a small child.

They were married two days later at Gretna Green. At first Hephzibah was uncomfortable with the idea of elopement, then she reminded herself that with her parents gone there was no family to stand witness to her nuptials. She would have preferred her friend, Mr Nightingale, to perform the ceremony – but marrying under the nose of the squire was out of the question according to Thomas.

As soon as the wedding was completed, Thomas told her they would return immediately to Ingleton Hall. Hephzibah was disappointed and upset that they were spending no time together on a honeymoon before returning to face Squire Egdon, but Thomas promised that would come later – the first priority was to let his father know.

Hephzibah had only a few items of clothing in her carpet bag – her trunk was still waiting for her back at Ingleton Hall. They took a train back to England just a matter of hours after arriving in Scotland. She was tired and felt grubby after all the travelling. The prospect of a warm bath and a change of clothing made a return to the Hall almost bearable, although she dreaded facing the squire.

Thomas slept during most of the train journey south and Hephzibah had to content herself with the passing scenery. She watched Thomas sleeping, still finding it hard to believe that this virtual stranger was now her husband. He looked, if anything, more beautiful asleep than awake and she raised a hand and ran it down his cheek, feeling the stubble on his face where he had not had a chance to shave.

A sudden recollection of the words of the gipsy fortune teller came into Hephzibah's head. *Married before summer comes*. The woman had been right. Remembering the rest of her prophecy Hephzibah shivered, then told herself it was just coincidence. The woman had probably jumped to conclusions about her being accompanied by Thomas to the horse fair. It was clear that it was the place that every courting couple in the surrounding countryside headed to each year, so natural enough for the gipsy to assume they were sweethearts. She wasn't going to think about it any more. Stuff and nonsense.

When at last Thomas awoke as their train drew into London, she suggested they break their journey in a hotel, but he was anxious to return to Ingleton Hall as quickly as possible. They took a train as far as Reading. Being too late for a connecting train to Nettlestock, Thomas hired a driver to convey them the rest of the way. Hephzibah tried valiantly to draw her husband into talking, but he looked preoccupied and, although answering her questions, failed to develop the conversation further.

'Are you worried about something, Thomas?'

He looked up. 'Sorry, my dear, what did you say?'

'I was asking if you were worried about something. You're not regretting marrying me, are you?' Her voice was quiet and she was terrified of his reply.

He must regret running away with her. It was such an

unplanned event. A crazy spur-of-the-moment decision. She herself had no regrets but she was terrified that he did. But Thomas turned to look at her and grasped her hands in his.

'Of course I don't regret marrying you, my darling. How could I?' He ran his hands over her hair and tilted her chin towards him, bending down and brushing her lips with his. 'I've just got a lot on my mind. I'll make it up to you very soon.'

When Hephzibah walked into the drawing room of Ingleton Hall that evening, she was holding Thomas's hand. The squire was reading *Sporting Life* and dropped the paper as soon as he saw them. His cheek was swollen and he was wearing a dressing where Hephzibah had bitten him.

'What's the meaning of this?' He looked at their clasped hands, then at Hephzibah. 'What are you doing here?'

Thomas answered. 'We are married, Father. I heeded your advice and decided it was time to take a wife and have found myself the prettiest one in the county.'

'Is this true?' The squire addressed Hephzibah, who nodded.

'Why? What the hell? You barely know each other. She's the damned governess. What are you thinking, you stupid fool?' His face was sclerotic with anger.

Thomas shrugged. 'You're never happy, are you? Tell me to take a wife then insult us both when I do.'

'But it's not possible. Where did you get married? When? She only left here a couple of days ago.'

'We eloped to Gretna Green. We wanted to do it as quickly as possible. It was the only way I could keep her safe from your disgraceful behaviour. You're a cad, Father, a complete cad. And if you ever try to lay a finger on my wife again you'll answer to me for it and I swear to God I'll kill you.'

Thomas strode across the room and rang the bell. When

a maid appeared, he asked her to bring tea. 'Mrs Egdon is tired after our journey, Betsy, so ask Mrs Andrews to arrange for a bath to be drawn for her after she has taken her tea.'

The maid looked startled and after saying, 'Yes, sir. Right away, sir,' ran out of the room, presumably anxious to spread the news of the newly-wed couple to the rest of the staff.

The squire was still red in the face. 'We have a guest tonight. I invited the parson to dine with me in order to discuss Miss Wildman's disappearance and seek his suggestions for a replacement governess.'

He looked at Hephzibah, his expression a mixture of anger and confusion. 'Will you be staying here? Do you plan to continue with Ottilie's education? She was very…'

Word of Hephzibah's return must have reached as far as Ottilie, as, before the squire could finish speaking, the door burst open and the girl cannoned into the room, rushing straight to Hephzibah. She flung her little arms around her teacher's waist and rested her head against her.

'You've come back, Miss Wildman! You've come back. I was so sad. I cried and cried when I read your letter. I've been sad ever since, haven't I, Papa? But I knew you'd come back to us if I said extra prayers every night and ate everything on my plate. So I did and you have. You have.' She jumped up and down.

Hephzibah pulled Ottilie towards her and stroked the little girl's head.

Thomas grabbed the child by the waist and swung her into the air. 'And the best news is that your Miss Wildman is now your big sister.'

Ottilie's eyes widened and her mouth fell open. Thomas put her down.

'Is it true? How is that possible?' Ottilie looked between Thomas and Hephzibah and back again.

'Miss Wildman – Hephzibah – and I were married this

morning. She is now my wife and that makes her your new sister-in-law.'

Ottilie jumped up in the air again, waving tightly curled fists. 'I'm so happy. I've always wanted a sister. You will be the best sister anyone has ever had. I loved you already and now I will love you more and more and more. Oh, Papa, isn't it wonderful?'

Richard Egdon scowled but then gave a grunt, 'I suppose so.'

Hephzibah asked the child what had happened in her absence.

'Papa fell off his horse and hurt his face. The doctor comes every day to dress it, doesn't he, Papa?'

This evinced only a grunt from Sir Richard.

The doors opened and instead of the maid, Mrs Andrews herself entered, carrying a large silver tray laden with the tea things.

'I hear congratulations are in order, Master Thomas. And my best wishes to you for a long and happy marriage, Miss Wildman, I mean Mrs Egdon.' As she placed the tray on a side table she raised one eyebrow at Hephzibah, who couldn't tell if she was amused or disapproving.

'So two more places for dinner tonight? Instead of the lamb chops I will propose to Cook that she prepares a joint of beef. And I imagine you'll be wanting some champagne up from the cellar, sir.'

The squire waved his hand in annoyance. 'Do whatever you think. You know the drill. But remember it's only the parson coming, not the entire county.'

'Can I stay up, Papa? Oh please say I can stay up and come to dinner.' Ottilie climbed onto the sofa beside her father and rested her head against his shoulder.

CHAPTER FOURTEEN

But love is blind and lovers cannot see
The pretty follies that themselves commit;

(from The Merchant of Venice, Shakespeare)

Merritt pulled up short as he entered the drawing room. Hephzibah was back. He felt his stomach lurch and his face broke into a wide grin. She looked more beautiful than ever, wearing a gown of shot silk that shimmered in the candlelight. He moved towards her, his hand outstretched.

'Miss Wildman, you've returned. This is indeed a happy occasion. The squire has been anxious about your sudden disappearance, as indeed was I.'

He stopped short in the middle of the room a few feet in front of her and his stomach clenched as Thomas Egdon put a proprietorial arm around Hephzibah's shoulders and intercepted the parson's outstretched hand with his own. 'You can be the first person outside the family to con-gratulate us, Reverend Nightingale. I am proud to present the new Mrs Thomas Egdon.' He shook Merritt's hand vigorously.

The squire handed a glass of champagne to Merritt and proposed a toast to the happy couple, but Merritt was oblivious to everything and everyone in the room except for Hephzibah. She smiled at him, but then turned her gaze upon her husband with a look of undiluted adoration, as though he were the only other person in the room.

Merritt felt unsteady on his feet. His face burned and he knew his complexion must be as flushed as the colour of Hephzibah's dress. He stammered his congratulations, his throat dry and his hands shaking. How was this possible? Hephzibah had given no sign that she was courting Thomas Egdon – apart from the way she had allowed him to monopolise her at the squire's dinner party several months ago. But how could they have been courting when Thomas had barely been in Nettlestock? He sipped the champagne but felt it catch in his throat. Speak, man. Say something. You must. They're all looking at you. All except her. She has eyes only for him. Breathe. Slowly. Now swallow. Now say something.

'This is all very sudden. I'm afraid you have taken me by surprise. I'm lost for words.' He tried to laugh, to make light of the situation, to disguise his embarrassment. His hand went to the back of his neck and he could feel his skin hot under his fingers. He ran his hand through his hair and tried to find something else to say, but it was as if his brain had been scrambled. He was delivered of his mortification and confusion when the doors opened and they were summoned into dinner.

Merritt tried not to look at Hephzibah during the meal, but it was no use. His eyes were drawn to her like the incoming tide to the shore. He struggled to eat, grateful that the squire's beef was at least tender, as the effort of chewing would have defeated him – but it still was hard to swallow. Hephzibah's eyes shone with happiness and he cringed to think he had imagined that they might one day gaze upon his own in just the way that she was looking at Thomas Egdon. Merritt was oblivious to everything else in the room, then realised the squire was speaking to him. He apologised, citing a headache that had beset him earlier that afternoon and had returned to torment him now. He sipped his water and waited for the squire to speak again.

'My daughter-in-law has offered to continue with Ottilie's education. I'm not convinced it's a good idea, Nightingale. Not now she's a member of the family. What do you think?'

Merritt caught a fleeting expression of annoyance on Hephzibah's face and said, 'If Hep… Mrs Egdon wishes to continue with supervising Ottilie's education I can see no reason why not. Unless…' He glanced at Thomas.

Thomas said, 'I think it's a good idea. It will keep my wife occupied when I'm away. At least until she has other things to distract her.'

'Other things?' said Merritt.

Thomas leaned over and planted a kiss on his new wife's head. 'Children of her own, of course. I hope it will not be long before she is kept busy on that score.'

Merritt looked down at the remains of food on his barely touched plate. Why had he allowed himself to walk into that? He felt his stomach lurch and he struggled not to gag. He put his hand over his mouth and turned away from the table, coughing.

'I'm sorry. I think I may have picked up a chill today when I was out and about. Please excuse me.'

Hephzibah looked at him with sympathy and his heart jumped again and he wanted to get up from the table and run out of the house. It was unbearable. Images filled his head of Thomas Egdon holding Hephzibah in his arms, kissing her, touching her, taking her to his bed, making love to her. He felt sick.

Merritt knew Hephzibah had made a mistake in marrying Thomas Egdon. Not just from a selfish point of view. It was apparent that while she was undoubtedly in love with the man, her feelings were not reciprocated. It was not just wishful thinking on his part – he had watched the way they looked at each other. There had been undiluted joy in her face, an unashamed pleasure in looking at her husband that pained Merritt like a knife slicing between his ribs. She was captivated, entranced, enthralled by Egdon.

Thomas Egdon looked at his wife with a different kind of pleasure. There was a sense of smugness about him, a proprietorial self-satisfaction and Merritt had not failed to notice that Thomas looked as often towards his father as at his wife, as though putting on a display for him. Merritt had an urge to punch the man in the face. Instead, he endured the spectacle and cursed his own stupidity for ever thinking that Hephzibah might feel for him the love she was showing to her new husband.

Thomas Egdon was a bounder, but probably no more so than many of his peers. He was one of a breed that Merritt despised – a vain man with no sensibilities, wasting his time gambling, drinking, and pursuing amorous adventures. For Hephzibah's sake, Merritt hoped that her influence would bring about a reform of his character, but he doubted it. He predicted that before long Egdon was likely to break her heart into as many pieces as his own was in now.

Squire Egdon presided over the dinner with increasing sullenness, occasionally throwing a barbed comment in the direction of his son, but mostly sitting in silence, watching everything from under his hooded, vulture's eyes.

'Reverend Nightingale, I do hope that you will let me accompany you again next time you visit the workhouse in Mudford,' said Hephzibah. She turned to her husband in explanation. 'We had a most interesting visit there and since then I have had an idea. It came to me the other day when I was visiting Miss Pickering and we were talking about books. I'd like to set up a lending library at the work-house. I realise that not all of them will be able to read but it would be a wonderful opportunity to teach them. We could organise volunteers. What do you think, Reverend? I know those poor people have precious little spare time, but I'd like to think that their days might be lightened a little if they had something to take them out of themselves, something that would allow them to escape into another world. I was even thinking we might also set up a lending library here in Nettlestock for the villagers to use. Those able to read that is.' Her voice trailed away as it became clear that both the male Egdons were looking at her in horror.

Thomas turned to Merritt. 'You took her to the workhouse? You let my wife be exposed to those pestilential people? The place is packed with vagrants, drunks and lunatics and full of disease. Are you mad, man?' Thomas thumped the table, rattling the cutlery and the glassware.

Merritt felt the anger rise in him but before he could speak, Hephzibah answered for him. 'I persuaded the Reverend Nightingale to take me. It was my choice. He warned me that it might upset me, but I insisted on going and I'm glad I did. I learned so much. The people in there are not bad, just unfortunate. Many have lost their jobs and struggle to feed their families. There are widows with no means of support and there are over eighty children. They need your help not your disgust.'

'They should lock 'em all up and throw away the key. They're a bunch of wasters and ne'er do wells. They certainly took you in, Hephzibah,' said the squire with a snarl.

'But you, sir, are one of the guardians,' said Merritt, struggling to control his anger. 'You must know that most of the inmates would far rather be in their own homes and earning their keep by the sweat of their own brows and by doing work that's more meaningful than picking oakum and breaking stones.'

'They're idle. Happy to live off the parish. They don't deserve to be supported. They're vermin,' said Sir Richard.

His son interjected. He took Hephzibah's hand in his and bent his head and kissed it. 'Enough of this. I'd like you to promise me, Zee, that you won't go back to the place again.'

Hephzibah pulled her hand away.

Thomas Egdon smiled. 'I can see we will need to talk about this later, my darling.' He turned to the parson. 'I am sure you meant well, Nightingale, and of course we were not married then, but I am trusting you never to take my wife to the workhouse again. I hope we understand each other?'

Merritt looked him in the eye and nodded. He realised that he hated Thomas Egdon with every fibre of his body. This emotion was only less than his feeling of shock and disbelief that Hephzibah had not only married the man but, based on the way she looked at him, was deeply in love with him.

The evening dragged on interminably and after Ottilie had been dispatched to bed, the squire insisted, over Merritt's protests, that the parson join them in a game of whist.

They had played only a few hands when, impatient at Merritt's lack of attention and their losing streak, the squire yawned and got to his feet. 'That's enough. I'm going to bed. I can't abide to play with a partner who doesn't care about winning.' He chugged back the contents of his glass then refilled it from the decanter beside him. 'A nightcap. Now if you've any sense you'll take your wife to bed, Thomas. Do your duty and give me a grandson.' He gave a coarse laugh.

Merritt wanted to punch him. He looked at Thomas, expecting him to say something, but the man appeared immune to the ribaldry of his father.

Hephzibah however was blushing to the roots. When the squire lurched out of the room, limping on his bad leg, she immediately changed the subject. 'How are you to get back to the parsonage, Reverend Nightingale? Thomas, can we sort out the carriage?'

'No need,' said Merritt. 'A brisk walk will do me good.'

'I won't hear of it,' she replied, looking anxiously at her husband. 'You have caught a chill, sir. You can't possibly walk back to the village. There's a heavy frost. Thomas, can you summon the carriage, please?' Her voice was hesitant.

Merritt could tell Hephzibah was uncomfortable and uncertain in her new role, catapulted from governess to member of the family, while unaware of the workings of the house and unused to the role of hostess. He started to say that walking would be a pleasure, when Mrs Andrews entered and asked whether now would be a good moment to send the carriage round for the parson. Merritt saw the relief on Hephzibah's face and noted that Thomas was already walking towards the hallway, evidently eager to see the back of their guest.

Taking advantage of a moment alone together, Merritt took Hephzibah's hand and pressed it. 'I hope and pray that you will be happy, Mrs Egdon.'

As he climbed into the carriage and set off for home, Merritt acknowledged that he had just passed the worst few hours of his entire life. When he retired to bed he clutched the pillow and groaned. 'Oh, Hephzibah, my sweet girl, what have you done?

CHAPTER FIFTEEN

[Ganymedes] was the loveliest born of the
race of mortals, and therefore
the gods caught him away to themselves,
to be Zeus' wine-pourer,
for the sake of his beauty,
so he might be among the immortals.

(Homer, Iliad Book XX, lines 233–23)

The curtains were open and the sunlight came through the windows and dappled the bedroom floor like a mosaic. Hephzibah turned over and looked at Thomas asleep beside her. She remembered what he had said about their having the rest of their lives to get to know each other. Watching him sleeping, she was filled with an overpowering tenderness. She had not believed she would ever find the capacity to feel love again after the death of her parents, but this was different. The love she felt for Thomas was like nothing else. It consumed her. It burnt inside her, filling her with a longing and desire she had never experienced before. She would walk to the ends of the earth for him. She prayed he felt the same, and was terrified that he might not.

The night before, after the departure of Reverend

Nightingale, Thomas had led her by the hand up the stairs and she had followed him, weak with desire and nerves. He had thrown her across the bed and taken her quickly, shooting a sharp pain through her that dissolved into a sensation of pleasure which ended too soon. She had lain underneath him, pinned to the bed like a specimen butterfly.

Lying now on her side, she examined his face. So handsome, beautiful even. She searched for a fault. If she could find one it would render him human, whereas now he was like an angel who might disappear as if in a dream. His features appeared carved from marble by a sculptor seeking to create perfection – a Ganymede, too beautiful for mortal life. She wanted to run a finger along his dark eyebrows, but feared waking him. His nearly-black hair was tousled on the pillow, soft to the touch and she remembered how last night she had known what it was to tangle her fingers in it as he made love to her. And his mouth. It was slightly hard about the edges so that he often appeared preoccupied and serious – until he turned his smile upon her and her world lit up. She wanted his kisses to go on forever. His eyes. When he had moved inside her, the limpid blue of those eyes clouded over and lost focus as he looked down at her, before he closed them and let out a long sigh. A shiver of desire went through her as she thought of the moment when he had entered her, taken her, and she had given herself to him.

She felt an unexpected rush of sadness. What they had done together in the night was not as much as it might have been. She knew nothing of such matters, but sensed that she had disappointed him in some way. When he was done with her, he had rolled off her and fallen straight to sleep, leaving her with an unfulfilled longing and a strange melancholy. She had lain there in the dark for hours, staring up at the ceiling, consumed with anxiety. Was he already regretting his hasty choice? Was he thinking of Abigail Cake?

She should have asked Thomas about his relationship with Abigail before she agreed to marry him, but she had been too afraid of what he might say. She had rationalised her decision by telling herself that the Ribbon Thief's conduct with the squire indicated that she was a woman of loose morals and doubtless Thomas had merely dallied with her. After all, hadn't his own father said that his son had slept with half the county? She had not liked hearing that, but brushed it aside. Most young men were inclined to sow their wild oats before choosing a wife. And it was, after all, she, Hephzibah, he had chosen. She was the one he had fallen in love with. Wasn't she?

Then her thoughts went back to the dinner and Thomas's anger that she had visited the workhouse. She was baffled and disappointed by his reaction but took some consolation that he must have wanted to protect her.

Thomas opened his eyes. He looked at her with a momentary expression of surprise, as though he had forgotten he had married her and had not expected to find her lying beside him in his bed. He leaned over and kissed her briefly then yawned and groaned and moved to get out of the bed. He fumbled for his watch on the night table. 'Gone eight o'clock already. Damn it.'

Hephzibah reached out for his arm, to stay him. 'Why the hurry? Don't let's get up yet.' She wanted him to make love to her again so that this time it would be better. This time she would know what to expect. This time she would try harder to make him happy. Maybe she could even ask him what she could do, how she should respond to him, how she could make herself more in tune with him.

He leaned over and dropped another kiss on her forehead and smiled at her. 'I've got to go, Zee. I have to be in town for lunch. I need to make the nine-thirty train.'

She sat bolt upright. 'The train? Why? Why do you have to go to London? I will come with you.' She swung her legs over the edge of the bed.

'You can't. I will be staying at my club. They don't permit women there.'

'You're staying up in London?'

'Just for a few days, a week at most. Don't fret, my darling, I'll make it up to you when I return. Perhaps then we will go away for a few days. Have our honeymoon.' He came back to the bed, leaned over her and tilted back her head by the chin. 'Yes, my wife is the prettiest woman in Berkshire. Now get some rest and take care of my little sister.'

When he was gone, Hephzibah began to panic. Didn't he love her? Had he only married her to anger his father? Was he planning to meet Abigail Cake rather than going to London? Did he have other mistresses? Was this the way things would be from now on?

Hephzibah had no way to answer these questions. She could barely remember her own father and had anyway been too young to know what kind of relationship he had had with her mother. She did remember though that he was away from home frequently on his botanical expeditions. Often for months. Her mother and stepfather had been inseparable though. Even in death. She gave in to the tears that had been threatening to come all night.

Merritt stared at his reflection in the mirror as he shaved. As he carved a path through the shaving soap he felt his emotions rising. Since he had walked into Ingleton Hall and faced the newly-wed couple, his world had crashed apart, as if he were being drawn into a vortex, spinning around, drowning, having his soul sucked out of him. A little blossom of blood spread into the foam on his cheek. He scraped at the last of the stubble then flung the razor into the basin and dabbed at the spot where he had nicked himself. His eyes stared back at him. Hollow, raw, empty, bloodshot. He couldn't go on. He couldn't continue to live here, to look upon Hephzibah each Sunday as he delivered his weekly sermon.

Last night had been a journey into hell. Her face swam before him now, her eyes filled with love and happiness directed towards that wretch. It was like a death. A death of his hopes, a killing of his soul, the destruction of all his dreams. Yesterday morning he had been working on his translation of Ovid – Philemon and Baucis, the old couple who loved each other so much that rather than be parted in death they had chosen to die together and the gods had transformed them into a pair of trees. As he had worked, his mind had filled with the idea of a life with Hephzibah, having children together, then growing old together. He had imagined taking her to Rome for their honeymoon, helping to assuage the pain she had suffered at the loss of her parents just before their planned trip there. He had pictured her walking hand-in-hand with him through the ruins of the Forum, exploring the narrow streets of the city, eating dinner together in some quiet hostelry off the beaten track, paying homage at the Spanish Steps.

Two hours later he was shown into the bishop's study.

'I want to give up my living. I have made a mistake. I'm not cut out for the ministry,' said Merritt after pleasantries had been exchanged.

The bishop peered at him over the top of his half spectacles but evinced no surprise. 'What has brought about this sudden epiphany?'

Merritt looked away.

'Why don't you begin by telling me why you have reached this conclusion now when just two months ago you were telling me how life as a country parson was the perfect job for you.' He paused then looked meaningfully at Merritt. 'And I suggest, young man, that you tell me the truth.'

Merritt found himself spilling out his devastation that

the woman he loved had married another man and confessed that he could see no way to continue to live in the parish where he would be forced to see her all the time.

'Ah! As I thought,' said the bishop. 'These sudden changes of heart in my experience usually trace back to the actions or inactions of the fairer sex. I can see, young man, that you have been hurt. I can understand why it is your instinct to flee. But I put it to you that you will get over this. You will meet a suitable lady at some point in the future and all will be well. It just requires patience. I am not ashamed to admit to you, Nightingale, that I believed myself to love another before I met and married my good wife – but I'd be grateful if you'd not ever let that little gem of information reach her. Three years before I met her, I was at Cambridge and when the object of my affections threw me over in favour of a fellow who rowed for the university, I thought my world had ended. I contemplated coming down and abandoning the tripos but I prayed for guidance and persevered until I got my degree.' He leaned forward, elbows on the desk. 'And I suggest, Nightingale, that this setback is for you also only a temporary one. It is a test from God and you must face it. You will come out of it a better man and a better minister to boot.'

Merritt tried not to show his irritation. How could the bishop compare a student crush to the way he felt about Hephzibah. He bit his lip. 'I have no desire to be a better minister. I told you I am not cut out for the church.'

'Nonsense. You are a great scholar and a good preacher. Just the kind of man the modern church needs. I have heard good things about the quality of your sermons. No, Nightingale, we can't afford to lose a man like you. Go back to Nettlestock and throw yourself into your work as a minister and fill the rest of the time with your studies. You told me you were working on a new translation of Metamorphoses. That should take up much of your time and stop you mooning over this woman. Now, talking of Latin scholarship, I picked up a copy of the Aeneid in a bookshop last week and I have been struggling over a difficult passage. My Latin's quite rusty. Perhaps you'd be so kind…' The bishop rose from his desk and signalled to Merritt to follow him into his library. 'Then of course, you will stay for luncheon.'

As soon as she had finished her lessons with Ottilie, Hephzibah went for a walk into the village. As she passed through the gates of Ingleton Hall, she decided to call upon the parson to apologise for the previous night and find out whether he had indeed caught a chill. When she arrived at the parsonage, Mrs Muggeridge informed her he was not at home, having left earlier that day to call upon the bishop and she had no idea when he would return.

Hephzibah headed down to the canal, disappointed. She hoped that the ban on her visiting the workhouse would not extend to her taking the occasional walk with the parson, as she had grown fond of his company.

The day was warm, the sky blue and cloudless. Hephzibah walked slowly, aimlessly, mulling over Thomas's behaviour, trying to find a cause for it. To her relief the towpath was deserted.

A short distance ahead there was a small brick footbridge that crossed the canal and she could see a figure on it, leaning over looking into the water on the other side. As she approached, she saw it was Merritt Nightingale. Hephzibah picked up her pace and half ran towards him. He had his back to her and didn't see her until she was already on the bridge. He turned towards her and his face appeared stricken with grief.

'Merritt! Are you still unwell? You looked so sad just now.' She went to stand beside him, against the parapet of the bridge.

He turned back to look at the water passing underneath them and threw a twig into the canal. 'I used to do this when I was a boy. Throw sticks into the river and then race along the bank to get to the weir faster than the sticks did.' He shook his head. 'I was probably responsible for dumping more wood into that stream than a whole band of beavers.'

'I called at the parsonage, Merritt. I wanted to apologise for last night. But Mrs Muggeridge said you were calling on the bishop.'

'It's better that we revert to our formal names, Mrs Egdon. I don't think your husband would approve of us being over familiar.'

'Mr Egdon isn't here.'

'It wouldn't be right to go behind his back. Besides, it would be awkward having to remember when and where to address each other that way. This way is easier. And there's no need for an apology. I don't even know why you want to offer one.' He continued to look down at the canal, avoiding her eyes.

'I want to say sorry for what the squire and my husband said to you about the workhouse and for the squire's rudeness in pressing you to stay for cards then going to bed and virtually showing you the door.'

'You have no need to speak on their behalf. And I am sure they would stand by every word they said.'

She shook her head. 'The squire has a tendency to speak out of turn when he's had too much to drink. He's not supposed to drink as he suffers from gout but I'm afraid he won't be told.'

'I know,' said Merritt.

'What's wrong, Merritt? I mean Reverend Nightingale. Just now you looked terribly sad. Have you had bad news? Your parents?'

'My parents are well.'

'I see. And there is nothing else?'

'Peter Goody is dead.'

'No! What happened?' She laid her hand on his arm.

'I've just returned from his cottage. I called on him when I got back from the bishop's palace.' He sighed. 'The rust from the mantrap caused an infection in the wound which hadn't cleared up. He was worried about his family after months without work and hobbled his way around several farms looking for some work. When he got home the wound had opened up again and he developed a fever. He died last night. I will be officiating at his funeral tomorrow.'

'I am so sorry. That's terrible. He had children?'

'Five and his wife was expecting a sixth.'

'What will she do?'

'What do you think?' His voice was harsh, bitter. 'She has no choice but the workhouse. They were already behind on the rent for their cottage. Cake, the squire's bailiff, won't tolerate arrears.'

The parson shook his head and stared into the water again. Eventually he spoke. 'Where is Mr Egdon this afternoon?'

Hephzibah swallowed and leaned over the parapet herself, struggling to prevent her emotions being revealed on her face. 'He's had to go to London. He's staying at his club. For a few days. Urgent business.'

'I see.' He picked up another stray twig from the top of the parapet and dropped it into the canal. 'Shall I walk with you as far as the gates?'

She nodded. 'If you have nothing else pressing?'

They skirted around the village, eventually leaving the towpath and arcing back along the edge of woodland, behind the whiting factory, towards Ingleton Hall.

'Did you mean what you said about starting a lending library?' he said.

'Of course. Do you doubt me?'

'Then we shall do it. Without you going again to the

workhouse, of course. Perhaps you could help me choose a selection of books and maybe help to set up the branch here in the village.'

'We must involve Miss Pickering. It was her idea. I'm sure she will want to work with you on the selection of the books. She is a true bibliophile – just like you.' She turned to him and smiled, reminding herself of her plan to push the pair together. Merritt looked unmoved.

Hephzibah pressed on. 'Maybe you and Miss Pickering could put your heads together. She was wondering where we could site the library. There's no room in the church.'

Merritt said nothing.

'I was wondering whether it might be a suitable project for a memorial to the late queen. We could erect a library in her name. What do you think?'

Merritt shrugged, then said, 'A good idea. I'll need to speak to Sir Richard. Do you think he'll agree?'

'He would of course prefer it if it were named for him – but I'm sure if he can be persuaded to chair the committee to raise the funds and then he is the one who cuts the ribbon and gets his name on a commemorative plaque he might be persuaded.'

The parson nodded. 'I am sure if anyone can persuade him, Mrs Egdon, you can. But it will take some time to raise the money and even more to raise the building itself. And I think that will be difficult unless we are able to show that people will actually make use of it.'

'Then we must find a temporary home for it.' She clasped her hands together. 'That would mean we can start very soon, and as soon as Sir Richard and his wealthy friends realise what a valuable and much-needed facility it is they will agree to fund a permanent structure. But where? It can't be the Hall. The squire would never agree to people traipsing through his house.'

'Could we use one of the outbuildings?'

'I could ask but I think it should be in the heart of the village. I doubt people would be prepared to trudge out here in all weathers to borrow a book.'

They were silent for a few minutes.

'The school?' Merritt suggested.

'Miss Pickering would never agree to keeping grown-up books in the schoolroom where the children might read them,' said Hephzibah. 'We need somewhere that people can visit any time and we can't expect Miss Pickering to keep the place open in the evenings.'

'There is one possibility,' said Merritt, his voice lacking any enthusiasm. 'The Egdon Arms – the public house. I suppose I could speak to the landlord later and find out if he's willing.'

Hephzibah raised her eyebrows. 'Really?'

Merritt shrugged. 'Why not? It might bring him some new custom.'

'He won't be too pleased if his patrons spend more time reading than drinking. But if you can convince him, I think it's an excellent idea.' She hesitated, sensing that the parson was lacking his usual energy. She touched him lightly on the sleeve and smiled at him. 'We make quite a team, Reverend Nightingale.'

She thought she saw him frowning, but decided she had imagined it as he suddenly took her hands in his and said, 'If ever you are in trouble, if ever you need anything… anything at all, remember I am here. I am always here for you, my friend, I promise you.'

He raised his hat to her and walked away briskly, heading back towards the village. They were still a good half-mile from the Hall gates.

CHAPTER SIXTEEN

"– when Pluto espied her,
no sooner espied than he loved her and swept her way,
so impatient is passion."

(from The Rape of Proserpina, Metamorphoses, Ovid)

About three weeks later, the coachman from Ingleton Hall arrived at the parsonage without warning and told Merritt he had instructions to bring him up to the Hall, where the squire wished to meet with him urgently. Merritt put aside his book, placing it on top of the pile that had accumulated in the drawing room since he had acknowledged there was no point in keeping up appearances for the woman who was now lost to him.

He was shown straight into the squire's study, at the side of the house, set apart from the finer rooms at the front of the building. It was accessed internally by a stone-flagged passage that led deeper into the house to the kitchens and servants' quarters, and externally by a door that opened onto the rear courtyard. This entrance was designed so that the bailiff, head gardener, gamekeeper and groom could access their employer without passing through the formal end of the building. Merritt had never been inside this inner business sanctum before.

The study was sparsely furnished, with just a couple of heavily stuffed leather chairs, a large oak table which served as the squire's desk, and a threadbare rug on top of the flagstones. The rug looked as though it had been in use since the squire's ancestors had fought in the civil war, no doubt with the Cavaliers not the Roundheads.

'Sit down, Nightingale. Care for a snifter?' Sir Richard pushed a decanter of whisky across the table toward him and pointed to an empty crystal glass.

Merritt shook his head.

The squire sipped at his whisky. 'I need some advice. Confidential of course. I'd ask my lawyer but he's in Scotland until next week. Damned inconvenient. I'd like your opinion in the meantime. You're a man of letters. You went to Oxford. Read this and tell me if I can do anything to stop my son getting his hands on this money.' He thrust a document into Merritt's hand and leaned back in his chair, expectantly. 'Read it, man, and tell me. Can I stop him?'

The parson put on his spectacles and read the document, which bore a large wax seal beside the signatures. When he had finished, he folded it again and handed it back to the squire.

'If I understand correctly, this documents a trust executed by your late wife's father in favour of her during her lifetime and thereafter, her sons, of whom only Thomas is surviving. It provides for an allowance to be paid to him out of the interest on the capital.' He looked up and removed his spectacles. 'So I presume Thomas has been in receipt of the interest since the death of your wife and his brothers?'

'Yes, yes. I know all that. It's the rest I want to be sure about – I want to check what happens to the capital if he marries.'

'It's unequivocal. The full control of the capital passes to your surviving son upon his marriage. He is free to do with it as he wishes.'

'Damn and blast. That's what I thought. Is there no scope at all to challenge it? What was all that gobbledygook on the last page about?'

'I'm not a lawyer, Sir Richard, but I believe that's just the usual legalese. You know lawyers – they never use one word where ten are available. But why would you want to challenge it? It's your son's inheritance.'

'Because my miserable excuse for a son has only married that Wildman girl to spite me and get his hands on the money. He's already almost had me in the poorhouse with his overspending and all the debts he's run up and now the ungrateful sod wants to burn his way through his mother's money too.' He splashed more whisky into his tumbler and took a large swig. 'He's brought me close to bankruptcy.'

Merritt felt sick. Sweat broke out on his forehead at the thought of Thomas Egdon only marrying Hephzibah for financial gain. He forced himself to respond. 'Then this is good news, Sir Richard. If your son is indebted to you he now has access to the funds to repay you.' He desperately wanted to leave and twisted in his chair, ready to rise.

The squire thumped his glass down. 'He'll not repay me a penny. I know my son. Although I doubt I know the half of his gambling debts. I've had to pay off his club bills or risk being expelled myself. I can no longer show my face to my tailor, and I'm sick and tired of bailing the boy out.' As he spoke, the surface of the table was sprayed with his spit.

'It'll be worse now he's married,' the squire went on. 'Gowns and jewellery for that governess. He'd already spent a fortune kitting her out for riding. The shop came after me to settle the unpaid bill. The woman doesn't even like riding.'

Merritt leaned back in his chair, to escape the spittle spray. 'I'm sorry.' He shook his head and took a handkerchief from his pocket to wipe his face while pretending to blow his nose. He didn't want to hear this. He didn't want to listen to anything more about Thomas Egdon and the way he had exploited Hephzibah. His brain was in tumult. Egdon didn't love her. Why had Hephzibah thrown her life away on that wretch? How could she possibly love him? Why didn't she see his shallowness and vanity? He, Merritt, would lay down his life for her and yet she neither knew nor cared. She was blind to all but Egdon.

The squire, oblivious to Merritt's distress was still talking. 'This used to be one of the richest estates in the county, before that boy set out to beggar me. My grandfather made a fortune when they dug the canal though our land. Then when the railway came my father made more money out of that, selling them land. Now, thanks to that son of mine and the collapse in rents and grain prices I'm struggling to keep afloat. Have you seen the state of the gardens? I had to get Cake to lay off half the gardeners. And when was the last time we had a ball here or even a shooting party? Not since long before you've been in the parsonage.'

The parson half rose from his chair. 'I must be getting along.' He was angry and impatient to be gone and his head was pounding.

'No. Stay for lunch. I insist. Now that I've dragged you all the way here.' Sir Richard looked at his fob watch. 'Time already. Come on, man. It will just be cold cuts and pickles.'

Merritt was unable to muster a believable excuse and followed the squire through to the dining room, like a man ascending the scaffold. Hephzibah filled his thoughts. Why hadn't he stopped her? Why hadn't he declared his own feelings? Fool. Idiot. Imbecile. He imagined punching the face of Thomas Egdon. On and on. Pummelling away until that habitual smug expression was obliterated.

'Come on, man,' said the squire. 'Stop dawdling.' He tapped Merritt on the back and pushed him into the dining room.

Hephzibah and Ottilie were already seated at the table.

Hephzibah looked up and her face broke into a warm smile when she saw Merritt. His stomach lurched. He had forgotten she would be present. She was wearing pale blue, which matched the colour of her eyes.

Merritt remembered the afternoon he had first seen her, as a young girl in a blue dress, eating an apple in the college garden. He ached to think of how young and innocent she had been then, how he had already sensed he would love her. His Proserpina, now captured by Pluto and descending with him into Hades.

A bitter taste filled his mouth. Hephzibah had been gulled by Thomas Egdon. He swore to himself he would never say anything to give the slightest hint that her husband had used her – but he had no power to prevent her finding out. He prayed it would never happen. While Hephzibah would never be his now, the one thing that was paramount in his mind was her happiness. The way she had looked at Egdon was incontrovertible – she loved the man with a passion.

CHAPTER SEVENTEEN

Even the dearest that I loved the best
Are strange – nay, rather, stranger than the rest.

(from I Am!, John Clare)

Hephzibah had been married for three months and had lived at Ingleton Hall for a year, before Thomas finally proposed they go to watch his racehorses training on the gallops. Thomas had given her a couple more riding lessons and had accompanied her once in a hack around the estate. She had also ridden out many times with Ottilie. While she felt slightly more confident, Hephzibah was only too aware she would never make a great horsewoman and sensed her husband's disappointment, although he never voiced any criticism and was always encouraging.

When Thomas announced the trip at breakfast one morning, Ottilie jumped up and down in delight, her face crumbling as soon as her brother told her she would not be included. While Hephzibah felt sad for the girl she was glad for her own part and excited about the prospect of spending a whole day alone with her husband.

Thomas's racehorses were stabled about ten miles away at Lambourn on the Berkshire Downs. The village and its surrounds had grown in popularity since the advent of the railway a few years earlier, which meant horses could be transported far afield to race meetings. The dry chalky soil was unsuited to farming but perfect for exercising.

They set out on horseback straight after breakfast, and Hephzibah, after a few minutes in the saddle, began to relax as they trotted along sedately, heading north along a leafy lane. Thomas said little as they rode, but kept looking towards her, checking she was comfortable and secure. She smiled at him, happy at his concern. After a while, he turned off into some pastureland and, without warning, pushed his horse into a gallop. Before Hephzibah realised what was happening she was galloping behind him, breathless, terrified but exhilarated, feeling the wind on her face.

When they eventually pulled up, he turned to her and asked if she'd enjoyed it. She nodded then said, 'But you should have asked me first.'

'You'd only have said you were too afraid, Zee. The best way to learn is to do it. Come on. No time to waste. We'll follow the old Roman road for a while. Not far to go now.' And without waiting for an answer he was off again, with Hephzibah following behind him.

When they reached the stables at Lambourn they spent two hours beside the gallops, watching Thomas's horses being exercised. They stood side-by-side while Thomas studied the animals through his binoculars and Hephzibah soon became bored. She had expected them to be thundering past in a race but the process of training involved lots of steady cantering up the slopes which Thomas told her was to build the strength of their muscles. It was a cloudy and chilly day for August and she couldn't see the horses clearly from a distance. Thomas was absorbed in discussing their form with the trainer as if she didn't exist. She wanted to share in his interests and passions but he took no time to explain and she wondered why he had wanted her to accompany him.

When at last the training session was over, they went to an inn for luncheon. At last she had an opportunity to talk to Thomas; at last a few moments when he wasn't in a hurry to be elsewhere, when they weren't surrounded by others, or their chance for conversation subsumed in the monologues of the squire.

She began by asking him how the training had gone but he had little to say on the subject – she sensed he felt there was little point in telling her much when her knowledge of racing was so limited. She was desperate to find a way to get closer to him, but it felt as if Thomas divided up his life and Hephzibah and horse racing were not in the same box. When it began to seem they were drifting into an awkward silence, she raised the subject of the death of Peter Goody.

'Did you know that your father's gamekeeper had left an old mantrap on the estate and a man died after being trapped in it? He left a pregnant wife and lots of children.'

Thomas bent his head to one side and gave her a look that betokened boredom rather than concern.

'It happened several months ago, before we were married. I've been meaning to ask you about it for ages.'

'Why? What's it to do with me?' He sounded bored. 'He should have known better than to poach on our land. You know what my father's views on poaching are. Everyone knows. If that fellow was daft enough to ignore that then he got what he deserved.'

Hephzibah gasped. 'Daft enough? Don't you mean desperate enough? And *deserved*? How can you say anyone deserves to die like that, just for trying to catch a couple of rabbits?'

Thomas sighed. 'Please don't preach to me like a parish do-gooder, Zee. It's such a bore. I have no interest whatsoever in the petty goings on in the village.'

Hephzibah looked at him in dismay. How could the man she loved be so uncaring? 'You call a man's death a petty going on?' She put down her knife and fork, all appetite gone.

'Of course I'm sorry the poor chap had to die and yes, I suppose it's a bit rough on his wife, but these people do know the score, Zee. If they choose to break the law they must face the consequences.'

Hephzibah was shocked at her husband's callousness. Something must have happened to put him in such a bad mood. It was too much for her to accept that he truly believed what he was saying. 'It sounds like you have more in common with your father than I realised. I expected more of you, Thomas.'

She got up and ran out of the inn, then realising she had no idea how to get home, and no means of mounting her horse without assistance, she took to pacing up and down in frustration, until Thomas emerged from the building. He came up behind her and placed his arms around her waist, pulling her close to his chest. He smelled of his familiar lemony shaving balm as he pulled her around towards him and went to kiss her. She jumped apart, shocked that he wanted to kiss her in public.

'Don't let's quarrel, Zee,' he said, and lifted her into the saddle, before springing up onto his own horse.

They trotted up the lane, Hephzibah still smarting from the argument. They entered a small copse of trees, following a track through the middle. Thomas rode slightly ahead so he could hold back the overhanging branches for her as she followed him. As they passed through one low-hanging obstacle he edged his horse close to hers and leaned over and kissed her full on the mouth. She gasped in surprise, but this time did not try to repulse him. He slipped off his horse and lifted her down from hers and carried her over to a mossy bank under an oak tree.

'I hate to fight with you, my darling,' he said as he lay down beside her and pulled her into his arms. 'But you're irresistible when you're angry.'

'We can't…' she said. 'Not here. Not like this. Someone might see us.'

'No one will see us.' Then he stopped her mouth with a kiss. He made love to her, there in the open air, as if they were a pair of peasant lovers. She was shocked, affronted, but thrilled to the core of her being, their argument forgotten.

As they rode back to Nettlestock, Hephzibah felt confused. Marriage was proving to be a difficult thing to get right and not at all what she expected.

CHAPTER EIGHTEEN

But when your heart is tired and dumb,
your soul has need of ease,
There's none like the quiet folk who wait in libraries–

(from Old Books, Margaret Widdemer,
The Old Road to Paradise)

When Hephzibah had first raised the matter of the village library at dinner one evening, Thomas had been scathing about the idea, declaring it a complete waste of time and money. Hephzibah wondered if that was the only reason the squire had chosen to support it. So far, Sir Richard had been assiduous in his efforts to raise the necessary funds for the building of the permanent library, convincing most of the neighbouring landowners to donate to the cause. The building was also to incorporate a social hall for the village. The linking of the building to the memory of Queen Victoria, and the opportunity for benefactors' names to be included on the dedication stone, had helped the money roll in fast. Work had already begun to clear the land, a small plot adjacent to the old silk mill, and an architect from Newbury had drawn up the plans.

The afternoon of the first Sunday in September was

set for the opening of the new temporary village lending library at the Egdon Arms. Hephzibah and the parson had persuaded the squire to pay for shelves to be built inside the village inn, and the parson, the schoolmistress and the squire had all donated books from their own collections.

Most of the village turned out for the occasion, from the gentlemen farmers to the shopkeepers, the station master, the estate workers, the manager of the whiting factory, the guardians of the workhouse – which would itself benefit from a monthly loan of thirty or so books from the collection to be delivered and collected each month by the carter. A group of volunteers had been recruited by the Reverend Nightingale to offer evening classes in the pub, to assist people with their reading.

The Egdon Arms was packed to the rafters and people had spilled out into the street. In celebration of the library's inauguration, the landlord was offering free cider to all-comers, while still making a tidy profit on the sale of beer, spirits and non-alcoholic drinks. In order not to offend the sensibilities of the parish council and the teetotallers, there was also a plentiful supply of homemade fruit cordial and ginger ale. Despite this, there were those among the population of Nettlestock who believed that a lending library housed inside a public house, even on a temporary basis, was not only a step too far, but a positive incitement for parishioners to take to drink. It had only been down to the strong advocacy of the parson and the influence of Mrs Thomas Egdon that the squire was eventually persuaded to enter the fray and weigh down in support of the project. Jacob Leatherwood, the preacher from the Nonconformist chapel had taken to his pulpit to denounce the enterprise and ban any members of his flock from attending. The previous cool but civil relationship between Leatherwood and Merritt Nightingale turned sour and the former now crossed the road to avoid his counterpart.

Despite the best efforts of the naysayers, Nettlestock had seen nothing like the library opening since the victory celebrations for the war against Napoleon and the coronation of the late queen.

Hephzibah was sitting with Miss Pickering and a group of women at a makeshift table just outside the pub, sipping their cordials and enjoying the September sunshine. She didn't notice at first when Abigail Cake slid into the seat beside her. The young woman prodded her in the ribs.

'Parson wasn't good enough for you then?' Abigail was speaking in a lowered voice but the venom in it was causing her to speak louder as she went on. 'You know Tommy only married you for money?'

Conscious of the other village women around them, Hephzibah got up from the table. 'I have no money and I have no idea what you are talking about, but I'm not going to stay to find out.' She began to move towards the door of the hostelry.

Abigail took hold of Hephzibah's arm with a grip so tight Hephzibah almost cried out. 'Not so fast, governess. You'll hear me out.' She shoved Hephzibah into the crowded pub, working her way through the throng, pushing Hephzibah in front of her. Ignoring a sign on a door banning entry, Abigail propelled Hephzibah into the snug bar, which was occupied only by the landlord's sleeping dog, seeking sanctuary from the crowded public bar.

The pair stood either side of the fireplace. The red-head had her arms akimbo. 'You must have known Tommy loves me but you married him anyway,' she said. 'What you happened to see that day between me and the squire has nothing to do with what Tommy and I have together.'

'How dare you drag me in here. I don't want to hear anything you have to say. If you loved my husband so much you'd never have dreamt of doing what you do with his father. You're disgusting.' Hephzibah spoke with force, but felt sick with fear.

Abigail moved towards Hephzibah, a finger prodding her in the chest as she spoke. 'We grew up together, Tommy and me. He saved me from drowning in the canal when were children. I held his head when he was sick after drinking the squire's sherry when he was only a wee lad. Promised to marry me when we were six. Kissed me for the first time when we were fourteen. Took my cherry when we were both fifteen. He loves me and I love him and there's nothing you can do about it. You may have married him but he doesn't love you.'

Trying to maintain her dignity, Hephzibah said, 'That's all ancient history – even if it's true, which I doubt. You can't equate what children do when they're playing games with love between adults.'

Abigail moved close to Hephzibah, crowding her space, her breath warm in Hephzibah's face. 'Love?' Her voice was scornful. 'You know nothing of love! You march into Ingleton Hall like the Queen of bloody Sheba and you're stupid enough to think Tommy cares for you. I've news for you, he doesn't give a fig for you and he never will. He might give you presents but they mean nothing.' She pointed at the mother of pearl brooch pinned to Hephzibah's jacket. 'That's payment for services rendered. And you did him a great service helping him get his hands on his mother's money.'

Hephzibah stared at her, unable to believe what she was hearing, paralysed from responding by a need to hear her antagonist out.

Tossing back her long curls Abigail put her hands on her hips and stared at Hephzibah, a smile on her face. 'You had no idea, did you? I get the last laugh then!'

Hephzibah swallowed, tasting bitter bile in her mouth. She raised her voice, summoning as much confidence as she could muster. 'I'm not listening to another word.' She stared back into Abigail's face in defiance. 'You have absolutely no right to speak to me like this.'

'What? Because I'm only the bailiff's daughter? Is that what you mean? Not good enough to address the wife of the young master? I'm every bit as good as you, governess.'

'It's nothing to do with whose daughter you are. It's because you're the squire's… mistress.' She hesitated a moment then gave way to her anger. 'Nothing more than a common whore.'

Abigail stopped Hephzibah as she tried to leave the room, placing herself against the door.

'Whore I may be, but I'm twice the woman you are. You know why he chose you? Because no other woman would have him. The word gets around in the circles he mixes in and every time he courted a girl I made sure they got to know of his ways before the engagement could be announced.' She held her hand in front of her and counted on her fingers. 'Let me see. There was Lady Anna Somerton, Agnes Delargy, Rosanna Bellamy, Rachel Burghley-Archer, Mary Bennett, Julia Harley-Smyth. Each of them with a fat trust fund so he'd have been sorted, until I showed them my collection of letters, the love tokens, the lock of his hair that I wear in the locket he gave me.' She put her hand up to her neck and touched the silver locket that hung there. 'It's inscribed. Gave it to me when I turned eighteen, three months after he did. Now you know why I didn't want yours.'

Hephzibah stared at the girl, in a state of shock and disbelief.

'I saw off all the eligible women in the county. He knew, but he couldn't blame me. He couldn't blame me because he was secretly glad. No matter how pretty or rich they were he always came back to me. But he needed the money badly.'

Abigail kept her eyes fixed on Hephzibah. 'It was a condition of his trust fund that he marry. Spending money has always been my Tommy's weakness. That's why he married you. Very clever of him. I didn't see it coming. Never thought he'd stoop so low as to marry the governess. He usually left them to his father – but he got in fast with you – just enough of a lady to stop the squire objecting and the county talking. He would never have got away with marrying a bailiff's daughter, no matter how much he wanted to.'

The young woman moved towards Hephzibah, her face practically touching hers, her breath hot. 'Just remember this, Hephzibah Wildman, my Tommy will never ever love you. You'll never really have him. His heart's mine and always has been and nothing is going to change that. I'm his true wife, in every sense of the word and I always will be.'

She turned to leave, then stopped in the doorway and looked back at Hephzibah. She put her hand in the pocket of her skirt. 'Here, you can have these back. I've no more use for your trash.' She flung the green velvet ribbons onto a table and left the room.

CHAPTER NINETEEN

But the voice of my beloved
In my ear has seemed to say –
'O, be patient if thou lov'st me!'
And the storm has passed away.

(from The Power of Love, Anne Brontë)

24th May 1904

After the bailiff's daughter told her about her long-stand-ing affair with her husband, Hephzibah tried to convince herself it was lies and jealousy. She was afraid to confront Thomas about it, rationalising her fear as a reluctance to imply that she doubted him. Every time she looked at him she felt a longing that was like a sharp pain. He behaved to her with perfect civility, brought her gifts, apologised for his frequent absences, blamed them on business matters and, when he was home, made love to her with an attentiveness that she told herself must signify that he did indeed love her. But still the claims of Abigail Cake haunted her as the months and years passed. Abigail's words stayed in her head where she could not shift them and repeated themselves like a rasping noise that set her teeth on edge or an exposed nerve that was raw and painful.

Whenever Thomas made love to her she searched his eyes for a sign of how he felt about her, hoping the love she felt for him would be reflected back. All she saw were the progressive stages of concentration, pleasure and release. He never opened up his heart to her; he never told her he loved her – just that he found her beautiful. He was affectionate, teasing her occasionally, bringing consolatory gifts after his lengthy absences and chatting about superficial topics such as the weather, what he read in the newspaper and the racing results. He never enquired about her life, her interests, how she spent the days and nights she passed without him. She often thought of how he had said to her, when he proposed, that they would have the rest of their lives to get to know each other – yet as the years passed she knew little more.

Hephzibah was spending her third wedding anniversary, without her husband: Thomas preferring to spend his time at his club in London. At least that's what he told her. When feeling low, which was increasingly often these days, she wondered whether he was holed up somewhere with Abigail Cake. As well as their wedding anniversary, today had been declared the first of what was to be an annual day to celebrate the glory and mighty heritage of the British Empire. The village school was closed for the afternoon and the evening festivities were to include the lighting of a bonfire and a small firework display. Thomas was unmoved by the prospect of the celebrations or the opportunity to also commemorate their anniversary – a race meeting took priority.

Feeling guilty, she searched the pockets of his favourite jacket, but found no love tokens, just a few crumpled bills and a number of race-course betting slips. The bills alone were cause for concern as they were all stamped in red with the words Final Demand. Raising the issue of his debts with Thomas was out of the question. She could hardly tell him she had been going through his pockets – and even if she found an excuse, he would never listen to her.

Thomas was even more resolute than his father in his views about the role of women. Any mention of women's suffrage caused him to rail angrily that women ought to know their place. He cited Hephzibah as a model whom other women could learn from. This made her uncomfortable as she had been nursing plans to get involved with the suffragette movement. She had discussed the aims and objectives with Miss Pickering and they had spoken about going along to a meeting of the newly formed breakaway, the Women's Social and Political Union, in Newbury. If only Thomas were at Ingleton Hall more often. She would be able to work on him, begin to open his mind to the importance of women gaining the franchise, make him understand the sacrifices so many women were making for the cause.

The best hope she had of encouraging him to stay at home was the hardest to achieve. She was certain that were she and Thomas to have a child he would spend more time at Ingleton Hall. She had failed to conceive in three years of marriage. It was not for want of trying – whenever Thomas was at home he wasted no time in taking her to bed. At first she had not worried about it, but during the past twelve months her anxiety had increased. The squire lost no opportunity to goad his son, constantly reminding him that he had always suspected he would fail to father a child. While Thomas ignored the barbed comments at first, the constant repetition, and the growing awareness that his father was right, made Thomas preoccupied and distant and his absences grew longer.

On the evening of Hephzibah's wedding anniversary, Ottilie, now thirteen, accompanied Mrs Andrews to the village to witness the Empire Day bonfire celebrations, leaving Hephzibah alone with her father-in-law. The squire drank little during dinner, then asked her to join him for a nightcap. The fire was roaring in the large drawing room and the squire's dogs, a pair of foxhounds, lay sleeping in front of it. Hephzibah picked up her book, a volume of poetry, and began to read.

The squire interrupted her reading. 'By now you must know my son is an uncontrollable spendthrift,' he said. 'He received a substantial sum when he married you, a bequest from his mother and grandfather, but it's all gone.'

Hephzibah felt a wave of fear pass over her. What Abigail Cake had told her was thus at least partially true.

'I had a letter from him today asking me to lend him a hundred and fifty pounds. Claims to be broke. That means he's managed to work his way through several thousand since your marriage.'

Hephzibah felt her face colouring. Did the squire also believe Thomas had only married her to get his hands on his inheritance? 'Where has the money gone?' she said, her voice so quiet she could barely hear herself.

'Dashed if I know. Horseflesh, gambling, trinkets and dresses for you and Ottilie, paying his tailor. Running up bills from entertaining his friends at his club. My son is a generous man. One thing I can't fault him for. But his generosity doesn't run to his father. Seems to think it's perfectly acceptable to bleed me dry.'

Hephzibah picked up the poetry book she'd laid aside when he began talking. 'I am not comfortable discussing Thomas behind his back.'

'It's time you got comfortable. You're his wife, damn it, you need to share some responsibility.'

'Responsibility?'

'If we don't put a stop to his profligacy there'll be nothing left of Ingleton Hall. I don't want to go to my grave knowing that this house and the estate have gone to wrack and ruin. I've worked hard to make the place profitable. I invested in the most modern farming methods; I drained ten acres of waterlogged ground; I put in limekilns so I could fertilise; I experimented with machinery; I built the carp ponds and the water gardens; I was the first man in the county to use a steam thresher. Every penny I spent on Ingleton was from money I earned or my father had earned before me. Every last penny. Thomas is draining me dry. I didn't know what a mortgage was until a few years ago. Now with the rents at rock bottom and the collapse in grain prices, I can barely get by. It breaks my heart.'

'Why don't you say this to Thomas, not to me? Why don't you involve him more in the running of the estate?'

The squire snorted. 'Involve him? He's never shown an interest in anything except his own selfish pleasures. He hates the countryside unless he's riding a horse through it. Why in God's name do you think he spends so long in town? I hoped that when he married you he might be here more often.' He drained his glass and poured himself another drink. 'He's more than a disappointment to me – I'm actually ashamed of him.' He leaned forward, his head in his hands, then reached for his balloon of brandy. 'His brothers were different, you know. Worth ten of him. Both of them. If either of them had lived they'd have worked with me to make Ingleton what I wanted it to be. You can't imagine what it's like to have your children die before you. And not one but two of them.' He took a slug of brandy. His big dark eyes were lachrymose.

'I'm sorry. It must have been very hard for you. Losing Lady Egdon too.'

He looked up at her. 'She was never the same after Sam's death. They died within a few months of each other. Thank God she never lived to know that Roddy would be killed too – and before he was of age. My youngest boy was in the army. Should never have signed up. Only seventeen. What a bloody waste…' His voice trailed away.

Hephzibah had never before witnessed the squire in such a melancholic state. She was lost for words, muttering that she was sorry whilst hoping he would pull himself together and move onto safer territory.

'I was to blame for Samuel's death,' he said at last.

'I thought he shot himself?'

'I might as well have pulled the trigger. I let him down. Did something I regret.' The squire narrowed his hooded eyes.

Hephzibah waited for him to elaborate but he lapsed into silence, staring into the bowl of his brandy glass.

Eventually, he spoke again. 'I've decided to redraft my will. I need to protect Ingleton Hall from my son.'

'Why are you telling me this? You need to tell Thomas.'

'It concerns you too. I want you to be the one to tell him. It will be better coming from you. I intend to leave the bulk of my estate to my first male grandchild. Ottilie is nearly fourteen and I hope she will be married when she's eighteen – so you and Thomas have very little time left to get on with producing an heir.' His dark hooded eyes bored into her. 'But you know as well as I do, Hephzibah, my son is incapable of fathering a child.'

Embarrassed and uncomfortable, Hephzibah's brain raced. Where was this conversation leading? She wished she had refused to join him in the library. Squirming with embarrassment she said, 'Why do you persist in saying that he can't father a child? Why do you blame him? It could just as easily be my fault.'

Her head pounded. *Stop him talking at me. I don't want to hear any more. How can I get away?*

Egdon raised his hooded eyes and studied her for a moment or two. 'You have been deceived in your choice of a husband, Hephzibah. He takes his responsibilities as a husband no more seriously than those as a son. If you didn't realise it when you married him, you must know by now that it's more than playing cards and trips to the races that keep him away from home.'

Hephzibah jumped to her feet, picked up her book and moved to the door.

'Stop. Please,' he said, his voice, quieter and more conciliatory.

She halted at the door but kept her back to her father-in-law, waiting to hear what he would say.

'I don't want to be cruel, Hephzibah. In fact I've become rather fond of you. You've a bit of spirit. I know I made it hard for you when you first arrived, but you soon put me in my place. And you have to admit I've not laid a finger on you since he married you. But you need to stop burying your head in the sand. He tomcats his way around London and is hardly ever here. If he wants to make babies he has to be in your bed. Now come and sit down.'

She stayed on her feet.

'When he is here, does he do what he's supposed to do? Does he make love to you?'

Hephzibah could feel her face burning. It was insupportable, having to listen to this gouty old devil lecturing her on the facts of life. The memory of his assault on her three years ago was still fresh. She was angry and humiliated. 'Mind your own business, Sir Richard. What happens between my husband and me is entirely *our* business.'

'Damn it, woman. It isn't. More than a hundred souls depend on Ingleton Hall and this estate for their livelihood, not to mention the tenant farmers and countless others from the smithy to the innkeeper, the thatcher and the undertaker. You need to face the facts. Make my son see sense. Do what you need to do to keep him here more and to get you pregnant. The way to make babies is to keep having sex.'

He paused a moment, studying her. 'You're wasted on that boy. A woman like you needs a real man. One who won't neglect you in the bedroom.' His wet lips shone in the candlelight and Hephzibah felt afraid.

'I don't want to hear any more. You've made yourself clear. Goodnight.'

When she got to her bedroom, Hephzibah was shaking with fear and anger. There was an implied threat in what the squire said. His obsession with carrying on the family dynasty was evident. A child of Ottilie's would only ever be second-best without the Egdon name. Yes, the squire had behaved impeccably towards her since her marriage but the stakes were high for him and his past behaviour left Hephzibah in no doubt that he would force himself upon her again if it meant he would gain an heir.

Opening the top drawer of her clothes chest she took out the green ribbons that she had bought for her cancelled trip to Italy. Hephzibah stroked the soft velvet and felt the tears welling. The ribbons had been stolen by the woman with whom her husband was probably still dallying. She stroked the thick velvet pile and ran her finger along the edges. Holding them up to her face she could smell Abigail Cake on them – a smell of wood-smoke and apples. She dropped them. She would never be able to use them now. Any pleasure she might have had wearing them had been spoiled by Abigail Cake. Yet something held her back from throwing them away. They were the last gift from her mother. Abigail had returned them to her – perhaps it would be the same with Thomas. If she was patient, would she win her husband back too? The words of the squire swirled around in her head. Was he right that Thomas was having affairs all over London? She couldn't bring herself to believe it. She folded the ribbons, wrapped them in tissue and put them back in the drawer.

It was three weeks before Hephzibah had an opportunity to speak to Thomas about what her father-in-law had said.

That afternoon, while walking in the grounds, she had seen Abigail Cake heading from the kitchens towards the cottage she shared with her father and siblings. As Abigail crossed the stable yard she was in profile and it was immediately obvious to Hephzibah that the bailiff's daughter was expecting a child.

Hephzibah's heart contracted. Who was the baby's father? Why was Abigail Cake, an unmarried woman able to conceive so easily? Was it Thomas's baby? The squire's? Hephzibah turned off the track and went into the woods, her head spinning. Bile rose in her throat and she bent over and was sick in the undergrowth. She wiped her hand over her mouth and felt the tears coming.

That evening when at last she was alone with Thomas, Hephzibah gave him a watered-down version of her conversation with the squire, merely stating that Sir Richard had expressed consternation at the lack of a grandchild and intended to alter his will, to permit Ottilie's eventual offspring to inherit his estate. She didn't mention that the squire's plan was to bypass Thomas altogether, but the implication was clear.

Thomas's reaction was not what she expected. He was lying, slumped on his back on the bed. He rolled over onto his stomach and at first she thought he was ignoring her. Then she realised he was crying.

Hephzibah rushed over and sat down beside him and began to stroke his hair. 'What's wrong, my darling? Please tell me. What's wrong?'

His voice was muffled. 'I've messed everything up, Zee. I should never have married you. I've not been fair to you.'

Hephzibah felt her stomach clench with fear. Was he going to admit his feelings for Abigail and tell her that he was responsible for her becoming pregnant? She closed her eyes.

Thomas sat up, drawing his knees up to his chin. 'It's hard for me to tell you this. When I was eighteen I had the mumps. Besides turning my face into a chipmunk's, it caused my testicles to swell up. The doctor said it could make me sterile. I took the risk that it wasn't going to happen and didn't warn you. Now we are suffering the consequences.'

Hephzibah climbed onto the bed beside him and wrapped her arms around him. 'Oh my poor darling. I'm sure we can still have a child. Why don't we go and talk to Dr Desmond? We can go together.'

He looked stricken. 'I will not humiliate myself by doing that. I won't have him prodding me about and feeling sorry for me. If we can't have children then it's too bad.'

'Tell me exactly what the doctor said when it happened.'

He closed his eyes. 'Just that there was a risk it might make it harder for me to father a child.'

'But not impossible?'

'No. It could turn out not to be a problem, or it might take longer. But there is a possibility that I may never be able to father a child at all.'

'There you are. A possibility only. And he did say it may take longer. So we will be patient and keep trying.' She stroked his hair and kissed the top of his head. Taking his face in her hands she looked into his eyes and said, 'No matter what, my darling, I will always love you.'

He sighed and whispered, 'Thank you, dearest girl.'

She tried not to dwell on the fact that he had still not told her that he loved her too.

'I married a good woman,' he said eventually, 'and the most beautiful I have ever laid eyes upon. I don't deserve you, Zee.'

'Hush,' she said and kissed him on the mouth.

He rolled her onto her back and murmured, 'Yes, let's keep trying, starting now.'

September 1904

The parcel bore an Oxford postmark and was addressed to Hephzibah in an unfamiliar hand. It was a rectangular shape and, judging by the weight contained one or more books. She felt strangely reluctant to open it, taking it up to her bedroom and leaving it there while she took Ottilie through her daily lessons.

It was only after dinner that Hephzibah sat on the bed and undid the wrapping, folding the brown paper and winding the string into a ball. Thrifty habits died hard.

Inside were three leather-jacketed notebooks and a short letter from the Dean who had replaced her stepfather at the college. He had found the notebooks inside a dusty shoe-box in a corner of the attic and, as they appeared to be the work of the late Mrs Prendergast, he thought Miss Wildman should have them. He hastened to state that he had not read the contents.

Hephzibah undressed, washed and then climbed into bed with the notebooks, overcome with excitement and anticipation. She felt as though she was about to hear from her mother from beyond the grave.

The diaries dated from 1884, when Hephzibah would have been two years old and her birth father still alive. The family were living in Oxford but, as was the case for much of her mother's first marriage, Hephzibah's father was away on one of his botanical expeditions to Africa. Hephzibah read eagerly, hoping that she might find out something new about her father.

She turned the pages with a growing sense of shock and disbelief. The idyllic marriage that she had always supposed her mother had enjoyed with her father, despite their long separations, appeared to have been a far from happy one. Walter Wildman had been cold and distant and prone to fits of melancholy that made his long absences a relief to her mother. As she read the words in her mother's familiar sweeping copperplate, Hephzibah gasped. Never once had her mother said a bad word to her about her father and yet reading her agonised words, it became clear that the marriage had been a bitter and miserable experience. On his rare visits home to Oxford he spent his time closeted away in his study. He paid no attention to his daughter and was critical of his wife, belittling her at every opportunity. Hephzibah felt a mixture of embarrassment and anger as she read her mother's heartbreaking disclosures, presumably meant for no eyes other than her own.

It was only in the last of the three books that the tone of the diaries changed. In 1886 misery was replaced by exuberance. Hephzibah's hand went to her neck and clutched at the locket that hung there. Everything she had ever thought she had known about her parents was a lie.

Her mother had embarked on a love affair with her stepfather some three years before her own father had died. She felt herself blushing as her mother all those years ago poured out the love she felt for James Prendergast, a visiting professor whom she had met while he was undertaking research in the Bodleian.

Hephzibah closed the last notebook and leaned back against the pillows she had piled behind her. Her mother and Dr Prendergast. The devoted couple. The late second marriage. She had always assumed they had been drawn to each other in mutual grief after the loss of their original partners and that love had only slowly blossomed, that such love was based on mutual respect and companionship – a mature marriage of shared interests and friendship. Yet reading her mother's words it was apparent the love she had found was *un amour fou*, a passionate love affair, viscerally physical.

Hephzibah hugged her knees. What would her mother

think if she knew that her daughter was reading her secrets years later and discovering that she had betrayed her father by having a love affair? She felt angry on behalf of her father, a man betrayed, cuckolded – to use that old but appropriate expression. She put out the light and curled her body into a ball in the bed. Lies, lies, all lies.

As she tried to sleep, images of her mother and stepfather filled her head. She couldn't even remember her real father. All she had known of him was a faded wedding photograph, in which he stood stiffly, wearing a top hat behind her seated mother. Dr Prendergast had been the only father she had known. The only father she had loved. Reading her mother's words she now understood why. He was a good man. Her own father had been a cold, cruel bully. Hephzibah told herself it was time to ignore convention and think instead about emotion, about love, about one person caring for another above all others.

Suddenly it all made sense to her. She knew what she must do. She must sacrifice herself for the love of her husband. Love was all that mattered and she would do anything for the love of Thomas Egdon.

CHAPTER TWENTY

And God blessed them, and God said unto them, Be fruitful,
and multiply, and replenish the earth, and subdue it; and have
dominion over the fish of the sea, and over the fowl of the air,
and over every living thing that moveth upon the earth

(Genesis 1.28)

Ever since he had recommended placing the temporary
lending library inside the village pub, Merritt Nightingale
had enjoyed improved relationships with most of his
parishioners – the exceptions being those who preferred
the stronger, sterner messages of Jacob Leatherwood, the
preacher at the Nonconformist chapel. Whether or not the
villagers could read, they saw the creation of the new library
as an act of generosity and the parson's short term siting
of it in the Egdon Arms a sign of his liberality. The shiny
new memorial library and village hall opened and were well
patronised, but Merritt felt sad that the casual nature of the
library-in-a-pub was lost.

This morning he had received a long succession of
petitioners, requesting his endorsement of their requests
for charitable aid, his witnessing of their wills, as well as
one or two illiterates asking him to write or read letters on

their behalf. The better-off petitioners brought him small gifts – a basket of eggs, a jar of honey or a nice fat cabbage. Merritt, for his part, had instructed Mrs Muggeridge to put a flask of beer and a jug of cider on a table in the lobby where the parishioners waited for their audience with him.

The requests for the parson's clerical services significantly outweighed any applications for spiritual guidance – although this morning he had been asked for advice by an elderly man who claimed to be increasingly troubled by his conscience regarding a brief episode of more than forty years earlier. The man confessed to having kissed another woman a week before he married his wife. Merritt tried not to smile as he assured him that, as long as he showed contrition for this minor long-ago infraction, God would be merciful and would allow him into heaven. The old man then enquired whether he should confess his infidelity to his wife.

'Have you had anything to do with this other woman since?' asked Nightingale.

'Oooh no, your reverend. Never.'

'Then I'd caution you against mentioning it to Mrs Carver. It was so long in the past that there's little point in raising it now.'

'You reckon, sir?'

'You've had a long and happy marriage with Mrs Carver. There's no point in raising doubts in her head after all this time. Better to let sleeping dogs lie.'

'A happy marriage? I'm not sure I'd put it that way meself. Only I was athinkin' that I might try my luck at kissing the lass again, seeing as how she's now a widow woman.'

Merritt sat back in his chair, surprised. 'I don't think I've understood. I thought you said your conscience was troubling you? Why then would you want to kiss this other lady? That would make matters worse. It would give you more to weigh your conscience down. And while your wife may not have known, or will have long forgotten about this past indiscretion, you run the risk that she'll find out and be much less forgiving if you try it again.'

'I don't see how as it would make my conscience worse,' the old fellow replied. 'I was athinkin' it might make it better.'

'How so?'

'I felt bad to have kissed the lass and then left her to marry the missus. She only wed old Sorrell because she couldn't have me. For forty years I've thought it a terrible mistake and now old Sorrell's passed on, so I was in a mind to put things right with her.'

'Why are you asking me, Mr Carver? What do you want me to say?'

'I just wants to know if I can do it.'

'Do what? Kiss her?'

'I'd in mind a bit more than just kissin' – my missus has had no truck with the sex thing since our last one were born and I gave up trying to convince her otherwise twenty year ago, but I've a mind to have myself a little fling before I meets my maker. Just want to know that there's still some life in this old dog before I kicks the bucket.'

Merritt was puzzled. 'It sounds to me as though you have already made your mind up. I'm not sure why you're asking me. If you expect me to give you some form of ecclesiastical dispensation for adultery then I'm sorry I neither can nor will.'

'But the Bible says "Go forth and multiply", so that means God wants us to procreate.'

'I suspect you've left it rather too late to be multiplying, Mr Carver. I imagine the lady in question is long past child-bearing age?'

Carver nodded enthusiastically. 'That's the beauty of it, Reverend. No chance of unwanted babies. Just a nice bit of slap and tickle.'

'And is this lady, er… Mrs Sorrell, aware of your intent? Do you think she feels the same way about you?'

'Ooh aye. Judging by the look she give me over the top of her hymn book when I winked at 'er in church on Sunday.'

'And Mrs Carver? What would she say if she knew you planned to have a last fling with this other lady?'

'I'm not telling 'er. She'd clobber us with an iron skillet. She's a temper on 'er, that woman. Down to sex frustration if yer askin' me. If she enjoyed a bit of the other every now and then, she'd be all the better for it.'

'In that case, Mr Carver, I believe you should direct your efforts to wooing your wife again. It sounds like you've each been taking the other for granted. Treat her the way you did when you were courting her all those years ago. Woo her and win her. Imagine you've just met. Never mind the other lady. After all, it was your wife you chose to marry. Make her want you all over again. If she'd hit you over the head with a frying pan if you told her about this lady then it shows she still cares for you.'

'Ya reckon?'

'I do. If you direct your desire and affection at her I'm sure you'll see the benefits and before long you could be enjoying a second honeymoon.'

'Yer a wise man, vicar. And you not even married. God must indeed speak through ya. Thanking you, sir.'

'Don't thank me now – you can thank me later when Mrs Carver has a smile on her face again.'

Carver gave the parson a slap on the back. 'Yer all right, you, sir. Yer all right.'

He left the room and another man took his place. Merritt looked at the clock and sighed.

The last of the long line of rustics had left the parsonage, Merritt had eaten his luncheon, or dinner as Mrs

Muggeridge insisted on calling his midday meal, and the parson was ready to retire to his study to work on his weekly sermon. This task was becoming increasingly onerous. Merritt felt uncomfortable when he witnessed the rapt attention bestowed on him by his flock, who nowadays hung on his every word. With a sizeable minority of them living in straitened circumstances, Merritt felt guilty at offering balm in the form of words when he knew they needed not prayers and piety but bread and the occasional bit of meat, and a chance to enjoy their homes without fear of eviction.

Before he could settle at his desk, there was a knock at the front door and a few moments later another knock on his study door and Mrs Muggeridge entered.

'Reverend Nightingale, there's Mrs Egdon here to see thee. Shall I ask her to wait in the drawing room or do you wish me to ask her to come back later. I can explain you're busy working on your sermon.'

'Show her into the drawing room, Mrs Muggeridge. I'll be in right away. And don't forget to offer her some refreshment.' The housekeeper nodded and bustled away.

No matter how long it was since he had seen his hopes for marriage dashed, Merritt still felt his heart race with excitement at the sight of Hephzibah, or even at the mere mention of her name. He took off his spectacles and hastened towards the drawing room, wishing he had not allowed the chaos of books to take possession of the room again.

The object of his frustrated desire was sitting in one of the fireside armchairs, from where she had removed a small pile of books and papers, which were now neatly stacked on the floor beside her. She looked up and smiled at him but Merritt thought her expression appeared nervous, perhaps even anxious.

The parson settled himself into the chair opposite. 'What an unexpected pleasure, Mrs Egdon.'

Hephzibah didn't reply. Her hands in her lap were restless. She kept rubbing the back of one hand with the other, then interlocking her fingers. They sat in silence for a few moments as the fire in the grate crackled and the long-case clock ticked.

'Are you well, Mrs Egdon? You seem distressed.'

She closed her eyes, then took a gulp of air and said, 'Do you remember, Reverend Nightingale… Merritt… you said to me once that I could ask you anything and you would not hesitate to help me?' Her face was suffused with blushes and she continued to fidget with her hands.

'I do,' he said. 'And I meant it.'

'I need to ask your help now, but I am too afraid to ask you.'

'Don't be afraid, Hephzibah. There's nothing you could ask of me that would be too onerous. I am here at your disposal.' He paused and looked up at her face, contorted with emotion. 'Tell me what's wrong. How can I help you?'

Hephzibah looked at him and Merritt felt as though she were seeing him for the first time, exploring his face, studying him, searching for something. It was so different from the usual way she behaved towards him – kind, indulgent, friendly, as if he were a family pet, a faithful dog, accepted and loved but taken for granted. Now she seemed to be trying to read him, fearful that she might have mistaken something in his character, anxious that what she was about to say might never be unsaid and would mark an irreversible change in their friendship.

Merritt felt his heart racing. He sensed she was about to reveal some confidence, show a level of trust that no one had ever shown in him before, but he also knew that it was fragile and that she might withdraw, pull away and the moment would be lost forever and their drawing together would not only not happen but they would move further apart. He moved off his chair and knelt on the floor in front of her and reached for her restless hands, anchoring them under his own.

She drew her hands away from his, placed them on the arms of the chair and leaned back, putting a distance between them. Merritt felt awkward, still kneeling at her feet, stranded like a polar bear on a drifting iceberg. He got up and went to stand in front of the fireplace.

He was confused – one moment she appeared to drop her barriers and the next to raise them higher than before. He was out of his depth, afraid. Something told him that they had reached a point where their relationship would change irrevocably and he was afraid that he might be unfit to offer the help she so clearly craved. This was not like his conversation with Mr Carver – he could not trot out platitudes or quote scriptures at Hephzibah. She was obviously distressed. His stomach churned as his brain raced through the possibilities, but his imagination fell short.

'This is very difficult for me,' she said, at last. 'I am afraid. I don't know how to tell you. How to ask you for help.'

Merritt fought the urge to kneel at her feet again – fought the urge to grasp her hands in his. He clenched his fists behind his back and looked at her, fixing his eyes on hers, trying to summon up the strength to help her, without giving away the fact that he loved her with a passion that would not abate.

The clock struck the hour and it was as if it had struck Hephzibah too, as she jumped to her feet. 'Do you mind if we go for a walk? I feel uncomfortable here. I don't think I can speak freely. I will be more able to talk openly if we are outdoors.'

They set off, walking in silence, following their instincts, heading away from the village and the well-trodden paths. After fifteen minutes or so they reached the boundaries of Nettlestock village where it adjoined the open parkland leading up the hill to Mudford. Merritt thought of the last time they had walked together here, when Hephzibah had spotted the herd of deer, just as he had been about to open his heart to her. He was glad he hadn't had a chance to speak then as he had saved himself the humiliation of her rejection. It had been just days later that she had eloped with Thomas Egdon.

There was still a little part of Merritt that wondered, if he had spoken up that afternoon, whether she might have listened and thought twice about Egdon's offer – but he knew he was deluding himself. The way she looked at her husband was enough to disabuse him of any illusions. The last time he had been in their company Merritt had looked in Hephzibah's direction and saw her gazing upon Thomas Egdon with a look of unmitigated love and admiration. He had kept asking himself why he didn't seek another parish, return to Oxford and resume his academic studies, travel abroad – anything to get away from here, get away from Hephzibah and the constant pain of watching her loving someone else.

It was a beautiful autumnal day. They stood at the top of a low hill and looked out over the farmland below, where men were hard at work in the distant meadows, making hay. They stood side-by-side, watching the men moving between horse and wagon, pitching, loading and raking hay. From time to time a man would break away and walk over to fill a tin cup from a large wooden bottle of ale to quench his thirst.

'I have come to love this place,' said Hephzibah. Her voice was tremulous.

'Would you like to sit down in the shade and then you can tell me how I can help you?' he said.

'No. Let's keep walking. I will find it easier that way. I don't think I can look you in the eyes.'

A rabbit ran across their pathway, disappearing into the long grass. Hephzibah sighed, then, staring straight ahead, started to speak. 'I am in a terrible predicament. You are the only person I can turn to, the only person I can ask for help. You did say once that you would do anything for me, but what I am going to ask of you may be too much and I will understand. Yes, I will understand… but I don't know what I will do.'

He rested a hand on her arm but she shook it off. 'Please don't touch me. Let me finish what I have to say first. When I have said it, you may want to have nothing more to do with me.'

Merritt was beginning to feel frustrated. 'Just tell me, Hephzibah. Nothing you could ask of me would make me like you any less.'

She gave him a sad smile. 'As you know I married my husband somewhat precipitately. His proposal was unexpected, but it was the fulfilment of my dearest wishes. I love Thomas with all my heart.'

Merritt's face twisted in pain but he stared ahead, grateful that she had wanted to walk and he didn't have to look her in the face.

'Have you ever loved anyone, Merritt? Loved them so much you can hardly breathe in their presence? Loved them so you would do anything to secure their happiness?'

He swallowed and mumbled that he had. He was beginning to wish he had not agreed to accompany her. It was too painful to listen to her avowals of love for his rival.

'In my experience, love is not always a happy state, a source of joy,' she said. 'For me it is more often a cause of pain. May I speak frankly?'

Merritt nodded.

'It seems to me that love is a very one-sided thing. And yet I know it doesn't have to be. My parents loved each other deeply and couldn't bear to be apart. My husband, however, is frequently away. By his own choice. His time spent in London and elsewhere outweighs the time he spends with me. I cannot understand that. When he is with me he is a good husband, but yet… I can't help but think if he truly loved me he would not choose to leave me so often.'

Merritt started to speak but she cut him off. 'Please let me finish or I will lose my courage,' she said. 'Our elopement was brought about by my father-in-law acting inappropriately towards me. He has appetites that he wishes to feed as soon as they occur. I have since come to know that he made advances to my predecessors and none of the other governesses lasted long as a consequence. I also understand that he takes advantage of some of the servants and women on the estate, who are afraid to resist him for fear of losing their livelihoods.'

'That is terrible. Who? When? I must speak with him.'

Hephzibah shook her head. 'There's no point. He'd ignore you and it would hurt your relationship with him and his support of your work in the parish.'

Merritt knew what she said was true. The squire's behaviour was not even unusual. 'Richard Egdon is like many landowners who seem to think the *droit de seigneur* is still in force and it is his right as the landowner to take his pick of any woman on his estates. I wish it were otherwise. Has he harmed you, Hephzibah? Tell me. I will kill him if he has laid a finger on you.'

She looked sideways at him, a little surprised. 'Ah, Merritt, ever the gentleman. I made it clear that he would get nowhere with me and he would come to wish he had never started if he tried to touch me. It worked at first, but then… he tried again. He was aggressive. He kissed me, touched me. It was horrible. I had to leave Ingleton Hall immediately to escape him. I was on my way into Nettlestock to seek your help when I met Thomas and he… he… swept me off my feet. I told him what his father had done and he offered to marry me. I was shocked but overjoyed. It was like a light breaking through the clouds and transforming my life. Until that moment I'd no idea he cared for me.'

Merritt bit his lip, knowing that Egdon's offer of marriage had more than his love of her at its root. Were she to know that Egdon had benefited financially from marrying her it would surely break her heart.

Hephzibah's voice was soft, hesitant, as she continued. 'I love Thomas with an intensity I never knew I would feel. Just to look upon his face moves my heart, swamps me, fills me with pain. Oh, Merritt, if only you could understand what it is to love someone when you are uncertain that their love for you is in equal measure. But let me get to the point. We have now been married for more than three years and have yet to conceive a child.'

Merritt felt a little flicker of hope inside him. 'You are trying to tell me that you and Mr Egdon have not consummated the marriage?'

'Of course we have.' Her voice was sharper, with a hint of exasperation. 'My husband has always been most attentive whenever he is at home. Yes, he may not be here as often as I would like, but when he is, he fulfils his duties as a husband without fail, if you understand what I mean. This is so embarrassing. I have never discussed such intimate matters with anyone else before. I suppose your being a clergyman means I see you as different from other men. I feel a little more able to talk to you – but it's still difficult. I hope you don't mind my frankness.'

Merritt stared ahead. Why was she so capable of twisting the knife into him? He knew it was unconscious on her part. He knew that she would not wish to hurt him, but the way she failed to see him as a flesh and blood man pained him almost beyond endurance.

'The squire is desperate to secure the future of Ingleton Hall and the whole village – I think you know that he and Thomas don't see eye to eye? They quarrel often and I believe that explains Thomas's frequent absences. I have suggested we move to live in London or even in Mudford but he won't hear of it. He doesn't appear to suffer the pain of our separations the way I do.'

The path narrowed in front of them and a tree overhung the pathway. Merritt stepped ahead and held back the branches so that Hephzibah could pass without impediment. They were forced to walk in single file for a while so he fell in behind her and she carried on speaking, calling back over her shoulder to him. She told him about the squire rewriting his will to favour his future grandchildren over Thomas and how he constantly taunted Thomas about his failure to father a child.

'Yesterday morning, after Thomas left, Sir Richard summoned me to his study. He spoke to me as if it were a business transaction. He asked me again if I was expecting a baby. Oh, Merritt, I am afraid if I don't conceive soon he will take matters into his own hands.'

Merritt stepped off the narrow track and pushed his way through the undergrowth, re-joining the path in front of her. He gripped her by the arms. 'He threatened to rape you?'

'Not in so many words. He spoke of disinheriting Thomas if I don't produce an heir and called upon my duty to his family and the future of Nettlestock and the community. He told me he believes Thomas to be incapable of fathering a child.' She flushed. 'I know he wouldn't hesitate to force himself on me if he felt it necessary. Having an heir is the most important thing in his life.'

'But you can't possibly mean that he would try to father a child on you himself? Did he threaten that?'

'When he attacked me before Thomas married me I had to use force to stop him from having his way.' She blushed. 'I had to bite him. Very hard. He has been forcing one woman on the estate for some years to have sexual relations with him or risk her whole family being thrown out of their home. I hadn't seen her for some time. She is an unmarried woman but I saw her last week – she is unmistakably with child. It is no doubt the squire's fault.'

'Abigail Cake.'

'How did you know?'

'Because I noticed she was expecting a child,' he said. 'She must be several months gone.'

Hephzibah nodded. 'The squire boasted about it to me yesterday. Said terrible things. About how Abigail had tried to avoid pregnancy by various methods…' She blushed. 'He compared himself to Thomas. It was horrible. He resents the fact that Thomas has a tendency to overspend and blames him for his inability to make the estate profitable. He has never come to terms with the death of his other sons and every time he looks at Thomas it's as though he resents the fact that it is he who stands before him, not Sam or Roddy. Did you know that Ottilie is actually his adopted niece?'

Merritt nodded.

'She may not be,' said Hephzibah. She told him what Thomas had told her about Ottilie's mother.

Merritt sat down on the ground and put his head in his hands. After a moment or two he looked up at Hephzibah, standing above him. 'There is a rumour that Samuel Egdon killed himself because he found his fiancée had had relations with the squire.'

Hephzibah gasped.

'I hate to participate in village gossip but there are some things I have been unable to avoid hearing. Mrs Muggeridge has a tendency to tell me things whether I want to know or not. She believes a parson must be aware of everything about his parishioners.' He took off his hat and twirled it around, restlessly, by the brim.

'Samuel was engaged to be married to a girl who was not from around here, the sister of one of his former schoolfriends. The squire didn't approve of the match believing that, as eldest son, it was Samuel's duty to marry for the advancement of the family and not for love. He wanted Samuel to marry one of the daughters of Sir Haverford Bellamy at Longstreet but Samuel refused. He invited the girl and her brother to a shooting party at the Hall, hoping that over the course of their stay they would win around his father. One morning, when the men were all out shooting, the squire went back to the house early, complaining of gout pains. When Samuel and the others returned, the girl was missing. She had drowned herself in the carp pond, leaving Samuel a note to say his father had forced himself on her. Samuel took his gun and shot his father then turned the gun on himself.'

Hephzibah gasped. 'What an absolutely horrible story.'

'The squire only took a flesh wound and the whole affair was hushed up. The only reason Mrs Muggeridge found out is that she is very thick with Mrs Andrews.'

'I'm all the more certain now that he will try to force himself on me.' She slumped to the ground beside the parson.

'Have you spoken to Thomas about this?' Merritt said.

'No. He would be mortified. I'm afraid of what he would do to his father. And he's all too conscious of the fact that the squire believes he is a poor substitute for his brothers.'

'Oh, Hephzibah, what a mess. What did you want to ask of me? How can I help you? Would you like me to speak on your behalf to the squire? To Thomas?'

She gasped and stretched out an arm. 'No. You must never speak of this to either of them. I haven't been able to sleep with worrying about what to do. I'd rather die than let the squire touch me. I can understand why that poor girl drowned herself in the lake. But if I don't produce a child Thomas will lose everything. He's already wracked with worry. His father has refused to settle his debts and he has spent all his mother's inheritance. Oh, Merritt, I love him so much that I'd do anything to help him.'

Merritt shook his head, more puzzled than ever about how she wanted him to help her.

Hephzibah swallowed, closed her eyes for a moment then told him about Thomas getting mumps. 'We have tried to have a baby for more than three years and I have come to the conclusion that the only way to resolve matters, and help my husband, is for me to become pregnant and the only way to do that is with another man.' Her eyes were wild, welling with tears, her voice cracking.

Merritt was so startled he jumped to his feet. 'The squire?'

'I told you I'd die first. Don't you understand what I'm asking you, Merritt? Must I spell it out?' Hephzibah reached her hand up for Merritt to pull her up to stand beside him. 'I will understand if you don't want to do it. I know it's too much to ask. I would never have dreamt of asking you, but you did say that you'd do anything to help me. I know you never had anything like this in mind, but I wouldn't ask if I wasn't absolutely desperate. I've thought of every other possibility. I've lain awake at night trying to think of solutions. There's no one else I can ask. And you are not married or – as far as I know – courting anyone. I did think you and Miss Pickering might…' Merritt put a hand up in horror.

'If it works and I have a child you would be able to see it whenever you wanted and were you to marry later I would never let your wife know what had passed between us. And of course the child itself would never know. Nor Thomas. Please, Merritt, can you do this for me? I hope it's not too horrible a prospect for you?' She looked up at him, her blue eyes large and filled with tears. Merritt swallowed, then put his hand up to the back of his neck, unable to credit what Hephzibah was saying.

'I had always thought you were at least quite fond of me, Merritt, and we are friends, aren't we? You probably think of me more as a sister but I hope you could at least give it a try. It may not work. The fault may, after all, lie with me.' She covered her face with her hands. 'I can't believe I'm saying all this, asking this of you. What has become of me?'

Merritt was dumbfounded, completely lost for words. He stood in front of her and stared at her in disbelief.

Hephzibah reached for his hands. 'You're going to say no, aren't you? Of course you are. It is a mad idea. To expect you to have relations with a woman you feel nothing for is to expect too much. I'm so sorry, Merritt. Please forgive me.'

She squeezed his hands between hers. 'I am doing this for love. Otherwise I would never betray my husband, never lie with another man.' She looked up at him, as if searching his face for validation of her words. 'In your sermon last Sunday you spoke of how love covers all wrongs. My love will surely cover this wrong. Won't it? When I'm doing it for all the right reasons. Doing it because of my love for Thomas. I have been reading *The Prince* by Machiavelli. He talks about the end justifying the means. God would understand, wouldn't he? The alternative would be much worse. If you can do this for me, Merritt, I will be indebted to you forever.'

Merritt shut his eyes and realised he was close to tears. He turned away from Hephzibah.

She grasped at his sleeve. 'At least think it over tonight. If you decide not to help me I will understand. I realise I am asking a terrible thing of you. If you decide you can't do what I ask, we will never speak of it again. But, if you are prepared to help me, I'll be waiting for you tomorrow afternoon at two. There's a place we can use – an abandoned cottage in the woods on the far side of the water meadows. No one goes there. No one will ever know. Please, Merritt, just think about it.'

That night, Merritt barely slept. He had never felt so torn. Here he was with the only woman he had ever loved – ever could love – offering her body to him on a plate. He thought of what it would be like to see her, to touch her, to possess her. He thought of her lying beneath him: tried to imagine what it would be like to make love with her. He had no frame of reference for this as he had never been with a woman. He turned over onto his back and stared at the ceiling. His only knowledge of sex was through the words of Ovid and he had approached the *Ars Amorata* as an intellectual exercise rather than a practical guide. All he knew was that the thought of being in Hephzibah's arms was almost too much for his brain to comprehend. Yet, as he lay staring at the ceiling, his body comprehended only too well.

He rolled onto his stomach and buried his head in the pillow, which was damp with his sweat. He was supposed to be a man of God: maybe his vocation was shallow, but he did have a moral compass and it was telling him that everything about Hephzibah's proposal was wrong. He had only that morning done his level best to dissuade Mr Carver from his proposed adultery and yet here he was himself, contemplating adultery with a woman who was only doing it because she loved her husband. Wrong, wrong, wrong. He beat his fists against the pillow in anger and frustration.

His scruples were not only moral. There was also his pride. Merritt felt humiliated: Hephzibah had implied that the prospect of making love with him was distasteful to her. She had spoken at length of her love for her husband. As for Merritt, hadn't she said she looked on him as friend and brother, not as an object of desire?

The situation was like Satan in the desert tempting a starving Christ to turn stones into bread. He had preached to his hungry parishioners about it – were he to succumb to temptation himself, he would be nothing but a hypocrite.

And yet... Merritt closed his eyes but could not efface her image from his brain. Trying in vain to sleep, all he could think of was the look of desperation in her eyes as she had asked him to do this for her. He had made her a promise and surely it would be a bigger sin to break that promise, to betray her trust. Could he deny her anything? He feared not. He was powerless where she was concerned. If Hephzibah asked him to cut off his hand for her he would ask her to hand him the axe.

CHAPTER TWENTY-ONE

Neither can the wave that has passed by be recalled,
nor the hour which has passed return again.

Ovid

They met on the path leading to the water meadows, then took a narrow plank bridge over a stream, passed through a small copse of trees and up a slope in the chalk hill on the other side. They walked in silence, both of them embarrassed and uncertain of what lay ahead of them, wondering whether there was any alternative and whether they should turn back. The thin soil was sparsely vegetated, but they were concealed from the village and the Hall by the copse of trees. When they reached the summit they descended the other side where a small shepherd's hut hunkered under the slope of the hill, concealed from view by an outcrop of bare chalk and a clump of scrubby bushes.

'No one comes here. It's not used any more. The journeyman shepherd who used to stay here died two or three years ago. And the road's half a mile away,' Hephzibah said.

Merritt nodded. His mouth was dry and his palms were sweating. He couldn't believe what they were about to do. His heart ached with sorrow. Everything that Hephzibah had said to him the previous day reinforced how she didn't see him. He was invisible to her. She saw only the costume of the local parson, a friendly man – someone to exchange pleasantries with, enjoy a walk with but not someone who merited more than the occasional passing thought. He had lain awake most of the night wrestling with his conscience and his pride. He had few religious scruples – despite his clerical profession, he saw himself as more of an agnostic or a humanist – but he did believe in marital fidelity.

How could he stand in the pulpit and lecture his parishioners about morality when he was committing adultery with one of them? And to know that Hephzibah was only doing this out of love for her husband. There was the rub. It was a humiliation to be used in this way, to be treated by Hephzibah like a necessary evil, something to be dispensed with as quickly as possible, like holding one's nose while taking medicine.

Merritt looked sideways at Hephzibah. She was clearly as nervous as he was. Her eyes were fixed on the path ahead as she walked briskly towards the small wooden structure. He wondered if she was filled with disgust at the thought of their coming congress – something to be got over with quickly, possibly with gritted teeth. He trudged on beside her, feeling like a condemned man approaching the gallows.

The place hadn't been used in some years. Woodbine was growing over the stone walls and there was a collection of rusting chains hanging on one of the outside walls. A pile of shepherd's crooks lay abandoned in the grass, beside a heap of woven fencing panels, beginning to rot away, their surfaces green with mould.

Hephzibah pushed the door of the hut open and they both started as the ancient hinges creaked. Inside, Merritt was grateful for the gloom – the two small windows were encrusted with grime and cobwebs, blocking out most of the light. He looked around him. There were old shepherding implements hanging from hooks on the wall, alongside a few moth-eaten linen smocks and a couple of hats. Against one wall of the tiny room was a narrow wooden box-bed without any bedding, save a neatly folded woollen blanket.

'I brought the blanket here yesterday in case it was chilly,' said Hephzibah. 'We can lie on it. It's clean.'

She looked away, avoiding his eyes. The pair of them stood there for several moments, neither knowing what to say or do.

Eventually Hephzibah spoke again, 'Have you done this before?' Her voice was shy, hesitant.

Merritt shook his head, frozen to the spot. For years he had longed for this moment, for the anticipation of at last possessing her, but instead of joy, he felt only pain and heartache.

'We don't need to undress,' she said. 'It won't take long. Shall we lie down together and then I can help you?' She was blushing again. 'I mean I can do my best to make it easy for you, as at least I know what to expect. We can get it over as quickly as possible.' She climbed up onto the bed, her back against the wall of the hut and motioned for him to join her. 'We could just lie here a while, until you're ready.'

Merritt started to move across the narrow space then stopped. He wasn't going to let it be this way. He was determined to make it mean something for him, if not for her. This afternoon might prove to be the only time in his life he made love. If he couldn't have Hephzibah, he wanted no other. He couldn't control whether or not she became pregnant, he couldn't control the fact she had chosen him just to impregnate her, but for these few stolen moments he could take control, he could do what he could to make it memorable and beautiful.

'Stand up,' he said, his voice husky.

Hephzibah looked surprised but slid off the bed. 'You're not going to back out are you, Merritt? Not now.'

He reached for her and pulled her towards him. He looked into her eyes, uncaring that he was giving away his true feelings. He reached up to stroke her hair and gently pulled out the pins that were holding it up, letting them fall to the floor. He kept his eyes on her as her hair tumbled loose around her shoulders. She looked up at him, her eyes wide with alarm.

'Don't speak,' he said, placing his fingers for a moment over her lips. 'If we do this, we do it on my terms. I am not a machine you can switch on and off. I have to feel something, see something, see *you*.' He looked into her eyes. 'And I'd like you to see *me* too.'

Carefully and slowly, Merritt began to remove her clothing. Hephzibah stood in front of him, shivering slightly, but she kept her eyes fixed on his, evidently accepting that she had no choice. As each item was discarded, revealing more of her, he ran his hands slowly over her body, feeling the alabaster smoothness of her skin. He could hear her breathing growing more rapid. When he touched her bare breasts her nipples hardened under his hands and he dropped his head and took one of them in his mouth, running his tongue over the aureole. She gave a little gasp. He raised his head to look at her, afraid she would tell him to stop, but she started to unbutton his shirt. Moving slowly, terrified that at any moment the other might call a halt to what they were doing, they continued to undress each other until their clothes lay in a heap on the floor.

Merritt drew her naked body to his, holding her against him and as he felt, for the first time in his life, the feeling of skin upon skin, he gave an anguished cry, then before he could stop himself, his mouth was on hers, his hands tangled in her hair. Her mouth opened to his and he felt her warm breath mingling with his, her tongue seeking his. He lifted her into his arms and moved with her to the narrow, hard bed. Her hands and arms were all over his body, touching him, stroking him, causing him to tremble with a joy and hunger he had never before experienced.

As he entered her, he looked into her eyes, drowning in them, feeling at last that he was whole, that until now a part of him had been missing. Her hands gripped his buttocks and she groaned with pleasure as they fused their two bodies into one entity. She moved under him, responding to him, matching her movements with his. Merritt had never experienced such undiluted pleasure before.

Sweat pooled on their skin between them. He felt her legs gripping his sides, then wrapping themselves around his back, squeezing him tightly, taking him deeper into her. He bit his lip, trying to hold back the release he knew would be coming and felt her hands reaching around his torso pulling him further into her, as if she wanted them to be joined like this forever. Their movements grew faster and more urgent. She was moaning now, little frantic gasps of pleasure. At last, when he could hold back no longer, he eased his head back and looked at her and she nodded and closed her eyes. As they climaxed, she clung to him like a drowning woman holding onto passing wreckage, and then she gave a long sigh as her body juddered under his.

They lay crushed together on the narrow pallet, as the sweat dried on their naked skin. Merritt pulled the blanket over Hephzibah and held her close. They lay there in silence, matching their breathing to each other's, trying to restore it to a normal rhythm. As he held her he stroked her hair and touched her face.

'Thank you,' she said at last. 'I know that has worked. I felt it. Just then when we… you know… I was certain that we have made a baby. It felt so different.'

'Different?' he looked at her, uncertain, unsure of himself now.

'I can't explain it. I just know. We have made a baby. I have never been so sure of anything in my life. Thank you, Merritt.'

Merritt turned away and lay on his back, looking up at the wooden ceiling, where a canopy of dense spiders' webs decorated the beams. 'But it was also pleasurable for you?' he asked, struggling to cover his nerves.

'You know it was. I didn't expect that. Not at all.'

He bit his lip. *Don't ask her to compare me to her husband.*

'I have never known anything like that in my life before,' he said. 'You must realise now that I love you. I have always loved you, Hephzibah. But you were blind to it. You were blind to me.'

Hephzibah nodded. Her eyes sad. 'You're right. I didn't think of you in that way. Lying here with you now I still find it hard to believe what we have just done. How it felt.' She smiled and stroked his cheek. 'You're an unexpected man, Merritt Nightingale. A man of hidden qualities and hidden depths.'

Merritt felt a surge of joy and turned over to face her, putting his hands behind her head to draw her into a kiss.

She started to respond, then pulled away from him, her body stiffening. She sat up and reached from the bed to her blouse where it lay crumpled on the floor, holding it in front of herself, covering her breasts from him.

'I am so grateful to you, Merritt, and I know with absolute certainty that I am now carrying a child, so that means we must never meet like this again. We must never speak of this again. Do you understand, Merritt? Once the child is born you may of course see it, but I beg you to give no cause for my husband or the squire to suspect what has passed between us.'

She scrambled about, gathering up her clothes as he watched her. 'Please, Merritt, look away. Don't look at my body. Please try to forget what we have done. You say you love me but I am not worthy of your love. I acknowledge that what has happened this afternoon is not what I expected. I didn't think we would… I didn't expect there to be such tenderness. I didn't expect there to be passion. There were both those things, weren't there, Merritt? For both of us. That makes it special. It will make our child special. Know this, my dearest friend, that while we will never repeat this nor speak of it, I will always treasure this afternoon in my heart. Now, please wait here for a little while before you leave. We can't risk anyone seeing us returning to Nettlestock together.'

She moved back to the bed, where Merritt lay, the blanket tangled in his limbs. She bent over him and dropped a light kiss on the top of his head and laid her hand against his cheek. 'Goodbye, my dearest friend.' Then she was gone.

Merritt lay on the bed, overcome with emotions. He had never dreamt that making love with a woman could be as sweet, as exciting, as emotional. The pleasure had swamped him like waves, a wonderful drowning. How was it possible that in a few short moments he could move from absolute joy to wretchedness, loss and sorrow? If Hephzibah had been blind to him before, she was now deliberately wiping him out. He wasn't sure which was worse.

He tried to take consolation from the fact that she had been as moved as he was, as swept up by the passion and pleasure. She had admitted she hadn't expected to feel that and he dared to think that it was not only because she had not expected it of him but also because it was something she had never experienced before. He dared to hope Thomas Egdon had never known what he had just known because if he had, how could he possibly bear to be so often apart from Hephzibah? But now having tasted that intoxicating pleasure, Merritt was to be deprived of it. He buried his head in his hands. She would drive him mad. How could he live without her now?

Merritt punched the wall in sudden anger, breaking the skin on his knuckles. He sucked at the blood and cursed his stupidity. He had known all along that he and Hephzibah were meant to be with each other, so why had he hesitated in telling her? Had he made his feelings clear she might have at least been willing to give him a chance, to find out more about him, to let him court her. Surely then, as they got to know each other better, the intensity of the feelings they had for each other would have surfaced, even in her. Instead, he had let his crippling lack of self-worth and fear of rejection master him.

He swung his legs over the side of the bed and quickly dressed, looking around the miserable little room before he shut the door. *Oh, Hephzibah, my darling Hephzibah, my love, my life, what am I to do now?*

Walking back to the village, he thought of the possibility that she was indeed expecting his child. Until now he had not really entertained that as a possibility. He had not thought past what would happen this afternoon. How could he bear not only being apart from her, but also from his own child? Merritt hadn't contemplated having his own children, other than as a vague and abstract possibility in some as yet undetermined future. Now he knew he might face the prospect of being a father without a child. *You fool, you complete and utter fool.*

CHAPTER TWENTY-TWO

And all her face was honey to my mouth,
And all her body pasture to mine eyes;
The long lithe arms and hotter hands than fire,
The quivering flanks, hair smelling of the south,
The bright light feet, the splendid supple thighs
And glittering eyelids of my soul's desire.

(from Love and Sleep, Algernon Charles Swinburne)

The following day, Hephzibah walked along the towpath. The past twenty-four hours had been a sweet torture. She had been unable to get Merritt Nightingale out of her thoughts.

Since her liaison with Merritt she had been unsettled, veering between guilt and excitement. She was not guilty at about what she had done – she had spent too many hours beforehand agonising over her plan and had come to the conclusion it was the right and only thing to do. She was guilty about how she had *felt* doing it. It had never entered her head that committing adultery in this way would have given her pleasure.

It had come as a shock, a blinding revelation that she had experienced what she could only describe as physical passion with him. Hephzibah had never thought of Merritt that way. Now every time she thought of him a little shiver went through her body.

It was difficult not to make comparisons between Merritt and her husband. She pictured their faces – Thomas with the cold beauty of a finely carved marble statue, while Merritt's face was different in some way each time she looked upon him. It was an interesting face, one that was animated, changing expression based on what was going through his head. And there was always so much going through his head. Thomas, on the other hand thought only of horses. He had the appearance of a man who inflamed passions, yet all he talked about was inflamed pasterns. Merritt was caring of others, fascinated by the lives of his parishioners and eager to help them. Thomas despised the villagers and thought their lives trivial and unworthy of his attention.

But to accept that her feelings about both her husband and Merritt had changed was to accept that she was an adulteress. Having experienced pleasure rather than pain from their encounter threw what they had done together into a completely different light. It was no longer feasible to classify what she had done as an honourable deed. She could no longer tell herself she had done it selflessly, out of love for Thomas. She knew she had been beguiled by Thomas Egdon. Acknowledging that made her ashamed. Was she as shallow as she now knew he was?

There were a couple of lads fishing close to the confluence with one of the tributaries that fed the canal, but otherwise the place was deserted. She nodded to them and passed by. She was intending to walk towards Mudford but, without consciously thinking about it, she turned off the path and found herself heading over the hill towards the abandoned shepherd's hut.

The sky darkened and she looked up, wondering if there

was a chance of rain – her umbrella was back in the house. But it was one of those days where one minute there was a blazing sun in a deep blue sky, then a passing grey cloud-mass blotted it out, casting shadows over the countryside before moving on.

The look in Merritt's eyes when they were making love had shocked her and she felt herself blushing as she walked. There had been such tenderness threaded through the desire and passion he had shown her. She'd never known that with Thomas, who was an enthusiastic lover but she realised now she had always been incidental to his pleasure. With a flash of understanding she knew they had never had a true connection the way she had with Merritt, emotionally and intellectually as well as physically. She pressed her fingernails into her palms, willing herself to forget what Merritt had made her feel.

Hephzibah walked on, telling herself that she would turn back in a moment, but her feet led her along the towpath and over the narrow footbridge, across meadows and fields, up and down the long chalk slope of the hill and then she was there, outside the shepherd's hut. Perhaps if she were to look once more on the scene it would force her to accept that what had happened was nothing more than a transaction, an expediency. The shabby surroundings of an abandoned shepherd's temporary resting place was hardly the stuff of romance. Revisiting it would show what had happened for what it was – a sordid act that she had forced the parson into.

As soon as she pushed open the door, despite the dark interior, she knew at once that there was someone inside – and then he was upon her, enveloping her in his arms, pressing her against the door, kissing her until she could barely draw breath.

'You came. I knew you would,' Merritt said. 'I've been waiting here for an hour.' As he spoke, his hands were

216

unpinning her chignon, his fingers weaving through her hair. 'I knew you couldn't mean what you said about us not meeting like this again. Not after what happened.'

Hephzibah tried to draw away from him, wanting to tell him that this was not her intent, but her body responded to him where her words didn't and she returned his kisses with a fervour that surprised her. 'I didn't mean to come,' she said at last, her voice low, 'but I couldn't help myself. My feet brought me here. I never thought to find you waiting.'

'I have thought of nothing but you since you left yesterday. Every waking minute and all my sleepless night. I love you, Hephzibah, and I know we are meant to be with each other. I have never been so sure of anything.'

This time they didn't pause to take their clothes off. Merritt took her in his arms and then they were against the door, fumbling with the openings in their garments. He lifted her up and she wrapped her legs and arms around him and let him position her against the wall of the hut for support. She lost herself in the abandon of kissing him and cried out when he entered her. Just when she thought she could take no more, he carried her to the bed where he took his time, until Hephzibah was at the point of screaming. What was this man doing to her? How could he have this effect on her? How did her body know his better already than it knew her husband's? Thomas's face swam before her eyes, but she pushed the image away and looked into Merritt's face, asking herself how she could ever have thought it ordinary and unmemorable.

Afterwards, they lay together in a mass of tangled limbs and dishevelled clothing. Merritt stroked her hair and kissed her again, this time softly, tenderly, lovingly.

'I have never before experienced what we have,' Hephzibah said at last. 'It is different with my husband. I had not imagined or thought it possible to feel such pleasure with another person.' Then, with no warning, she burst into tears.

Merritt fumbled in his pocket for a handkerchief and wiped away her tears. 'Don't cry, my beloved. Don't cry.' He folded her in his arms.

'It's such a mess,' she said. 'I've made it a mess. I'm an adulteress. You are a man of the church. I've ruined both of us. I thought I was doing the right thing. I wasn't supposed to feel this way.'

'Tell me,' he said, 'Tell me how you feel.' He covered her face with kisses.

She pushed him away and sat up. 'It's torture. Complete torture. I did what I did out of love for Thomas and now I know I don't love him any more. What does that make me?'

Merritt said nothing, just held her, stroking her hair and looking into her eyes.

Hephzibah was sobbing. 'What have I done, Merritt? What have we done? I am ashamed.'

Still with his eyes locked on hers, he said, 'I love you, Hephzibah and I will never be ashamed of that.'

She raised her face to his and this time let him kiss her again, returning the kiss, drowning in it, her arms gripping him tightly as if afraid he might disappear.

'I was rash and impetuous in marrying Thomas.' She gulped and buried her head in his shoulder. 'I should have waited. I would have realised in the end that I love you, wouldn't I? You would have made me realise it. I am such a stupid fool, blind and shallow. How can you possibly love me, Merritt, when I have been so foolish?'

'Blame me, not yourself, Hephzibah.' He stroked her hair and kissed the top of her head. 'I was too slow to declare my feelings.' He shook his head. 'No, worse than that. I didn't declare them at all. We might have gone through life without ever knowing what we could mean to each other if you hadn't asked me to do this.'

She sat up. 'Oh God! Do you believe I asked you to do this as an excuse to seduce you? What must you think of me?'

'Of course I don't think that. I know you were surprised at what we feel for each other,' he said.

'It's not just about doing this, though. About making love,' she said. 'This is the way it is only because there was already a strong feeling between us. I just hadn't realised it. I have always loved being with you, Merritt. Our walks in the woods and by the canal. Our conversations. The work we did together on the lending library. Whenever you tell me anything I'm fascinated. I could listen to you talking for hours.'

He said nothing.

'Oh, Merritt, I only came here today in the hope that it would make me see sense. That looking at this place again would make me think differently about what happened between us. I hoped that seeing this sordid little place would make me see what happened as sordid too. I thought it would help me to forget how I felt being with you. I hoped it would make me see again why I did it. Why I asked you to do it. I hoped it would make me love my husband again. But it's no good. I don't just love being with you, Merritt, I love you.'

Merritt gasped and Hephzibah saw his eyes were misted over.

'You love me too?' he asked. 'You really love me?'

'I think I fell in love with you when you told me how the books in your house were out of control. I just didn't know it at the time. My husband has never read a book in all the three years I have known him. He speaks only of horses and racing results. I fell for his good looks and his air of excitement. He was so different from everything I had ever known and that cast a spell on me. I was enchanted. You however are so *like* everything I have ever known and everything I have ever cared about, so that talking with you is like slipping on a well-worn pair of favourite gloves that have moulded to the exact shape and size of one's fingers.'

'I'm flattered,' he said, laughing. 'It's not every day I get compared to a pair of old gloves.' He was overwhelmed with joy to know that she felt the same way about him as he did about her. He pulled her towards him and started to kiss her again, but this time she pulled back, her hands on his shoulders to keep him at arm's length.

'None of this helps our situation though,' said Hephzibah. 'Everything I said yesterday was true. I made a bad choice when I married Thomas Egdon but now I must live with it.'

She looked at Merritt and saw the shadow of pain disfigure his face.

'It doesn't have to be so. Come away with me, Hephzibah. We could go to Italy, to France, find an island somewhere, have our child and spend our life together. Let's just go. We can disappear. Who cares what people say if we are far away and cannot hear them?'

She gave him a rueful smile and laid her palm against his cheek. 'Oh Merritt, Merritt, Merritt, if only – but it would never work. You would lose your living. Your reputation would be destroyed. We would be the talk of the county and our reputation would follow us wherever we went. We can't live on love alone.'

'We'll find a way. I could become a tutor to a family.'

'Tutors are single men. No family would take in a man with a wife and child in tow. Not that I could be your wife when I am married already. That would make me your mistress. And our child a bastard.'

Merritt was about to protest when she spoke again, her voice brisk and practical. 'Do you have any idea what tutors earn? Obviously more than governesses – but, believe me, that's not saying much. And people would expect references. They'd want to know why you walked out of your living in a country parish. It would not be long before they discovered the reason, and what respectable family would entrust the education of their children to a man who had fathered a child with a married woman, one of his parishioners to boot?'

Merritt put his head in his hands.

'I don't want to be apart from you,' she said. 'I have never felt pain like this before. But this is the price of love. These past two days I have known the greatest joy of my life and the greatest sorrow. We must be strong, Merritt. I need you to help me be strong.' She stood up and straightened her clothes. 'You leave first this time. Don't look back. Say goodbye now and know that you will have my heart forever.'

'I want you with it,' he said, his face contorted with pain.

'I know, my love.'

'But the baby?' He looked at her in anguish. 'Our baby, if we have conceived it.'

'We have – I told you I am certain,' she said, her voice solemn. 'The child must never know you are its father but I will ensure you get to spend time with him or her. Lots of time. I promise, my darling. I will find a way. Now go. I beg you.'

He kissed her again and she clung to him, then taking a deep breath, she pushed him through the door. When he had gone, she watched his retreating figure through the small filthy window, her eyes misted with tears. When he had vanished over the brow of the hill she dried her eyes and left the hut and headed back to Ingleton Hall.

An old woman with a black eye-patch was watching the shepherd's hut from a clump of trees. She was on her way back after collecting rushes for the basket-weaving that supplemented her income as a washer-woman. Her name was Mercy Loveless and the surname was a better fit than her given name. She'd never had time for people and her temperament had worsened in the ten years since she lost one of her eyes in a haymaking accident.

The reeds were heavy on her shoulders and Mercy stopped to rest for a moment. Laying them down, she stepped behind a bush to relieve herself. She was rearranging her undergarments when she saw Parson Nightingale emerge from the old shepherd's refuge.

'What's 'e bin doin' in there?' she said to herself. Mercy often talked to herself. Many in the village called her mad; more were afraid of her; all gave her a wide berth. She watched the parson stride away in the direction of the village. 'Can't be no good as comes from a man 'anging about where 'e don't belong. Fancy I'll wait and watch 'ere a while. Happen 'e's bin up to no good with summat or someone.'

Mercy's patience was rewarded within ten minutes, when Hephzibah Egdon stepped out of the hut. The old woman waited until she had disappeared over the brow of the low hill, then shook her head. She muttered, 'Bloody outsiders – and them doing the naughty.'

There was one person in Nettlestock who neither feared Mercy Loveless nor cared whether or not she was a mad woman. Abigail Cake had always found Mercy to be that most useful of individuals – someone prepared to share privileged information in return for a half side of bacon, a sack of coal or a bag of potatoes. Trouble was, Mercy hadn't had any news worth sharing. Not in a long while. But now her luck had changed. Mercy knew Abigail Cake was acquainted with the two male Egdons rather better than was fitting for the daughter of their bailiff. If anyone was going to go in for playing at handie dandie in Nettlestock they'd better understand that Mercy Loveless would know all about it.

Half an hour later Mercy was sitting in the kitchen of the bailiff's cottage, smoking her pipe and swigging from a mug of ale, while Abigail stirred a stew on the range.

'And 'im as is meant to be a man of God. And 'er as is meant to be married to squire's son. 'E were grindin 'er corn. Bold as brass.'

Abigail wiped her hands on her apron. 'You saw them doing it?'

'Not exactly. But what else would a man and a woman do inside an empty ol' building which 'asn't bin used since Dick Farthing died three Michaelmas ago? Only one reason to go in there. And them with the door shut tight. Up to no good, I say.' She bounced one fist against the palm of her other hand. 'Reckon if I'd got there a few minutes sooner I'd 'ave 'eard them moanin' and groanin' and taking a turn among the cabbages like a pair o' pigs.'

Abigail smiled and turned back to the pot of stew.

'I said to mesel I did, that Abby Cake will find this interestin', she will. She'll make it worth my while to spend my time trailin' all this way to share such useful information. She's a good girl is that Abby, I said.'

'Times are hard, Mercy Loveless. It'll have to be turnips.'

'Turnips! Who do thee think I am, Abby Cake? I can dig turnips out the soil mesel. Na! I want a nice side o' bacon or a barrel of ale.'

Abby reached up to the shelf above the cooking range and took down a tin box. She opened it and pulled out a handful of coins and dropped them into the old woman's palm. 'There. Best I can do now. But you bring me more information about those two and maybe I'll see my way to letting you have a brace of pheasants.'

'Thou's a good lass, Abby Cake. Smart like ya mother afore ye. Now lemme have another ale afore I go. To see us on me way.'

CHAPTER TWENTY-THREE

What likeness may define, and stray not
From truth's exactest way,
A baby's beauty? Love can say not
What likeness may.

(from Babyhood, Algernon Charles Swinburne)

As soon as her baby boy was placed in her arms, Hephzibah forgot all the agony of delivering him. She looked down at his small, squashed-up face, red and wrinkled, the tiny bud of a nose, his head with hardly any hair, and she fell hopelessly in love.

Thomas was at home when the child was born, pacing the landing outside her room while she laboured. He grinned with pride when presented with his son.

Even the squire was forced to acknowledge that his only surviving son had finally done something right, but showed little interest in the baby once he knew it was safely delivered. 'They're all the same, babies. Can never tell 'em apart. All bloody ugly. Look like little piglets and make a hell of a lot more noise.'

Thomas, once he'd got over his relief that at last his manhood would no longer be questioned by his father, slipped back into his usual habits, with long absences in London and at his horse trainer's. He now had five young horses being trained in the stables at Lambourn. Two of them had been competing for a season, but so far the results had disappointed and Thomas used this to justify his spending more time watching them train on the gallops, as well as going to every race meeting in which they ran. Hephzibah now accepted his absences with relief: all her misty-eyed illusions about him had vanished since she had fallen in love with Merritt.

In the early months of her pregnancy she saw Merritt at least once a week when he took the Sunday service in Nettlestock. She tried to refrain from watching him, keeping her head bowed as though in devotion, but inevitably her gaze would lift and she shivered with desire and longing when she looked up. With her eyes closed she luxuriated in the sound of his voice. Every Sunday was a beautiful torture.

As the evidence of her pregnancy grew, she had stopped appearing in public and hence had a break from church-going. She felt thankful that she was able to avoid the pain of seeing her erstwhile lover, mixed with a desperate longing to be near him.

One afternoon, she bumped into Merritt when walking beside the water meadows. She had believed herself safe from any risk of seeing him as it was within the grounds of the Hall, so he must have walked that way deliberately in the hope of seeing her. She was seven months into her pregnancy and it was the first time the parson had seen her this way. Trying to avoid him, she turned back and walked away into the woods, but he ran after her. He wrapped his arms around her then placed his hands over her bump, crying out when he felt the baby kicking. Overcome, she pressed her own hand over his, before pulling away from him and walking briskly back towards the Hall.

Now that Edwin was born, she knew she had to fulfil her promise to Merritt that he would have plenty of opportunity to see his son, even if none to acknowledge him. The parson had called at Ingleton Hall to enquire after her and the baby's wellbeing, but Hephzibah was unable to face him, and was wary about his reactions on seeing his son, fearful that he would give himself away in the presence of Thomas, Mrs Andrews or the squire.

She waited until a month after the birth then, recovered from her confinement and the weather being mild, she took the baby out in the carriage to call at the parsonage, purportedly to arrange the christening.

Mrs Muggeridge showed them into the drawing room and went to summon the parson who was reading in the garden. Hephzibah was tempted to follow the housekeeper outside to join Merritt in the garden but this would risk their being overlooked from the road, over the hedge, or by Mrs Muggeridge from the kitchen window. She didn't want anyone other than herself to witness Merritt's first sight of his son.

She settled into a chair with the sleeping Edwin in her arms and waited nervously. Merritt appeared in the doorway, his face flushed, his freckles prominent from exposure to the summer sun. He ran a hand through his hair, then stepped back and called over his shoulder to his housekeeper. 'Mrs Muggeridge, please give Mrs Egdon and me half an hour to discuss the christening arrangements and then you can bring us in a tray of tea.'

He closed the door and leaned against it, looking across the room at Hephzibah and the baby, as if afraid to move closer.

Hephzibah beckoned him. He gulped a lungful of air, then went and knelt at her feet. She parted the shawl to reveal the sleeping child's face and Merritt gasped.

'Merritt, meet Edwin. I have named him for my stepfather.'

'May I hold him?' he said, his eyes brimming with tears. She nodded and placed the little bundle in his arms. He bent his head down and breathed in the smell of the baby, then kissed its head. Hephzibah untied the cap from the boy's head so Merritt could better see his son. He cupped his hand around the small head, then kissed the baby again. He looked up at Hephzibah, and shook his head, unable to speak.

Eventually he said, 'He's beautiful. I am overcome. We made him, Hephzibah. Our little boy. I love him so much. I love you so much.' His voice broke and he brushed a tear from his eyes. 'I'm sorry. I didn't expect to feel this way. To feel so much love for him.'

The baby opened its eyes and looked straight at his father. Edwin gurgled and smiled at this strange new person, then his face reddened, transformed into a scowl, and he began to bawl.

'I need to feed him. Do you mind?' She held out her arms and Merritt gently placed the howling baby in them. He watched, fascinated as she undid her blouse and gave the baby her breast. Hephzibah looked up at him and could see the tenderness and longing in his face. She was the cause of so much pain. It was clear he wanted to protect her and the baby, to be with them, to care for them, to love them. She had denied him that possibility. Yet she knew that if faced with that terrible choice again she would do exactly the same. Edwin was the result of what they had done and it was impossible to imagine life without him. And as for Merritt – they could never be together but nothing could take away the sweetness of her memories of being with him.

'Oh my darling girl, how I have missed you,' Merritt said, as if reading her thoughts. 'Not a day has passed when I haven't thought of you, when I haven't relived what happened in that miserable hut. To see you in the distance or among the throng at church on Sundays has been the most terrible agony, knowing that I can't speak to you, touch you, kiss you, experience again the joy of being with you. I can't do it any longer. I can't go on living like this. We are a family. We must be together. We have to leave Nettlestock. We have to go somewhere where no one will know us, where no one will find us.'

Hephzibah wanted to say yes. She wished there was a way she could wave a magic wand and turn back time to that fateful day when Thomas Egdon had found her on the way to the village. If she had left the house only a few minutes earlier or later they would never have run into each other. She would have walked on into the village, knocked on the parsonage door and told Merritt everything and he would have felt able to declare his feelings for her. Her eyes stung and the tears welled up in them.

'We've been through this, Merritt. You know it's not possible. I feel the same as you do. Just now, seeing you holding our son. You can't imagine how that felt to me. You can't imagine how it has felt pretending that he is Thomas's child.' Her voice broke.

The baby began to cry again and she moved him onto the other breast. 'Thomas doesn't like me feeding him. He says it looks as though I'm a common villager. He wants me to have a wet nurse or to feed him with milk from a tin. He got Mrs Andrews to try to persuade me to have the bailiff's daughter come to take care of him.'

'Abigail Cake?'

'Yes. Her child is now ten months old. Oh, Merritt, you have no idea how horrible my life is there. I don't want that Cake woman anywhere near Edwin.'

'Then we must run away together. Please, my darling, let me make a plan. Just give me a little time.'

Hephzibah eased the baby off her nipple and the child immediately went to sleep. She laid him on one of the fireside chairs, making a nest for him out of cushions and covering him with his shawl. She and Merritt stood side-by-side for a moment watching him sleep. Merritt's hand reached for hers and she turned towards him.

There was a loud knock on the door and they sprang apart as Mrs Muggeridge backed into the room, bearing a large tray. When she had laid out the tea things, the woman said, 'May I take a peek at the baby?' Without waiting for an answer she was across the room and bending over the child. 'He's a bonny little thing, isn't he? He has your colouring, Mrs Egdon, rather than Master Thomas's, but I can see he's going to be as handsome as his father. Now if you'll excuse me, I have some gooseberries to preserve.'

When the door was closed behind her, Merritt and Hephzibah fell upon each other. He held her face in his hands and kissed her tenderly at first, then with mounting urgency. Hephzibah extricated herself from his hold. 'We can't. We mustn't. We're only making it harder for ourselves.'

'You have to understand, Hephzibah, everything's different now. We are a family. We need to be together. I don't want my son growing up under the influence of the squire and his spendthrift son. I can't stand aside any longer.'

He ran his hands through his hair and shook his head. 'I should never have agreed to you living this lie. I can't sleep at night for thinking about you in Thomas Egdon's bed, his hands touching you where only my hands should be, your body under his, able to have you whenever he wants to, to use you without loving you. It's a sham and I can't stand it any longer. I won't tolerate it, Hephzibah.'

She bowed her head, unable to find any adequate words.

Merritt looked down at the sleeping baby. 'As soon as I held my son, I knew I'd made a terrible mistake letting you keep this a secret – but there's no reason to continue with that mistake when we have the power to redress it. We can't reclaim the past months, but we can live the rest of our lives as a family. That is what's right.'

Hephzibah looked at him in anguish. 'Merritt, we can't. I love you with my heart, my body and my soul. I too lie awake at night thinking of you, of us, of being in your arms, of feeling everything you make me feel when we're together.' She paced up and down the room. Merritt moved towards her his arms outstretched, but she held up her hands to block him.

'You have to understand I couldn't live with myself if I were to do what you ask of me,' she said, her palms extended in front of her as a barrier. 'Thomas Egdon rescued me from his father. I married him willingly. I thought I loved him and I was wrong about that, but it's not his fault.' She closed her eyes and took a deep breath, hoping that what she was saying didn't sound rehearsed. She tried not to look at Merritt's face. Get through this, Hephzibah. Don't look at him. She raised her hands and covered her eyes. 'Yes, he may be away from home more than I'd expected of a husband, and he may spend more money, but in every other respect he has behaved decently to me.'

Merritt took advantage of her covered eyes to move to her, but as soon as he touched her she stepped sideways. 'Let me finish, Merritt. I do believe Thomas loves me in his way. I promised before God to be with him until death do us part.'

Merritt opened his mouth to speak, then appeared to think better of it. She allowed herself to look at him at last, studying his face. 'You do understand don't you, Merritt? God knows, I hate this as much as you do. I love you now and will always love you. Only you. I beg your forgiveness for unleashing this upon us both. If I'd had any inkling that I'd fall desperately in love with you, I would never have asked you to do what we did. At the time I wanted to save my marriage, save the husband I thought I loved. I was naïve, stupid even, blind certainly. I may not love Thomas but I can't hurt him.'

'But you're hurting me!' Merritt's voice broke with anguish.

'Don't you think I don't know that, my darling? I'm hurting you and I'm killing myself.'

The clock on the church tower began to chime the hour. Hephzibah looked at him, her mouth set in a straight line. 'I have to go. Ottilie is expecting us back for tea. She is besotted with Edwin.'

She replaced the bonnet on the baby and was about to take him back into her arms, when Merritt reached for the child.

'Let me hold him again. Just for a moment.' He walked with the baby in his arms to the window which looked out onto a patch of lawn and a small orchard of fruit trees that screened this side of the house from the road. He bent his head and kissed his sleeping son again. Then he turned and handed the boy back to Hephzibah. Neither of them noticed the old woman with the black eye-patch standing among the apple trees.

Abigail Cake was angry. Her father had hit her again: bounced her off the kitchen walls and she'd caught her head on the corner of the cooking range. All because the baby wouldn't stop crying.

Ned Cake hated the baby and had done ever since he'd noticed Abigail was pregnant and punched her in the gut – doubtless hoping to remedy that fact. The punch must have been in the wrong spot because it hadn't worked. Little Rosy was a stayer. Tough, like her mother. She wasn't going to be so easily disposed of.

Ned Cake had moaned about the cost of feeding another child, as if it were Abigail's fault she had found herself in the family way. Ironic. After her being so careful all the time. She was fairly sure it wasn't the squire who was responsible for knocking her up. She hadn't taken any chances, preferring to take him in her mouth or getting him to pull out of her before it was too late. And she kept out of his way altogether at the dangerous times. She'd read an article in a medical magazine when she was cleaning Dr Desmond's surgery for a spot of extra cash. It was all about which were the most fertile times of the month and ever since, she'd scribbled her dates on a piece of paper she kept inside an old biscuit tin under her bed. No, she didn't think it was the squire who had got her into trouble. That hadn't stopped her telling him the baby was his though. He'd been angry at first and accused her of sleeping with half the village, even though it wasn't true. In the end he'd paid her three guineas and told her to keep out of his sight in future. Abigail wondered how long that would last. Dirty old bugger.

She looked in the bit of broken mirror she kept on the shelf over the range. Her right eye was puffy. She was going to have a shiner. But better that the old man take it out on her than on the baby. As it was, she had to make no end of effort to stop her father hearing the baby cry. Rosy had a hell of a pair of lungs on her so Abigail tried to be ready for when she woke during the night so she could clamp her to the breast before she cried. Often, if her father was around, she'd wrap herself and the baby up and go outside and sit in one of the pheasant sheds so he wouldn't hear the crying.

The truth was plain. Her own father was her baby's father. Ever since her mother had died he had used Abigail when he was unable to persuade one of the many destitute widows in the village to service his needs in exchange for a bit of cash for food. It happened every few months. He'd come home roaring drunk from the Egdon Arms or the Cat and Canary and climb into her bed on top of her, clamping his hand over her mouth so she couldn't cry out and wake the other children. When it was over – which was usually mercifully quickly – she'd slip out from under his sleeping body and climb into bed beside her younger sisters. The first time he'd done it she had cried for days afterwards and refused to do the cooking and cleaning. Then he'd been full of remorse.

'I dunno what came over me, Abby, love. It's just you're the living image of yer mother when I first courted her. I miss her and a man has needs as must be satisfied. It's different for women. Just remember ya old da loves yer and means well. It won't 'appen again.'

But it had happened again. Not often. But it only takes one time to make a baby. Ned Cake refused to entertain the possibility that he might be the father of his own grand-daughter – yet his extreme aversion to the baby and her crying spoke clearly that her very presence was a reminder of his part in her conception.

Abigail looked at her sleeping child in the cradle. She struggled to feel much fondness for the baby herself. She was filled with a near constant anxiety that she would develop some terrible defect as a result of her perverted origin. Rosy didn't live up to her name – she was a pale, scrawny child, prone to sickness and undersized – apart from her well-developed lungs. While Abigail failed to experience the expected maternal love, she still felt fiercely protective of the baby. It wasn't the child's fault that she was the product of incest. Although sometimes she did wonder whether it might be kinder to all concerned if she placed a pillow over the baby's head and put Rosy out of the misery that Abigail was sure lay ahead of her.

She moved across to the stove and put a kettle on to boil. This was probably the only time she'd have time for a cup of tea – before her father came home and the kids came in from the fields. She had stolen a few pinches of tea from the kitchen up at the big house. Mrs Andrews usually watched her like a hawk on the days when she was up at the

Hall to polish the silver, but yesterday the housekeeper had been distracted by the squire summoning her to his study.

A loud rap on the cottage door made her jump. She opened the door to find Mercy Loveless standing on the threshold, chewing on the stem of her clay pipe.

'Is that a kettle you've got a-boilin' there, Abby Cake? Let's take the load off our feet and 'ave a cup of something, then I'll tell thee what I found out this very day about a certain couple as is of interest to thee and the folk up there at the Hall.' She shoved past Abigail and plonked herself into a chair, putting her feet up on a low wooden stool.

Abigail stood with her back to the room, preparing the tea. She wasn't about to reveal that she had some real China tea and have Mercy drinking her meagre supply, so she made them each a cup of nettle tea.

'Afore I drink this and tell thee the tidings, I want to know what the reward is. Me old legs are getting bad and it's a long walk out here from the village.'

Abigail tutted. 'It's five or ten minutes' walk, Mercy, and you know it. And you spend half your day walking anyway. You'll walk twenty mile if you think there's something in it for you.'

'What will you pay?'

'That depends on what you're selling. If it's good enough I'll give you the brace of pigeons I promised. Otherwise, it'll be an egg.

'T'wasn't pigeons thee said, 'twas pheasants. And I think a dozen eggs too when thee hear the tale I'm goin' to tell.'

Abigail groaned and told the old woman to get on with it, adding that pheasant was out of season.

The old lady snorted then said, 'I was passing by the parsonage earlier when I sees the carriage from the Hall stopping and that Mrs Egdon, her from out the village, she gets down with that new baby of hers and goes inside the 'ouse. Now since I caught 'er and the vicar doing the dirty down in Dick Farthing's old hut I was curious and so I puts off me trip to Saddlebottom where I goes to sell me baskets, and waited to see what'd 'appen.'

'What did happen?'

Mercy Loveless raised her black piratical eye-patch and rubbed a fist over the hollow spot where her eye used to be, then repositioned the patch.

'For nigh on an hour, bugger all. Couldn't see inside the 'ouse from the road, even though I walks round the side, down that little gulley as leads to the canal, but I couldn't see far enough inside the room. I could tell they was there but that was all.'

Abigail sighed and put down her cup. 'You'll have to do better than that, Mercy Loveless, or that cup of tea is all you'll be getting from me.'

'I'm coming to it. 'Old yer 'orses. Just as I was about to give up and go, the parson hisself comes up and stands in the window and 'e's 'oldin 'er babby. 'Er from the Hall. 'Er what used to be governess and married the squire's lad. Then 'e kisses the babby – the parson does. All over its little face.'

Abigail gasped. 'I knew it.'

'It weren't a normal thing for a parson to do with some-one else's babby. Parsons pour water over a babby's 'ead, but they don't go round kissin' 'em. Sure as those eggs thou's going to give us is eggs, Parson Nightingale is the daddy of that Egdon woman's child.'

Abigail went outside to one of the sheds and returned a few moments later, carrying two woodpigeons which she placed on the table in front of Mercy Loveless. Without a word she moved over to a shelf under the window and counted out a half dozen eggs from the basket there and put them in a cloth bag. 'Here's half a dozen. It's as much as we can spare and more than you need.'

The half-blind woman peered inside the bag. 'I 'opes

they's not cracked.' She slipped the bag inside her wicker basket. 'So what's thee going' to do on it? Goin' to tell squire?'

'Now that I've paid you for the information it's my property and if I hear you've told anyone else about it I'll take out your other eye. Understand?' She yanked the old woman's head back by the hair. 'Understand?'

The woman squealed and then said, 'Lemme go, Ab, I'll not breathe a word. I swear.'

Abigail released her grip then returned to the pan she was watching on the stove. 'You'll do well to forget all about it, Mercy. And don't be waiting and watching for what I'll do. I'm a patient woman. I'll be waiting for my moment – no matter how long it takes.' She reached over and took the teacup from Loveless. 'Now get on your way, old woman. And remember not a word if you value that eye.'

The woman scrambled to her feet and scuttled out of the door. Abigail took a cloth and wiped down the seat of the chair she had been sitting upon. 'Filthy old witch,' she said, under her breath.

CHAPTER TWENTY-FOUR

The means were worthy, and the end is won—
I would not do by thee as thou hast done!

(from Lines, on Hearing that Lady Byron was Ill,
Lord Byron)

March 1908

Edwin was two and a half and running around. The older he
got, the more he resembled Merritt Nightingale. Hephzibah
took care to cover his head with a bonnet most of the time,
but as he grew she knew it would become an increasing
problem. The little boy's hair was fair, much lighter than
her own, almost blonde, but with a slight reddish tinge to it.
She was certain she could detect the beginnings of freckles
on his nose and was careful to keep him out of the sun.

Thomas was seemingly oblivious to his son's lack of
resemblance to himself. He was relieved that his adolescent
mumps had not destroyed his manhood and confident that
the birth of the boy had removed any possible objections
by his father to him and, eventually, Edwin, inheriting the
estate. Yet the new addition to the household did nothing

to reduce the hostility between the squire and his son. Sir Richard appeared increasingly irritated and isolated.

One afternoon the squire came upon Hephzibah reading in the library. Edwin was taking his afternoon nap and Ottilie was riding. Sir Richard pulled an upright chair across the room and placed it in front of Hephzibah, and sat down.

'Thomas is not getting another penny from me,' he said without preamble. 'I'm going to alter the terms of my will in favour of Edwin. I'll create a trust so that if I die before the boy reaches majority – and you won't get good odds against that happening – I'll make you the trustee. I expect you to ensure that your wretch of a husband doesn't get his hands on the cash or try to raise a mortgage against the estate.'

'You can't expect me to do that. I have no influence over Thomas.'

'I do expect you to do it. For the sake of Edwin. I can tell that since the baby was born you've started to see through the charms of my son. I've seen how you look at him and it isn't the way you looked at him when you were first married. All marriages are like that – the passion never lasts. But you're different. It's more than the fact that you're no longer in the first flush of passion. You sometimes look at him as if you can't stand the sight of him.'

Hephzibah sat upright. 'I don't know what you're talking about.'

'The scales have come off your eyes. You know now that he's a good for nothing wastrel that cares for nobody but himself. You'd be well shot of him. And it hasn't escaped my notice that if he was barely here before, now he hardly ever darkens the door.'

Hephzibah felt the blood drain away from her face. She didn't want to have this conversation.

The squire went on. 'You have to think of the boy now.'

She shut her book and slammed it on the table. 'I don't want to talk about this. You can't expect me to act as policeman or banker to my own husband.'

He studied her for a moment, then leaned back in his chair, adjusting his bad leg with his hands. 'Perhaps you're right. So here's what I'll do. I will pay a small allowance directly to you and the boy. Thomas can have a lump sum of five hundred guineas to settle his debts, then I want no more to do with him. I won't be bled dry any more. He will no longer be welcome in this house. You and the boy will remain. I will make Nightingale the trustee of the boy's trust fund. He seems fond of Edwin and is a decent fellow. He'll look after the child's best interests.'

Hephzibah felt her face redden. 'That doesn't seem right. Thomas will never agree.'

'It's not up to him to agree.'

'But this is his home.'

'Then he should not have treated it with contempt and absented himself so much.'

'I don't think you should do this, Sir Richard. Thomas will be angry. I dread to think what he will do.'

'He can't do anything.'

'But Ingleton Hall is his birthright.'

'Then tell him to sue me. But as soon as any judge sees that he's worked his way through over twenty thousand pounds in just a few years, has no interest whatsoever in this estate or its affairs, and rarely so much as crosses the threshold, he'll laugh him out of court.'

'He's your son. Talk to him. Make him see reason.' She paused. 'I'll talk to him. I'll try and persuade him to spend more time here. Maybe he can help you and Mr Cake in the management of the estate. Perhaps if you gave him some specific responsibility?'

The squire lit a cigar and drew on it, watching the smoke spiral up in front of him. 'I tried that before. I offered him

Middledown Farm. He was never there. He waited too long to get the spring barley in and the crop was ruined. He almost lost me the barn when he left a lamp burning in the stable block. If it hadn't been for Cake seeing the smoke and acting quickly we'd have lost a season's hay, two plough horses and a three-hundred-year-old barn. All he cares about are his damned racehorses. He's never stopped asking me to turn this place into a stud farm and a training centre for racehorses.'

'Is that so terrible?'

'He knows as well as I do that the ground isn't right to create practice gallops. Too waterlogged, too uneven. And as for breeding – it takes knowledge and experience and more money than sense. I don't have to remind you about Bess – she lasted all of six months before pegging it. Ingleton has always been arable land with sheep and a few head of cattle. I'm not turning centuries of tradition on its head for the sake of his half-baked fancies.' He puffed on his cigar, creating rings from the smoke as he exhaled.

'Do you have any idea what a mess he's made of his ventures with racehorses? Have you ever asked him?'

Hephzibah blushed again. 'He took me just once to see the horses and became impatient when I asked questions. I have avoided enquiring since.'

'He's never had a winner in his life. Not even a placing. He thinks he knows horseflesh, but he knows less than I do and I'd describe myself as ignorant. He pays too much for animals that can't run – cracked hooves, long backs, constantly lame, overly jumpy – he's had them all. When he does find a nag that has promise, he's impatient and over-stretches it, runs it before it's ready. But he won't be told. He never learns from his mistakes. He's badly advised. His trainer is bleeding him dry and he's bleeding me dry.'

This was news to Hephzibah and she felt slightly ashamed that she had let herself become so ignorant about the business of the man who was still, after all, her husband. 'I didn't know,' she said. 'We never talk about the horses. I suppose he assumed it was a part of his life that I wouldn't be interested in.'

The squire snorted. 'Are you interested in any part of his life? Does he even have anything else in his life?' He ground his cigar into an onyx ashtray and pulled himself upright, using the arms of his chair. 'I'll talk to Nightingale about the trust. We'll all be better off without Thomas turning up here whenever he feels like it. I'm sick of him using this place like his club.'

'But you can't bar him from his own home. What about Edwin? He needs to see his father.'

The squire hobbled towards the door, where he paused, his hand resting on the handle. 'The lad will do better without his influence. I'll be as good as a father to him. It will be enough.'

The regular walks Hephzibah took with Edwin in his perambulator had at first raised a few eyebrows in Nettle-stock. The villagers were not used to the lady of the manor trundling around the lanes this way, rather than employing the services of a nursemaid. She curtailed possible criticism by turning a beaming smile upon anyone she met along the way, and after a while the villagers took her eccentric behaviour for granted.

She varied the route, each time agreeing in advance with Merritt where they would cross paths. It was not difficult to find quiet spots on the myriad country lanes around Nettlestock. Sometimes she took the pony and trap and she and the baby went into Mudford or further afield to other towns and villages in the area where she was not known. On those days, Merritt would use his bicycle and cycle over to meet them at the appointed time and place. During these arranged meetings Hephzibah insisted on there being no physical contact between her and Merritt. Being so close to him yet unable to touch him, to kiss him or show any sign of affection was heart-breaking, but she told herself the meetings were for Edwin and Merritt. Mostly she left them alone together but from time to time, Merritt insisted on her staying with them, telling her that being with her and the child was the nearest he got to feeling part of a family and Hephzibah felt unable to deny him.

Today they were sitting on a bench on the towpath on the far side of Mudford. It was a mile or so out of the town and there was no one about, despite the unseasonable March sunshine. Merritt's bicycle was leaning against a nearby tree and they had a good view of the canal in both directions so that he could make a quick escape in the unlikely event that anyone they knew should approach. A pair of swans glided past and a few moorhens were swimming close to the far side of the canal. Red campion flowers grew around the hedge behind them and the air was fragrant with the scent of bluebells. Edwin was lying asleep on his stomach on a stretch of grass beside them, safely away from the canalside, exhausted after a long walk through the woods with the parson.

Merritt reached for her hand. 'I don't think I can take any more of this, Hephzibah. All the furtiveness and snatched moments. It's killing me.'

'You're right,' she said. 'As Edwin gets older, meeting like this will be impossible. We can't risk him mentioning it to Thomas. I'm worried sick that his colouring is so like yours and it can only be a matter of time before Thomas and Sir Richard notice and put two and two together. I even thought of dyeing his hair darker, but when I asked at the dispensary in Newbury the chemist told me that I'd have to do it every week or the roots would show and putting chemicals on a little boy's head would harm him.'

'Enough, Hephzibah, this is insane! We should have known it would be impossible to keep it a secret. We have to tell the truth.'

Hephzibah chose not to hear. 'Obviously we need a way for you to continue to see Edwin regularly but you and I must stop meeting.'

Merritt looked anguished, and she stroked his hand. 'I have found a way for you to have free access to him.'

She explained how Sir Richard planned to cut Thomas completely out of his will in favour of Edwin and how he wanted Merritt to act as trustee. 'It gives you an excuse to spend more time with Edwin, then when he's old enough to start lessons, I'm going to propose that you become his tutor – so you can see him almost every day. He can come to the parsonage for lessons. What do you think?'

'Does Thomas know about this? That he's to be disinherited?' Merritt was frowning.

She shook her head. 'The squire wants me to tell him. But I can't face it. I dread to think how he will react.'

'Making me trustee and entrusting Edwin's education to me is likely to rile him further.'

Hephzibah looked down and twiddled her fingers. 'I know. But there's more. Sir Richard intends to ban him from Ingleton Hall altogether.'

Merritt twisted round to face her. 'Does he plan to exile you too?'

'No.'

'How can he do that? It's tantamount to saying you have no marriage.'

'We don't. It's in name only. Thomas is rarely here and, since Edwin was born, he no longer sleeps in my bed.'

Merritt gave a little gasp and took her hand in his. 'Why didn't you tell me this before, my darling? You've no idea how much pain you could have saved me.'

She looked away, ashamed. 'I'm sorry, but I knew if I did

tell you, you'd start to hope we could be together.'

'Of course I would. And wouldn't you?'

She looked at him, her eyes filling with tears, unable to find words to respond.

He squeezed her hand. 'He must let you go.'

'Why would he do that? He would have to accuse me of adultery and risk public humiliation. Thomas would never stand for that. He's too proud. And he would have custody of Edwin. I can't abandon our child.'

'You could ask him for a divorce.'

She tilted her head on one side and gave him a mirthless smile. 'Merritt, you of all people know better than to suggest that. It's thanks to the Church of England that a woman is chained to her husband, no matter how badly he behaves.' This conversation was proving harder than she had hoped. Why was Merritt being so unrealistic, so impractical, so stubborn?

She stood up and began to pace up and down in front of the bench, trying to control her rising frustration. 'Unless I can prove that Thomas has not only committed adultery but has been physically violent towards me there is no hope of my winning a divorce. Do you have any idea of the cost and the time involved? And even if I were to succeed, Edwin would be taken from me.' She sat down on the bench beside him again.

'But Thomas has effectively deserted you!' Merritt put his hands on her shoulders and turned her so he could look into her eyes.

She shook off his hands, avoiding his gaze. 'That's not grounds for divorce and anyway he is there occasionally. Once he finds out what the squire is planning, he will likely be there all the time. The squire can't evict him from his own home while allowing his wife and son to remain. Think of the scandal that would create.'

Edwin stirred in his sleep and rolled over. Hephzibah

took a shawl from a basket on the bench and draped it over the sleeping child. They were quarrelling. Why were they quarrelling? It was the last thing she'd wanted. She felt the tears rising and bent over Edwin, her back to Merritt while she brushed them away.

Merritt watched her tend to their child, then, as she returned to the bench, he said, 'Edwin isn't Thomas's son. Look, Hephzibah, we've done enough of this dissembling. It's wrong, plain wrong. We must face the facts. We love each other. We have a child together. Your husband is absent. If you can't escape from him legally then we will run away together.'

So much of what he was saying made sense to her. She squeezed her hands until her fingers hurt. Taking a deep breath she placed her hands around his. 'Please, Merritt, try to understand.' She told him the squire would never consent to Edwin leaving. 'The one thing that matters more than anything to Sir Richard is protecting the future of Ingleton. Edwin is his heir. He will never let me take him away.'

The exasperation in Merritt's voice was evident. 'Why are you being so stubborn? Edwin isn't even his grandson. We must tell Sir Richard and the world that he is *my* son.'

Hephzibah shook her head rapidly. 'No. That would make Edwin a bastard. How can I do that to him? My priority now is my son. Ingleton Hall is his future.'

Merritt took her hands in his again and knelt down on the grass in front of her. 'He's *our* son. *We* are his future. He doesn't need to inherit a country estate. He needs to be loved by his own parents, given a chance to flourish, to be educated, to find his own path, not be saddled with the responsibility of managing an unprofitable estate and a country mansion that's seen better days.'

Hephzibah put her head in her hands. 'I don't know what to do. I'm full of fear. I wish to God I'd never done what I did. I've dragged you into this mess, Merritt. I have ruined both our lives. I've made things worse for Thomas as well. At least before Edwin was born he tried to rein himself in a bit in order to keep in with his father. Now it's as if he doesn't care. And it will kill the squire.'

Merritt jumped up, his face now angry. 'Why do you even care what it will it do to the squire? He's the man who chased you round the house with his hands up your skirts. He's a complete blackguard. If it hadn't been for him you'd have never gone running into the arms of his useless son.' He banged his fist on the back of the bench.

Hephzibah started to cry. 'Don't say that about Thomas. He did what he thought was the right thing at the time. He cared for me. He wanted to help me.'

'No he didn't.' Merritt's mouth set in a hard line.

'What do you mean?' Hephzibah looked at him, afraid of what he was about to say.

Merritt walked away from her, towards the canal bank, speaking with his back to her. 'Thomas Egdon married you so he could access the funds in his mother's estate. His inheritance was held in trust until his marriage. He was no longer able to survive on the income and wanted to get his hands on the capital.'

Hephzibah was silent, numb with shock, remembering the words of Abigail Cake in the Egdon Arms the afternoon the lending library opened. Eventually she said, 'How do you know this? What makes you say such a terrible thing?'

He turned to face her. 'I saw the deed of trust. Just after you were married, the squire showed it to me.' Merritt told her about what he had seen in the document and its implications.

Hephzibah stared at him, numb with shock. Abigail Cake had told the truth. 'So Thomas didn't care a fig for me. I was just the means to him getting his hands on more cash?'

Merritt was silent, staring out over the canal.

'I was duped,' she said eventually. 'I believed Thomas loved me and I thought I loved him. The fact that I didn't know I would love you more is immaterial. I married him in the belief that he and I loved each other.'

'Why do you care? It doesn't matter now. Not now that we love each other.'

'I have been cheated, lied to, used, abused. It's a matter of trust.' Her voice was quiet. 'I trusted Thomas. I would have done anything to keep his love, to make him happy. When I sought your help, I had no idea that I would fall in love with you. I saw it at the time as a way to keep my husband and save my marriage. If I had known that he only married me for money I would never have done what I did.'

'Then thank God you didn't know.'

'You should have told me.'

'What?'

'You knew the reason he married me and yet when I told you I wanted you to sleep with me as a means of saving my marriage, you let me do it, without telling me.'

He looked at her, aghast.

'If I had known that Thomas only married me to secure his inheritance I would have walked away from him then and there. I don't know where I would have gone but I wouldn't have asked you to make love with me. You knew that. You knew that if you'd told me I wouldn't have done it. I trusted you, Merritt…' Her eyes brimmed with tears. '*You* have betrayed me too. I thought you were my friend. You took advantage of me.'

Edwin woke up and began to cry. Hephzibah rose from the bench and went to pick him up. Calming the child's wailing she set him down and, holding his hand, walked over to Merritt and said, 'I am weary of lies. Even my own mother lied to me, letting me believe that my father was a good man when all the while he was a cruel and cold one.

She lied. My stepfather lied. Sir Richard lied. Thomas lied and now I find out that you have kept this from me. I am the fool. I must be so easy to gull.'

Merritt started to protest, but she turned away and said, 'Don't try to see me alone again, Merritt. You have disappointed me beyond measure. I don't think I will ever be able to believe anyone in this world again.'

Hand-in-hand with her infant son she headed back along the towpath to where the pony and trap were waiting in the shade of a tree. It was only when they were out of sight of Merritt, and the little boy had been lulled to sleep by the motion of the trap, that she allowed her tears to flow. Her life was ruined. Worse, she had ruined so many others'. Most of all, she had hurt and been hurt by Merritt Nightingale. She cursed her stupidity, her susceptibility to the charms of Thomas Egdon, but most of all she wept for Merritt: for the chance of love and happiness she had thrown away and for the disappointment that he too, the love of her life, had lied to her.

CHAPTER TWENTY-FIVE

So you must wake and call me early, call me early, mother dear;
To-morrow 'll be the happiest time of all the glad new-year;
To-morrow 'll be of all the year the maddest, merriest day,
For I'm to be Queen o' the May, mother,
I'm to be Queen o' the May

(from The May Queen, Alfred, Lord Tennyson)

The annual May Day fair was a long-standing tradition in Nettlestock. Most of the village would be present for the festivities on the village green. Maypole dancing by the children was the prime attraction, culminating in the crowning of the Queen of the May. The celebrations were more modest than they used to be – the decline in the fortunes of the village and the departure of so many villagers to the cities had taken its toll on many of the old traditions of rural life. Nonetheless there was always a good turnout and if the morris dancing and mummer plays were long gone, the maypole, the May Queen's parade, the children's races and the village picnic were all still big draws.

Abigail Cake had been chosen as queen when she was fifteen and it was often said around the village that there had never been a prettier one. It had been after the ceremonies ended that year that she had lost her virginity to Thomas Egdon, in the stable loft at Ingleton Hall. Her floral crown had been completely crushed and Thomas, in his urgency to get her clothes off, had managed to tear two of the buttons off her dress and afterwards, despite a hunt through the straw, they had been unable to find them. When she eventually arrived home, late, bedraggled but happy, Abigail's mother had been angry and her father had taken his belt to her. Abigail had thought it was worth it.

Now was the time to put her long-prepared plan into action. The moment had come and her patience would at last be rewarded. Abigail had always believed the old axiom that revenge was a dish best served cold. There was something pleasing about choosing the May Day celebrations with the happy memories of the days when Tom Egdon had had eyes only for her – before Hephzibah Wildman had come along and stolen him from her. Now it wouldn't be long until she had him back again.

When Abigail arrived at the green there was already a crowd of people. The air was thick with the smell of burnt sugar and roasting pork and full of the cries of children running sack races organised by Miss Pickering, the schoolmistress, assisted by the parson. As usual the squire had provided the pig for the roast and the landlord of the Cat and Canary had laid on a supply of cider. Abigail walked around, nodding to people as she went, stopping occasionally to talk to some, but her eyes always alert to spot her target. It was good to be out and about again on her own, without Rosy to worry about and keep out of her father's way. She wouldn't ever have to worry about Rosy any more.

Hephzibah Egdon was sitting on a deckchair under the shade of an elm tree, her small son upon her knee and Ottilie beside her. They were watching the progress of the sack races and the little boy was wriggling with excitement, eager to participate himself. The squire was perched on his horse, slowly walking the boundary of the green, as though desirous of keeping his distance from the village hoi polloi. Thomas Egdon was sprawled on a rug on the grass next to his wife and child. Abigail studied the family group from a distance. Thomas looked bored. Not surprising. That jumped-up governess looked so smug and self-satisfied. Not for much longer.

Abigail waited until the sack race was finished, then took a deep breath and marched towards the family group. She held out her hand to Edwin and said, 'Come on, little 'un. There's a running race about to start now. Come and have a go.'

As she expected, Hephzibah Egdon held on tightly to her son and shook her head, but the little boy was determined not to be prevented from joining in the fun.

'Please, Mamma, let me go. Want to play.' He struggled to free himself from her grip.

'No, my darling, you're still a little young for that. Maybe next year.'

Abigail stood in front of her, 'This race is just for the little ones. The under-fives. The lad'll be fine.' She looked at her with defiance, then turned towards Thomas Egdon. 'Ain't that true, Tommy?'

Hephzibah still clung on to the wriggling boy.

Tom Egdon looked up and said, 'Let the boy run, Hephzibah. It'll do him good. You're too protective. He needs to toughen up a bit. It's only fifty yards.'

With a triumphant smile, Abigail took the child by the hand and led him over to the starting line where Miss Pickering was struggling to organise a group of toddlers into some semblance of order. As Abigail handed the child over to the teacher she brushed her arm against his head and knocked off his hat, revealing his shock of gingery blonde hair. She bent over, picked the hat up off the grass and said, 'I'll keep this for you until the race is over – it'll only blow off while you're running.' She strode away, hat in hand towards the finishing line which was being manned by the parson.

Merritt Nightingale blew a whistle and the line-up of small children began to race up the green. Two of them started late and, realising they were left behind, began to cry. One boy tripped up and managed to bring down several others in a heap in the middle of the course. Edwin, a little girl and another boy were running neck and neck towards the finishing line. In the excited throng of cheering parents no one noticed that it was Abigail Cake sticking a foot out that sent Edwin flying just before the finishing line. He landed face down and was silent for a moment, then began to howl as the realisation hit him that not only was he not going to win the race but he'd grazed his knee. Merritt Nightingale swooped down and scooped the boy up in his arms and brushed the grass from his knees, holding the little boy tenderly against his shoulder and patting him on the back. Edwin clasped his hands around the parson's neck and nuzzled against him.

A small crowd had gathered around them and instead of congratulating the girl who had won the race, they all stared in surprise at the parson and the little boy. The two were clutching each other tightly and their likeness was remarkable and unmistakable. It was the first time, the christening apart, that anyone in the village had seen the parson and Edwin in close proximity to each other. The child's hair was the same tone as Merritt's, but lighter and he had the same skin tone and a light dusting of freckles.

Abigail moved forward and put the hat on the boy's head, her mission complete.

Before Merritt could set his son down on the ground Thomas Egdon pushed his way through the fascinated crowd and grabbed the child from the arms of the clergyman.

Egdon dragged the now-wailing child by the hand behind him and marched up to Hephzibah. 'You. Home. Now.'

He jumped on his own horse which was grazing nearby and Hephzibah went with Edwin and Ottilie to the horse and trap. She looked around but could see no sign of the squire.

Thomas was waiting on the stone steps at the entrance of the Hall when Hephzibah, Ottilie and Edwin arrived back. Egdon told Ottilie to take her nephew upstairs to the nursery and stay there. He walked into the drawing room and Hephzibah followed him, her heart thumping against her ribs.

As soon as she had shut the door behind her he struck her across the face. The blow was of such force that she fell sideways and landed on her knees. He grabbed her arm roughly and pulled her to her feet then pushed her into an armchair.

Her face was burning and she felt tears of shock and pain smarting in her eyes. She wanted to be sick. Where was the squire? Where was Mrs Andrews? But she knew the whole household would still be at the fair.

Thomas turned his back on her and went to the fireplace. He leaned his head against the marble mantel for what felt to Hephzibah like an eternity, then he swept the collection of ornaments off the top and turned back to face her.

'You have humiliated me in front of the entire village. How long has that spineless vicar been screwing you? Did you think I would never notice the boy wasn't my son?' His words reignited his temper and he moved towards her, pulled her up from the seat and hit her again around the head.

Hephzibah screamed in pain and fell back into the chair.

She put her hand to her head and felt the wetness of blood on her forehead where his signet ring had caught her. The room was spinning. She couldn't think. Thomas leaned over her, his face in her face, his breath hot. The pain came again. A blow to her face. Then nothing.

She must have passed out for a moment. Then he was tearing at her clothes in a frenzy. The blows to her head had made her dizzy and disorientated. Sound of cloth ripping. Head throbbing. Face on fire. Blood in her eyes. Blinded.

'Stop, please stop, Thomas!' Her own words echoed from far away. Everything muddled. Large woven roses in the carpet bloomed, went fuzzy and faded away. Room spinning. Eyes won't focus. Nausea constricting her throat. Hard to breathe.

She was on her back on the sofa when he punched her again, then a searing pain as he forced his way inside her, tearing her, brutalising her. The last thing she was aware of was the gold paint on the cornicing around the ceiling before she passed out.

When Hephzibah came to, she was covered with a blanket and the squire was standing over her with a glass of brandy in his hand.

'Drink this. You fainted.'

She drank the brandy in one slug, feeling the heat of the alcohol kick-starting her senses. She looked around. 'Where is he? Where's Thomas?' Her voice was tremulous.

'I neither know nor care. As far away as possible. If there's one thing I won't tolerate it's violence to women. He'll never set foot in this house again. Now, suppose you tell me what's been going on.'

Hephzibah stared at him, uncomprehending. Who was the squire to defend the rights of women? He had shown scant regard for them until now. Sir Richard sat in silence watching her as she sipped a second brandy.

Her skin warmed with the alcohol and she felt

light-headed. All she wanted to do was sleep, but the squire was intent on finding answers.

'Now tell me what happened,' he said. 'It's clear from the pantomime on the village green that my son is a cuckold and our good vicar has been behaving in a less than godly manner. I must admit, I never thought the fellow had it in him. I never thought you had it in you, either, Hephzibah. I wouldn't have put you down as the unfaithful wife, although, God knows, that wastrel gave you cause enough.'

Hephzibah looked at him without really seeing him.

Sir Richard leaned over her and fixed her with his dark eyes. 'The sooner you tell me what's been going on, the sooner you can go to bed and get some sleep. You look done in.'

The prospect of lying in her bed, letting the brandy lull her to a deep sleep where she could dream none of this had happened, was irresistible. She told him everything – how she had persuaded Merritt Nightingale to have sex with her in order to get pregnant. She stressed that she had taken advantage of a promise once made to her by the parson to help her if she was ever in trouble.

'But why did you want to have another man's child?'

She told him her motivation had been her love for Thomas and a desire to save her marriage and Thomas's inheritance. She didn't tell him that she and Merritt had fallen in love. She'd done enough harm to everyone without adding that.

'I should never have done it,' she said, her voice weak and little more than a whisper. 'I know that now. I've made everything bad for everyone. And it didn't work. Once Edwin was born Thomas grew cold towards me. You saw it yourself.'

The squire studied her for a moment with his coal-dark eyes. 'He realised the child wasn't his?'

'He never said anything about that. Just that he was

happy. He said he was proud that at last we had a son.'

'He may not have realised it consciously. But a man knows.' Sir Richard looked away for a moment as if weighing something up. 'When Thomas was born I knew at once there was something about him that was different. As soon as I held him in my arms. I didn't feel the same way about him as I did about Sam and later about Roddy. I said nothing to my wife, wouldn't even acknowledge it to myself, but as the boys grew up I became more convinced that Thomas wasn't my own son.'

Hephzibah sat upright and swung her legs onto the floor, pulling the blanket around her. 'Who was his father?'

The squire shrugged. 'I don't know. I had my suspicions but no evidence. I watched her like a hawk after that and she never gave the slightest indication that there was anyone else. I think it must have been a brief affair. He was from outside the area. He's no longer around.'

'You never confronted your wife?'

He dropped his head. 'I was too afraid. I thought if I did, she might leave me and go to him. I loved her. I really loved her. Hard as that might be for you to believe. I know you think only ill of me. A year or so later Roddy was born. His arrival made me even more certain about Thomas. I knew Roddy was my son as soon as I saw him. And it was clear Jane loved Tom more than the other two. He was like her shadow. I tried to conceal how I felt about him but I couldn't. In truth, Hephzibah, I loathed the boy. There's a kind of poetic justice that what happened to me has happened to him.'

He stopped and lit a cigarette, inhaling it deeply. 'I blamed myself. I tried to make sure Jane would never regret staying with me.' His eyes misted over for a moment then the hardness in them returned. 'Sometimes I think Thomas dislikes women. The only one he had any time for was his mother. I on the other hand adore them. Yes, I may try to take advantage of them, but I would never harm any woman.'

'Harm is about more than physical blows. It can also be caused by forcing yourself on someone.'

He looked away. After a moment he stood up and went to stand in front of the window, looking out over the garden. Eventually he returned and sat down opposite her again.

Hephzibah looked at him and said, 'What about that woman, the bailiff's daughter? She told me Thomas loved her. I saw them kissing once. Before we were married.'

The squire snorted. 'Thomas loves only Thomas – and his horses. Yes, he and the Cake girl were inseparable as children and I know they had relations – but he had his way with half the girls in the village whenever he got the chance. She was no different from any other, no matter what she might like to think herself.'

He got up and began to pace the room. 'You and the boy may stay here. I've grown fond of you both. As far as I'm concerned, Edwin will be raised as my grandson. You will both always have a home at Ingleton Hall.'

Before Hephzibah could answer there was a knock at the door and Mrs Andrews entered. 'Sir Richard, there's trouble in the village. I think you'd better go. They've turned on the parson. It's that Jacob Leatherwood from the Wesleyan chapel. He accused Mr Nightingale of carnal acts and called him a hypocrite and a fight broke out. They pelted the poor man with vegetables and there's a gang of them going to march on the parsonage. They're carrying pitchforks and clubs. I thought I'd better come and get you – I'm afraid what might happen.'

The squire got to his feet. He told Mrs Andrews to run a bath for Hephzibah and treat her cuts and bruises, then left the room. Hephzibah had kept her head turned away from the housekeeper until the squire left, then she turned around and faced the woman.

Mrs Andrews put her hand to her mouth. 'Oh, madam, what have they done to you? Who did this? Did someone attack you on the way home? And where's the wee lad?'

'Edwin is safe upstairs in the nursery with Ottilie. What of Mr Nightingale? Have they harmed him?' She tried to disguise the fear in her voice.

The housekeeper shook her head. 'I don't know, madam. If the parson has any sense he'll have got out of the village. I always knew that Leatherwood was no true man of God. He's a mischief maker and a rabble-rouser.'

She told Hephzibah to stay where she was while she went to the kitchen for water and dressings. When she returned she washed the blood off Hephzibah's face and treated the bruising with witch hazel.

'You need to tell the squire who did this to you. Being a magistrate he will see to it that they're punished for it.'

'It was my husband.'

Mrs Andrews drew in her breath, then shook her head. 'Does Sir Richard know?'

Hephzibah nodded. 'He threw him out of the house. I don't know where he's gone, but I don't ever want to see him again. And Mrs Andrews, I can't stay here. The squire has asked me to stay but I can't. Not any more. Not after this.'

CHAPTER TWENTY-SIX

When I am dead, my dearest,
Sing no sad songs for me;
Plant thou no roses at my head,
Nor shady cypress tree;

(from Song, Christina Rossetti)

Abigail Cake was running. She had searched the grounds of Ingleton Hall and could see no sign of Thomas Egdon. She was starting to think she had made a terrible mistake. Thomas had taken Hephzibah by the hand and dragged her and the child away with him, heading back in the direction of the Hall. She hadn't banked on that. Her plan had been for Hephzibah to have to slink away in shame with that carrot-headed parson and their bastard child.

She ran to the back door of the Hall where Eliza, one of the scullery maids, told her that Master Thomas had been yelling at Mrs Egdon in the drawing room then, when the squire came home, he had saddled up his horse and ridden away. The girl had overheard the squire shouting and saying Mr Egdon could never come back to Ingleton again.

'Where's *she* gone?' Abigail asked.

'Up in her room. Mrs Andrews has been cleaning her

up. Looks like Master Thomas gave her the thrashing she deserved. She were all bloody and she'd been crying. None of us was 'ere when it 'appened.'

'In which direction did Mr Egdon ride?'

'He was headed the back way down towards the canal and the railway.'

Abigail turned on her heels and ran across the lawns. She jumped off the ha-ha and half ran, half stumbled, her way through the familiar paths around the woods towards the village.

She headed along the main street, which was deserted, as everyone was still at the green for the May Day festivities. She ran past the Egdon Arms, past the smithy, the Cat and Canary and the schoolhouse and round the corner towards the church and the parsonage. She heard the noise before she saw the crowds. There must have been almost fifty people standing in the street outside the parsonage, shouting and banging sticks on tin cans. There was no sign of the Reverend Nightingale.

The Nonconformist preacher, Jacob Leatherwood, was standing on top of the flint wall which separated the parson's garden from the street and the churchyard.

'I tell you this man is not fit to wipe the shoes of the people of Nettlestock. He is a creature of the devil and not a man of God. I say to you he is a hypocrite, a Pharisee. Heed the words of Matthew, Chapter 23 verse 27 *"Woe unto you, scribes and Pharisees, hypocrites! for ye are like unto whited sepulchres, which indeed appear beautiful outward, but are within full of dead men's bones, and of all uncleanness".*' As he said the words the crowd roared their approval.

Abigail paused for a moment, curious as to what would happen next. She had never felt any particular animosity towards the parson, but she didn't feel he warranted her sympathy either.

A man, whom she recognised as Leatherwood's brother,

shouted to the assembled mass. 'Let's teach him a lesson. We don't need 'is sort in Nettlestock. Outsiders with city habits and low morals. Let's drag 'im out here and tell 'im what we thinks of him. The crowd bayed their assent, surged forward and pushed open the gate.

Abigail elbowed her way past the few people who remained in the street and ran on down the hill towards the canal and the railway. Her heart was pounding in her chest and she was almost out of breath when she saw Thomas Egdon ahead of her, tying his horse up under a tree, close to where the railway line crossed the road. She ran down the hill, calling out his name.

Egdon turned his head when he heard Abigail's voice. He moved towards her and they met at the roadside, a short way from the station platform.

'You knew,' he said. 'You engineered everything. You planned this afternoon, didn't you?'

'I wanted you to know what they'd done to you. How they tricked you. Going behind your back. I didn't want them laughing at your expense.'

'You chose to do it in front of the whole village. You showed everyone that the boy wasn't my son. You humiliated me.'

'I tried to warn you before that she was no good, but you wouldn't listen to me. I told you she was wrong for you. I pleaded with you to leave her. I'm the one you love, Tommy. I'm the only one you've ever loved and I love you too. That woman had no right to come between us. She should have married the parson but oh no, she had to steal you away from me. And then she went and slept with him behind your back. But now you know everything you can leave her, divorce her for adultery and marry me.'

'Marry you? Are you mad, Ab? I'll never marry you.'

Her voice turned into a wail. 'But you love me. You've always loved me. You said we'd be married. You made a promise.'

'We were fifteen. We were children.'

'But you and I are meant to be together. You always said that. You said there was no one else like me. All those times we made love in the hayloft and down behind the silk mill. It was good. You wanted me all the time. You had me all the time. You just had to flick your fingers and I was there for you. You couldn't keep your hands off me. She never loved you at all. She only married you because you were the squire's son. I'd have loved you even if you were just the butcher's boy.'

She raised a hand to stroke his cheek but he pushed it away.

'Come on, Tommy, don't be like that. You know you love me. We can be together properly now. You can't stay with her. Not after what she's done to you.' She flung her arms around him and buried her head in his chest.

'No I can't stay with her now. Not after what you've done. Not after what you made me do to her.' He looked down at her, his eyes narrow slits of anger. He removed her arms from behind his back and pushed her away.

'Don't be like that, Tom. Don't let that woman get to you. You only married her so you could get your inheritance. You've always wanted to be with me. I've been patient. I've waited for you. I love you. You love me too. Now's our time.'

He grabbed her arm and jerked her towards him. 'I don't love you. I never have. We had some good times, but that's all it ever was. You were always good in the sack, Abigail, I'll give you that. But that's all. It was only sex.'

She looked at him, her eyes wide open in horror.

Egdon twisted her arm and practically spat his words at her. 'I broke you in, like a colt, when we were fifteen and I've always loved to ride you, to thrust myself into you, to make you scream, like the little slut you are. And don't think I didn't know that you did it with Roddy the night before he went to war. And with my father. You're just a good-time girl. An empty vessel to give men pleasure.'

He walked away along the platform to the far end. She ran after him, clinging to him like a limpet to a rock.

'You don't mean it, Tommy. You're only saying it because you're angry about what's happened. But once she and her bastard child are gone we can be together. We can get wed.'

He turned back. 'Do you honestly think I'd ever marry you? A village girl. A trollop who sleeps with any man who looks at her, even it's been said, her own father.'

Tears were flowing down her cheeks now and she wiped the snot from her nose and grabbed hold of him again. Thomas stood rigid as a rock. 'I married Hephzibah Wildman because I wanted her. Wanted her like I'd never felt before. I ached for her, lusted for her, couldn't wait to have her in my bed. She is a lady. Something you will never be. I suspected that child wasn't my own, but I said nothing, did nothing, because it suited me, because I didn't want to face the fact that my own wife had been with another man. Now I have faced it and I know she's as much of a whore as you are. You made me face that, Abigail, you made me see what I'd chosen not to see. But you made the whole damned village see it too and I will never forgive you for that as long as I live.'

The approaching train whistled in the distance. 'I'm going to London,' he said. 'I'm going to stay there and I won't be coming back to Nettlestock. My father has barred me from my own home. This is your doing and I never want to see you again.'

A number of people had arrived on the platform and were standing some yards away from the pair, keeping their distance while watching the unfolding spectacle. Abigail was hanging onto Thomas but he was unmoved, a statue of indifference.

The train slowed down as it approached the station. The waiting people began to spread themselves out along the platform.

It happened so fast that no one afterwards could be quite sure whether Abigail Cake slipped or jumped deliberately. They couldn't agree either whether Thomas Egdon had reached out in a vain effort to save her or whether she had pulled him over the edge of the platform with her. The whistle sounded its high pitched alarm and there was a crunch and a scream of brakes as the driver tried to pull up short. They had given him no room to stop, slipping over the edge in the split second the train was passing and their bodies were dragged under the wheels.

CHAPTER TWENTY-SEVEN

It is only when one has lost all things,
that one knows that one possesses it

(from De Profundis, Oscar Wilde)

Miss Pickering arrived at the back door of Ingleton Hall in a pony and trap that Mrs Andrews had sent to fetch her. The housekeeper explained what had happened to Hephzibah and asked the schoolmistress if she was willing to take her in for a while.

'It's just till things are sorted out. Mr Thomas must have struck her several times. I don't think there's any real damage but she's got some nasty cuts and her face will likely be very bruised. The squire has told her she can stay here but she won't hear of it. I think she's afraid of Mr Thomas coming back. She says she wants to go away, back to Oxford and take the boy with her. But she's not fit to go anywhere yet.'

'Of course I'll take her in. Edwin too. But please don't tell Mr Egdon where she is. I don't want him hammering at the door in the middle of the night. Does the squire know?'

'Not yet. He's gone into the village to try and calm things down. When I left they were gathering on the green ready to march on the parson's house.'

Miss Pickering said, 'The parson's alive, thank God, but only barely. A mob surrounded the parsonage and dragged him outside and beat him.'

Mrs Andrews gasped and put her hand to her mouth.

'He's alive thanks to the squire. Sir Richard took him to the doctor's first and then to Reading to the hospital. Poor Mr Nightingale looks in a very bad way. And that Leatherwood claims to be a man of God.'

'Is the squire with the parson now?' said Mrs Andrews.

'I imagine so. It will take a while to get to Reading and back.'

The housekeeper shook her head. 'I had no idea. I don't condone what must have gone on between the parson and Mrs Egdon, but the rule of the mob is no rule at all.'

'Mr Carver and the blacksmith helped the parson to get away from the green and back to the parsonage. Then the trouble began when that Leatherwood man stirred the crowd up. Poor Mrs Muggeridge was in a state of shock. They dragged the parson out of the house in front of her.'

'No man deserves to be hunted down in his own home, Miss Pickering. No matter what he's done.'

Thomas's funeral took place three days later. The service was conducted by the temporary vicar, who had been drafted in to replace Nightingale. Everyone in Nettlestock was in shock at what had happened on May Day and the church was packed. One notable absence was Hephzibah. Despite the urging of Miss Pickering, she refused to attend, caring not how people might interpret her nonappearance.

Abigail's funeral was held not in the parish church, but in Leatherwood's Nonconformist chapel. Ned Cake had long been a follower of Leatherwood and, while Abigail had remained a parishioner of St Cuthbert's, Cake was determined her daughter would not be laid to rest in the same place as Egdon, the man Cake held responsible for her death.

Hephzibah hadn't spoken in days and hadn't touched a morsel of food. Not even Edwin could revive his mother's spirits. She remained in her bedroom, or sat in the parlour, staring out of the window, and went for solitary walks, refusing company, even Edwin's.

This withdrawal and isolation worried Miss Pickering, who blamed herself for Hephzibah's state. Hephzibah had listened in silence when Miss Pickering told her what had happened at the railway station. She remained silent when her hostess told her that after the crowd pelted Nightingale with rotten vegetables, Jacob Leatherwood had incited them to riot and they had broken into the parsonage, dragged him out and beaten him savagely on the lawn. It was only the intervention of the squire that had prevented him being beaten to death.

'Thank heavens the squire got there in time,' said Miss Pickering. 'Sir Richard had him taken to Reading and admitted to hospital. He's paid for his treatment but told the doctors that should he recover he must be told he would not be welcome again in Nettlestock. But I understand that the prognosis is not good.'

These tidings appeared to pass over Hephzibah's head. She continued to stare blankly into space and passed no comment and asked no question.

Miss Pickering sought the help of the squire, who called at the house. When he was shown into the parlour, Hephzibah was sitting beside the window staring blankly at the lawn, where a strong wind had shaken all the petals off the dog roses that grew against the garden wall.

'Miss Pickering tells me you've stopped eating,' he said. 'You can't go on like this, Hephzibah. Come back to Ingleton Hall. Mrs Andrews will take care of you. You and Edwin will always have a home there with me.'

It was as if she hadn't heard him. She just sat there, hands in her lap while he paced up and down.

'You must stop blaming yourself. None of this is your fault. You did what you did because you thought it was right. You married Thomas because you loved him. You conceived a child with Nightingale because you thought it would help Thomas. If anyone's to blame for the whole damned mess it's me. I was the one who put it in your head that Thomas would be disinherited. It was I who kept taunting him. It was I who was looking for an excuse to deprive him of his inheritance. I never forgave him for the fact that he wasn't my own son, I never forgave him for the fact that my wife loved him more than she loved me and I never forgave him for the fact that he blamed me for his mother's death.'

Still she sat in silence, her hands fiddling with the fabric of her dress, her eyes empty of all emotion, seemingly deaf to his words.

Sir Richard pressed on regardless. 'Did Thomas tell you that Ottilie is my daughter?'

She remained unresponsive.

'It's true. I slept with my wife's sister. I suppose you might imagine it was a kind of belated revenge on Jane for her past infidelity, but it wasn't like that. I don't think Jane ever knew. Her sister died a few years before she did, when Ottilie was a baby. We only did it once. After a shoot. Jane didn't like shooting parties and always stayed at home, but Edith, her sister, was a bit of a crack shot. Her husband was away. He was in the army and was overseas a lot of the time. I don't know how it happened really. We were probably both excited. Full of adrenaline after bagging a lot of birds. We got separated from the rest of the party and found ourselves by the old ruined chapel beyond the carp ponds. I only meant to kiss her but somehow one thing led to another.'

He took a cigarette out of his breast pocket and lit it,

inhaling deeply. 'When Edith died, Jane suggested we adopt the girl, as Ottilie's father showed no interest in her and was always away with his regiment. My feelings for the child were the opposite to what I'd felt with Thomas. As she grew older I felt a growing conviction that she was mine. It's impossible to explain. When Jane died and then my firstborn son, Samuel, caring for Roddy and Ottilie kept me going.'

He lapsed into silence then moved across the room and sat down. 'You can't blame yourself for what happened to Thomas and the Cake girl. They had a history. He used her for years. She was convenient – whenever he was at Ingleton she was ready and waiting for him. Before he married you, of course.'

She turned back to look at him and spoke at last. 'You used her too.'

He looked down. 'I'm not proud of that. But she was there and she was willing. I've always had a weakness for a pretty face and that girl certainly had one. I've told you before, Hephzibah, a man has needs. It's like an itch and I need to scratch it.'

She looked at him, her eyes cold. 'You're a hypocrite. Don't try to justify yourself to me. You'll have to justify yourself to God one day.'

The squire coughed then decided he could put off the inevitable no longer. He had agreed with Miss Pickering that he would break the news to her. It was better coming from him. And better to get it over with quickly so that once Hephzibah came to terms with it she might eventually agree to come back to live at Ingleton Hall.

'There's something else you need to know, Hephzibah. It's about the Reverend Nightingale.'

She didn't move.

'It's bad news I'm afraid. He didn't make it. His injuries were too severe. I'm sorry.'

Her face showed no emotion.

'Please, Hephzibah, will you reconsider and come back to live at Ingleton? Ottilie misses you and Edwin. She is devastated by her brother's death. She has lost three brothers and now you have taken Edwin away from her too. The poor girl doesn't deserve that. With Thomas gone and Nightingale too it's time you thought of Edwin and what's best for him.'

'Don't tell me what's best for my own son. I will be the judge of that. And what's best for him is that he never sets foot in Ingleton Hall again.' She paused. 'I'm sorry about Ottilie. But she will be grown up soon. All this will pass.'

'Very well.' He gave a long sigh of resignation. 'I understand that Miss Pickering is happy for you and Edwin to stay on here indefinitely, but I beg you, Hephzibah, please stop blaming yourself. Everything you did, at the time you believed to be right.'

She looked at him for a moment, then got up from her seat. 'The road to hell is paved with good intentions,' she said and left the room.

The day after Sir Richard's visit, Hephzibah went to visit her husband's grave. It was dusk and there was no one around to witness when she entered St Cuthbert's churchyard. Thomas's grave was under a ewe tree at the side of the church, close to the path down to the canal. It was immediately evident as it was still piled high with floral tributes. She stood in front of the stone headstone and placed on top the sprig of white heather given her by the gipsy at the Mudford horse fair. The gipsy had been right about her marrying before the summer came and right about the rest of her prophecy. She played the old woman's words back in her head over and over. *Two men will love you. Both will pay the price for it.* The pain and grief at Merritt's death was mingled with the constant torment that it was all her fault. She had been the cause of their deaths and indirectly the

Cake woman's. Miss Pickering had told her that Abigail Cake's baby had died too. Abigail had told no one, but buried the child in a shallow grave which the dogs had dug up soon after Abigail died. Everyone in the village said that grief at the death of her child caused Abigail to throw herself under the train. Hephzibah was unconvinced. At the May Fair she had looked anything but grief-stricken. It was possible that the baby had died after Abigail's death and been buried by Ned Cake.

Hephzibah stared at her husband's grave. Was she cursed? What was it about her that everyone she loved died? Her mother and Professor Prendergast, Thomas, Merritt and even her own father. Death seemed to follow everywhere she went. Try as she might though, she couldn't find it in her heart to forgive Thomas. It was impossible to believe that he had ever loved her after what he had done to her after the May Fair and choosing to marry her to get his hands on his inheritance. She couldn't blame him for her falling in love with him. That was her own immaturity and susceptibility. She had mistaken physical attraction for love and only discovered the difference when it was too late. It seemed to her that life and human relationships were more unfathomable than ever. Everyone dissembled in some way. Everyone had secrets. Dirty little secrets. Was she any worse than anyone else?

Walking away from the country churchyard, Hephzibah came to the conclusion that no one was blameless. Everyone had played a part in the tragedy that had led to the deaths of Merritt, Thomas and Abigail Cake. The only innocent in all of this was Edwin. He was also the greatest gift she had ever received. Hephzibah increased her pace as she thought of him waiting for her back at the Pickerings' house: his chubby face, his emerging freckles, his reddish blonde hair, his winning smile. While he was in her world she had everything to live for. She would protect her boy with her life. She was determined that he would grow up in a way that would have made his father proud. They only had each other. Hephzibah had an overwhelming need to shelter him from the vicissitudes of the world. They would present a united front.

That evening Hephzibah started to eat again. Every time she looked at Edwin she saw some aspect of Merritt's features gazing back at her and was stabbed by love and sorrow. She thought of their last time alone together on the towpath when they had quarrelled. She would give anything to be able to relive what passed between them and make it different this time. She struggled to believe why she had been so angry then. It was so trivial in comparison with what had happened since. Was what Merritt did so bad? He had known he loved her before she had known she loved him. Had she been in his place, wouldn't she have done the same? It was too late now to tell him she forgave him and to beg him to forgive her. He was dead and it was her fault. She had brought about his downfall, cost him his life and, even in death, his good name.

Knowing she was unable to make things right for Merritt, Hephzibah determined to try to make things a little better for others around her.

The first day she went to visit the workhouse in Mudford was a sunny one. She walked hand-in-hand with Edwin along the empty road, past meadows bright with poppies. There was a light breeze and the whole countryside looked fresh and new and bursting with life, as though challenging Hephzibah to raise her spirits. She pulled a little hat onto Edwin's head to protect him from the sun, although she no longer needed to hide his pale coppery-golden hair. The secret of his parentage was widely known and she no longer cared for her own part, but she worried increasingly for Edwin. It would not be long before he must attend school and she was afraid he would be the object of taunts and abuse. If only she knew how to protect him. If only she had somewhere to go where no one would know either of them and they could begin again. As she trudged along the road she told herself that as soon as she had fully regained her strength she would seek a post somewhere else in the country. But what kind of position would be open to a widow with a small child?

It took them almost an hour to reach the grim-faced workhouse building. When she arrived and asked to speak with the matron she was shown into the same meeting room she had visited before with Merritt. Hephzibah went to stand again at the same window and a wave of loneliness washed over her. She turned back into the room, half expecting to see her lover once again sitting at the table, deep in conversation with the Master, but there was only Edwin, waiting patiently.

Her request to be considered for the part-time role of assistant teacher at the institution met with disapproval from the matron, who had evidently heard about what had happened in Nettlestock.

'I am not a person to judge others, Mrs Egdon, but I have to ask myself if you are a fit person to be employed here. We set the highest moral standards. All our staff need to be role models for the inmates.'

Hephzibah swallowed and looked down, tempted to take her son and walk out of the room and head back to Miss Pickering's. Then she told herself that the whole point of doing this was to try to make amends, to try and find some peace and salvation.

'Mrs Wilson, I am not proud of what I did and I seek to make no excuses. If I could undo it, I would. I have damaged the lives of many people. My son is fatherless. My husband is dead. I contributed to the disgrace and death of the Reverend Nightingale. Not a day passes when I don't castigate myself and I wish I could turn the clock back. But I need to support myself and my son. I have two letters of reference here, one from Sir Richard Egdon, my father-in-law, who is one of the guardians and who, prior to my marriage, employed me as a governess for his daughter, and the other is from Miss Pickering, who runs the school in Nettlestock and has been kind enough to welcome my son and me into her home. It was Miss Pickering who suggested I apply for the post here, which I understand has been vacant for some time. I will do whatever you ask of me. I just want to make myself useful and earn enough to support myself and Edwin.'

The matron looked from Hephzibah to Edwin, sighed then said, 'We are very stretched. And you're right, there has been a vacancy for some time. We would need you three days a week. You could start by hearing the children's reading. On a trial basis only. It will, of course, depend on the approval of the guardians and Miss Fletcher who is the full-time teacher. I know you helped set up the lending library here and that has made a great difference. I can't promise anything as the guardians often take a dim view of those who have low morals, but I'll see what I can do.'

A year passed and Hephzibah had grown used to the workhouse, but familiarity did not make it seem any less bleak to her. She did get pleasure from teaching the small children and from the hope that perhaps one day their learning might place them in a position to do more than their parents had been able to achieve.

Hephzibah and Edwin continued to live with Miss Pickering. The young woman would not entertain the idea of mother and son living anywhere else and claimed to enjoy their presence.

'Since Mother took to her bed, I've had little or no company. Of course I'm at the school during the day, but having someone to dine with and to sit with in the evenings has been a real joy.'

'You have never wished to marry, Miss Pickering?'

The school teacher dropped her eyes and gave a little cough.

'I'm sorry. I don't wish to pry,' said Hephzibah. 'I'm just surprised.'

'There was someone once.' The teacher's eyes misted and she looked away, embarrassed. 'I had to care for Mother after Father died when I was eighteen. She took his death badly and has been a semi-invalid ever since. It was hard enough for her to accept my teaching at the school, but marrying and leaving her here alone was out of the question.'

'You said there was someone once?'

Miss Pickering sighed. 'I trust you, Mrs Egdon, so I'll tell you, but I beg you please not to tell another soul.'

Hephzibah nodded.

'I have loved another ever since I was a girl. His name is Robert and he lives in a cottage just the other side of the old silk mill. We hoped to marry but my father wouldn't permit it.'

'Why not?'

'He did not consider it to be a suitable match. Robert is an agricultural worker and Father believed that he was far below our station.'

'But when your father died? Weren't you free to marry him then?'

'It was too late. By then Robert was married to someone else. He is five years older than me. A single man earns significantly less than a married one and his income rises in line with the number of his children, so it was imperative for him to marry and start a family. He was not bringing enough money home and was under constant pressure from his parents to take a wife.'

'How very sad. How terrible for you. Do you still see him? Does he still live in Nettlestock?'

Miss Pickering nodded. 'I see him every Sunday in church and his two eldest children are in my school.'

'Oh, Miss Pickering. I am so sorry. That must be hard to bear.'

'He has been blessed with his children. His marriage is a good and stable one, but once in a while I have met his eyes, coming or going from church, or passing on the towpath and…' Her voice broke and she dabbed at her eyes with a handkerchief. 'When I look in his eyes I know he still loves me. It's a comfort in a strange way. At least I can say I have loved and been loved.'

Hephzibah looked at the woman, seeing her in a new light. She reached out and took her hand. 'I know what you mean, Miss Pickering. It is the same for me, I too must seek consolation in knowing that I have known love. And at least I have Edwin. I can't imagine how hard it must be for you to see Robert's children every day.'

'No. In a way it is comforting. They are such good children and I can see him in them. And I bear no ill-will to Robert for not waiting for me. He had no choice. And his wife – she's a good-hearted woman. She married him in good faith and she knows nothing of what was between us.'

The evening was growing darker and Miss Pickering rose to light the lamps. Hephzibah reflected how fortunate she was that she had found a friend and such a haven of tranquility after what had gone before. She had Edwin, a constant source of joy and comfort and she was able to get some satisfaction from teaching at the workhouse and, like Miss Pickering, she had the consolation of knowing that once she had loved and been loved.

Miss Pickering leaned forward. 'I have never asked you this before, Mrs Egdon. I have never wanted to pry either, but is it true what they say that you only went with the parson so you could have a child? That Mr Egdon had to have a son in order to inherit the estate?'

'Is that what they say?' She got up and went to stand by the window. 'It seems strange for me to admit that now, but yes I went to Merritt Nightingale because I was desperate to save my marriage. At the time I believed I loved my husband but I know now I was only infatuated with Thomas Egdon.' She sat down on the window seat and turned to face Miss Pickering.

'Thomas Egdon was like no one I had ever known. I think that was why I believed I loved him. He was exotic compared to all the bookish types around me in Oxford. Of course, he was handsome too. The moment I looked into those blue eyes I was lost. When he paid me attention I fell completely under his spell. I stopped thinking straight. I married him even though I knew he had been having a love affair with Abigail Cake. I pretended I knew nothing. I brushed it away. I acted as if it hadn't happened and that it would not continue.'

'And did it?'

'I thought so, but now I'm not so sure. That's one of the things I feel most guilty about. That I might have misjudged him. I assumed he was unfaithful to me with Abigail Cake when in truth he was more interested in his horses, his gambling and his friends. I blame myself for his death.'

'You mustn't do that. If anyone's to blame for that it's likely Abigail herself. She's the one who threw herself under that train. So whether he tried to save her or she dragged him with her makes no difference. It would never have happened if she hadn't jumped.'

'If I hadn't done what I did she'd never have been in that position in the first place.'

'That's not true. That girl had a pretty hard life. Her father beat her all the time. And losing her baby must have hit her hard. She was probably out of her mind with grief. She tried once before to kill herself. Jumped off the bridge in Mudford, but someone fished her out.'

Hephzibah moved back to sit in the chair beside Miss Pickering. 'I didn't know that.'

'And Mr Nightingale? Did he know why you did what you did with him?'

Hephzibah nodded.

'I see.'

Hephzibah smiled and shook her head. 'Do you know, Miss Pickering, I once thought you and Mr Nightingale might marry. I thought you would have been a good match. But of course I knew nothing of your Robert. And…' She got up and looked out onto the darkening garden. 'And at that point I didn't know that I was in love with Merritt Nightingale myself.'

Miss Pickering gave a little gasp of surprise.

'If I had known we would have fallen in love I would never have done what I did.' She covered her face with her hands. 'Can you understand that? I thought it was a way to save my marriage. I thought I was making a sacrifice, but then when I discovered how I felt… When I saw how he felt…'

The clock had just struck eight when there was a knock at the door and they exchanged a glance. The knocking must have disturbed Mrs Pickering, who began to hammer on the ceiling with her walking stick.

'It must be the squire. I'll go and settle Mother if you'll be kind enough to let him in, Mrs Egdon.'

When Hephzibah opened the door, at first she didn't recognise the figure standing in the shadows. The man took off his hat and moved towards her and she gave a little gasp. For a moment she was glued to the floor, paralysed with shock and disbelief. She was aware of the scent of honeysuckles in the garden and felt the chill of the evening on her skin, then before she could think or speak she was in his arms and he was holding her until she thought he would press all the breath out of her.

Her hands went up to his face and she ran her fingers over it, unable to trust herself that this was Merritt. He had grown a beard and she touched it with her hand then pressed her mouth against his, seeking the familiar sensation of his lips on hers through the unfamiliar feel of his beard. They stood there on the doorstep locked in each other's arms, kissing with all the passion of that first afternoon together.

Eventually Merritt pulled back and held her at arm's length. 'Oh my dearest Hephzibah, I have missed you for every second of every day since I lost you. Can you forgive me?'

'Forgive you? It is I who must beg your forgiveness.'

'But after what you said by the towpath in Mudford that day. You said you never wanted to speak to me again. That I'd lied to you.'

'I was wrong, my love. I was very stupid and very wrong. I was the one who heaped trouble upon you. It's thanks to me that you lost your parish, your home. You lost everything for me. I've ruined so many lives. They told me you were dead.' As she said the words she began to cry and he gathered her into him again.

He bent down and kissed her. 'Not dead. Very much alive. Although I have felt I was dead all the time I have been apart from you.'

She clung to him, unable to believe he was standing there, flesh and blood. 'They said you were beaten so badly you had died in the Reading infirmary.'

'I was seriously ill. When I was in Reading they wrote to tell my parents I was dying so my father came to visit. He was not satisfied with the prognosis and had me transferred to the hospital in Birmingham where he could supervise my recovery. I was unconscious for days. My injuries took a long time to heal.'

Hephzibah looked up at him, her eyes full of tears. 'What kind of injuries?'

'Concussion. A collapsed lung and a ruptured spleen. They took part of my spleen away and I became very ill afterwards. And a broken leg, arm, four ribs and my collarbone. I walk with a limp now – the leg will never be what it was.' He smiled ruefully. 'But I recovered. I owe my life to my father. When I was released from hospital my parents took me back to their home. But when the story of what happened came out and Father realised I could never return to the living here, we quarrelled and I left.'

'I'm so sorry, Merritt. It's my fault.'

He shook his head. 'Of course it's not your fault. The differences between my father and me have always run deep. It's all for the best.' He looked into her eyes and stroked her hair. 'You liberated me, Hephzibah. I was in the wrong job and what happened forced me to confront that. And most important of all, you gave me the gift of your love, even if only for a brief while, and the gift of my child. Where is Edwin? Is he with you? Is he well? Will you let me see him?'

She buried her head in his chest and gripped the lapels of his coat. 'Of course you can see him. You are his father. And, Merritt, he looks so like you. Every day when I look at his little face my heart is filled with love for him – and for you. I can't wait for you to meet him again. To get to know your son.' Then she stopped and stiffened in his arms. 'You are going to stay aren't you, Merritt? Oh please say you are. Don't leave us. I don't think I could bear it.'

He shook his head. 'I can't stay in Nettlestock. I am lodged for tonight at the inn in Mudford and I leave tomorrow. I thought you would be at Ingleton Hall but they told me in the inn that Thomas Egdon was killed and you were living here and teaching at the workhouse. I came here only to see you and Edwin and to say goodbye and ask your forgiveness. There's nothing else here for me now.'

She felt the tears rising and her happiness ebbing away.

She looked up at him in bewilderment. 'I can't bear it, Merritt. To see you and lose you again. Why must you go? Will you return to Birmingham?'

'No. There's nothing for me there. I'm going to live in Rome. I've secured a position at the university there as Professor of Latin and Ancient Civilisation.'

'Rome?' she said, eyes wide with surprise. 'I was due to go to Rome the day I buried my parents.'

He looked at her with hope in his eyes, but his voice desperate. 'I know, Hephzibah. You told me once you would not go there because of that. But please come with me to Rome, my love – you and Edwin. Marry me, my darling. If you still want me? Do you think you can love me again?'

'Love you again? I have never stopped loving you. Even when I thought you were dead. I have thought of you every minute of every day. I have prayed for you. I told Edwin that his father was a great man and that he should always be proud of him.' She looked up at him, hesitating, unable to believe that he was alive, standing there in front of her. 'Oh, Merritt, I have never been happier in all my life. I don't deserve such happiness.'

Instead of answering, Merritt pulled her into his arms and kissed her tenderly. 'You are the light of my life, Hephzibah and *my delight is in you.*'

Hephzibah and Merritt set sail from Newhaven. They stood on the deck hand-in-hand watching the white chalk cliffs fade into the mist of the English Channel. Merritt was carrying Edwin on his shoulders so the little boy could see the receding coastline. The child was brimming with excitement about this new adventure and his first sea voyage.

Hephzibah didn't know what lay ahead of them, but with her new husband and her son beside her she was ready to face anything. She thought back to the day, eight years ago, when her trip to Rome had been cancelled by the death of her parents. Since then she had known grief, fear and unhappiness with moments of joy, but now she was wrapped in a cocoon of love and contentment, with a growing excitement and anticipation she hadn't experienced since she was a little girl. She reached a hand out and brushed the hair from Merritt's eyes where the wind had blown it. It was time to go below deck – but first she had one more thing to do. She put her hand in her pocket and pulled out the pair of green ribbons and released them into the wind, watching them dancing like streamers behind the ship until they floated down, touched the surface of the waves, then disappeared under the wake.

The End

ACKNOWLEDGMENTS

With thanks to my editor, Debi Alper, who is a fount of wisdom, encouragement and insight and whose words of advice have me frantically nodding. She is quite simply a joy to work with.

Thanks to Helen Baggott, my eagle-eyed proofreader who went way beyond proofreading to spot inconsistencies, correct sources and who saved me from playing fast and loose with the seasons.

To my merry band of beta readers who read an early draft and told me when I'd said too much – as well as when I needed to say more. Your support and encouragement is invaluable. Thank you all – Jo Ryan, Clare O'Brien, Anne Caborn, Sue Sewell and Anne-Marie Flynn.

Thanks to Jane Dixon-Smith of JD Smith Designs for another fabulous cover.

While Nettlestock is a fictional place, I borrowed aspects of it from the very real village of Kintbury in Berkshire. I am indebted to the authors of *Kintbury Through the Ages* for useful background on the history of the village and its surrounds – although it should be apparent to anyone who knows Kintbury that it is not Nettlestock. I also drew on the fascinating writings of Alfred Williams in *Round About Middle Thames, Glimpses of Rural Victorian Life* edited by Michael Justin Davis, *Rural Life in Victorian England* by G.E. Mingay and David Raeburn's translation of *Ovid's Metamorphoses* (Penguin Classics).

Get a FREE short story

Get an exclusive short story from Clare Flynn, set in Victorian London during the Great Exhibition of 1851.

Not available elsewhere.

To get your FREE short story go to Clare's website, www.clareflynn.co.uk or use the QR code below. You will be the first to know about new book releases, special offers and freebies.

ABOUT THE AUTHOR

Clare Flynn was born in Liverpool and has lived all over the UK with spells abroad in Paris, Brussels, Milan and Sydney. After eighteen years living in West London she has recently decamped to the seaside in Sussex, where she can see the sea from her windows and where she is already finding inspiration for her next novel.

For more information on Clare and her books visit www.clareflynn.co.uk

If you enjoyed reading *The Green Ribbons* do please leave a review. Authors rely on good reviews and welcome them – even just a few words – and readers depend on them to find interesting books to read.

You'll also find regular news and updates on Clare's Facebook page – AuthorClareFlynn

ALSO BY CLARE FLYNN

Kurinji Flowers

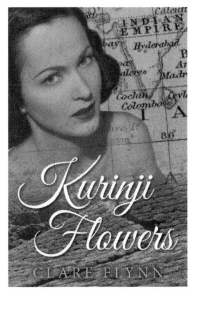

PRAISE

"A sweeping, lush story – the depiction of India in all its colours, smells and vibrancy is pitch-perfect in its depiction. You will be grabbed from the first chapter." *The Historical Novel Society*

"You would enjoy Kurinji Flowers if you are drawn – as I am – to stories of individual human relationships." *The Review Group*

"A beautiful story of betrayal, love, sacrifice and redemption all framed by the gorgeous countryside of India." *A reviewer*

"Kurinji Flowers is a lovely, joyful, heartbreaking novel. Oh, how I wished this story could go on and on!" *A reviewer*

"This is a brilliant book, Clare Flynn has recreated the atmosphere of pre-, and post-, war London and India really well – it is as if you are actually remembering it, instead of reading about it." *A reviewer*

ALSO BY CLARE FLYNN

Letters from a Patchwork Quilt

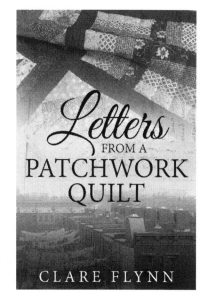

PRAISE

"The story is different, original and touching. It's interesting to read how the lives of Jack and Eliza unfold in different countries. The plot is powerful, the characters are well sketched, memorable, and their personalities will remain in the minds of readers even after they finish the story. It's a story of love, loss and tragedy; a heartbreaking and moving tale where readers will wish to see Jack and Eliza reunited and happy together. The narration is descriptive; it also speaks about the society that existed during that age and pulls readers into the story. It's well written and the story is not predictable, making it an engaging read." *Reader's Favorite 5 Star Medallion*

"The author has a great talent for weaving romantic and heart rending tales that give us a glimpse into life in the past." *A reviewer*

"A heart wrenching and gripping story of love lost between Eliza Hewlett and Jack Brennan. When Jack is wrongly accused of fathering another woman's child this leads to a series of ill-fated events for the young lovers, which span over a twenty-year period. From Bristol to Middlesbrough, Liverpool and America, Flynn's evocative and beautifully crafted prose is addictive and I found myself becoming immersed and emotionally involved in the lives of Eliza and Jack." *A reviewer*

"Tugged at my heartstrings from cover to cover. Exactly the kind of book I love to read. It's a sad heartbreaking tale of consequences and unfulfilled love. You'll cry, I promise you." *Ashley Lamar, book blogger.*

"A wonderful story…If Ms Flynn's other novels do for Australia and India in the early decades of the 20th century what Letters does for England and the United States, I will be packing my bags and traveling far from home very soon!" *Book Porchervations book blog.*

Printed in Great Britain
by Amazon

70775589R00175